NIGHTS AT MATA HARI: BOOK 2
LYING EYES
ROBERT WINTER

Books by Robert Winter

Pride and Joy series
September
Asylum (coming in 2018)

Nights at Mata Hari series
Every Breath You Take
Lying Eyes

Vampire Claus

Discover more about the author online:
Robert Winter
www.robertwinterauthor.com

NIGHTS AT MATA HARI: BOOK 2

LYING EYES

ROBERT WINTER

An Original Publication from Robert Winter Books
www.robertwinterauthor.com

ROBERT RW WINTER
Incurable Romantic

Lying Eyes
© 2017 Robert Winter

Cover Art
© 2017 Dar Albert

Author Photo
© Brad Fowler, Song of Myself Photography

Cover content is for illustrative purposes only and any person depicted on the cover is a model.

First Publication, July 2017
v. 1.0
Print Edition

ISBN-13: 978-0692907078 (Robert Winter Books)
ISBN-10: 0692907076
Printed in the United States of America

Dedication

To the community of storytellers, writers and readers alike,
who believe in happy endings for two men.

Chapter One

THERE IT WAS again.

The back of Randy Vaughan's neck prickled as he polished a glass, and he peered sharply around the almost-empty bar. It was a typical weeknight, and only a handful of patrons remained amid the deep couches and inviting club chairs grouped around cocktail tables of dark wood. He'd designed Mata Hari so that his customers would feel that they were guests at a cocktail party rather than a bar, and he even hung the walls with pieces from his personal art collection. Usually the homelike environment gave him a sense of satisfaction, but he drummed his fingers on the bar rail as midnight came and went.

None of the customers appeared to be paying him the slightest bit of attention. Yet he couldn't shake the sense of being watched—and not in the usual way of guys sizing up his muscular build and deciding whether to make a pass.

As the night wore on, Randy tried to tell himself it was just stress, but twenty-five years of law enforcement left him with an instinct for wrongness he didn't want to ignore. Surreptitiously, he checked to make sure that the .357 Magnum he kept under the bar was accessible. Then he shook his head at his own paranoia. At least whatever was off seemed to present no immediate threat, so he focused on serving drinks to the last stragglers.

At a few minutes before two, he sent his assistant Malcolm to deal with the back area in preparation for closing before he came out from behind the bar to begin his walk-through. In one of the side rooms off the main bar, he suppressed a chuckle. "Guys, time to take it elsewhere."

The two men pawing at each other in the corner jolted apart, and Randy snorted at their wide eyes and swollen lips. He turned away to pick up a few stray glasses and napkins from a nearby table, allowing them some privacy to adjust clothing and tuck away obvious erections. When he turned around again, the younger of the two would-be lovebirds ran hands through his hair as he scanned up Randy's six-foot-three frame.

His red-faced partner, or partner-of-the-moment, caught Randy's eye and muttered, "Sorry. Didn't realize it was so late."

The younger one raised a suggestive eyebrow. "Is it just the three of us here now? Maybe we could—"

"Malcolm will let you out the front," Randy said pointedly. The men hurried away then, hand in hand. Well, at least someone was getting laid tonight. He hoped they didn't try to get it on in the alley or the parking lot. There was little worse than a bare ass mooning him through a windshield at two in the morning.

He finished gathering glasses, then wiped down the tables. The cleaning crew would wash up and run a vacuum in the morning, but he never left the place messy. He ran a hand over the gleaming wood of the bar as he left a stack of glasses for Malcolm.

When he was strongly invited to take early retirement from the Secret Service because of the fiasco that was Trevor Mackenzie, he was left at loose ends. Barely fifty years old, he'd been aimless and despondent until his best friend, Thomas, came up with the idea of running a bar.

"We've got enough dance places around DC, but there isn't a

good place anymore to have a drink and just enjoy conversation," Thomas had said. "What about a piano bar?"

Randy had warmed to the notion immediately and threw himself into finding the right building, refurbishing it, and opening the doors. Now here he was with a place to call his own. Mata Hari had been open less than a year, but he'd built a good base of loyal regulars already. They talked the bar up, and on weekends Mata Hari was usually packed.

Tuesdays and Wednesdays though, not so much.

Randy walked through the main room again and stopped to adjust a picture frame that had been knocked askew during the evening.

The painting was a small pastel he'd bought in Kyoto, one that featured cherry trees lining a small stream. A single blossom had detached and drifted down toward the water. The elegance of the lines and delicate shading of pinks and blues pleased his sense of composition. A small tap on the frame's edge squared the painting again.

"Anything else, boss?" Malcolm called. The tall black youth waited for Randy to send him home, but he already had his jacket in his hand and a baseball cap over his fade.

Randy passed a hand over his bald scalp as he considered. "The side rooms are all empty, so we're good, Mal. See you tomorrow."

"Uh, boss?"

"Yeah?"

"Tips were a little light tonight. You think you could give me a small advance on the weekend?"

Randy grinned. "Got a hot date, kid?"

Malcolm preened back. "I'm meeting Sarah at Tryst after this, and then there's an after-hours club we're going to hit up."

Randy didn't carry a wallet while working but just shoved

cash into his pockets. Reaching in, he found two twenties and held them out. "Is this enough? If not, I'll reopen the till."

"Forty's great. Thanks, man." Malcolm smiled as he took the bills. "Don't want Sarah to think I'm sponging off her. You remember how it is, right?"

Randy shook his head. "Honestly? No. The last time I took out a girl, you could probably still get a movie and dinner for ten bucks."

Malcolm reeled a bit and flashed wide eyes, then laughed. "Fuck off, Randy. You never dated girls, did you?"

"I had my moments, back in high school."

"Yeah? Were you the big man on campus or something?"

"Girls kind of went with the territory, playing football. At least until I wised up and ditched the cheerleaders for the tight end."

Malcolm's white teeth shone in his dark face as he grinned. "I'm disappointed in you, boss. Couldn't you have banged the quarterback at least?"

"Nah, he was too easy. But Mickey Evans, now, he really did have a tight end."

Malcolm shook his head and laughed as he put on his jacket. "I'd like to see what kind of man you go for. You get these guys wanting up in your muscly, growly business, but in all these months I've never seen you take up even *one* of these dudes on their offers."

"Aah, it gets old. Everybody wants to fuck the bartender."

"Whatever you say, boss. But we'd get better tips if you'd play it up a bit instead of snarling. And since you give us your share of the tips, there'd be more to go around, you know what I'm saying?"

"I know what you're saying," Randy rumbled in mock outrage. "You want to pimp out your employer."

"A little smile, a wink here and there—it goes a long way in filling the tip jar!"

"Does Sarah know how much you flirt with these guys and lead them on?"

"C'mon, you know I don't ever get anyone's hopes up. I'm just friendly. If they get handsy, I let them know I'm all about the vajayjay and most of 'em drop it."

"And the ones that don't?"

"Well, then I holler for you." Malcolm gave him a huge smile. "Nobody's messin' with the boss bear!"

"Get outta here before I remember I don't need an assistant bartender on Tuesdays." Malcolm chuckled and waved a goodbye as he left through the front door.

Randy smiled to himself as he took a last walk around the place for the night. He stopped by the piano, raised the cover on the keyboard, and plinked a few keys. The tone was clear and the notes seemed to hang in the air of the quiet, empty bar. Even as the sound faded away, the hair on his arms stood. He just couldn't quite shake his unease.

I need a drink and a good night's sleep. That's all.

He closed the keyboard lid and pulled on his leather jacket, only then remembering the hand-addressed envelope he'd stuffed in there earlier as he left his house. The thick stationery of the Kensington Museum of European Art had an address in London, England.

Dear Mr. Vaughan,

I am employed by the Kensington Museum. We are renowned for the scope of our collection of the most important European artists of the eighteenth and nineteenth centuries. My personal area of expertise is in the works of the post-impressionists, including Vincent van Gogh, Paul Cezanne,

Georges Seurat, and Jean-Pierre Brousseau.

I am led to understand that approximately four years ago you purchased an oil painting from the Gates Gallery in London. I am very keen to see this painting for myself as it may shed light on some scholarly work I have undertaken.

My job brings me to Washington, DC, in the near future. If you would consent to allow me to see the painting, I would be very grateful.

Please contact my assistant at the number or email address below to arrange a convenient time, as I will be traveling and possibly unreachable until I arrive in Washington.

Sincerely yours,
Jack Fraser, Assistant Curator

Well, that was interesting. Randy knew exactly which painting the guy was referencing, because not four months earlier, he'd received a letter from Bernard Gates of the Gates Gallery in London about it as well. Except in that letter, Gates had offered to repurchase the painting for the price Randy had paid.

Four years or so previously, Randy had been shadowing Senator Grace Gibson, Democrat, Washington State, while she attended an economic conference in the UK. As the then-majority leader in the United States Senate, she was entitled to Secret Service protection, and Randy and his team had gone along as a protective detail. Whenever he had a free afternoon during such official trips, he'd liked to stroll through museums and art galleries. That particular rainy afternoon, he'd wandered past the Gates Gallery in the Whitechapel district.

The subject of the letters from Gates and Fraser wasn't a particularly beautiful or well-executed canvas, but it had captured Randy's attention through the gallery window. Trees filled the foreground, dominated by two larger ones that tilted left and drew the eye toward the stone towers of the ruins of a nearby church or perhaps abbey. Wildflowers dotted the slopes down into a valley, while clouds shaded from purple to red to orange against a sky of cerulean, suggesting sunrise. It was the choice of a particular progression of blues in the sky, a light cyan shading in hue almost to cobalt, that had intrigued Randy.

He'd gone inside to inquire, and Bernard Gates himself had greeted him. Gates was a little, pear-shaped man who wore his white hair swept back off his forehead.

"Hallo, sir. Not the best weather to be strolling the galleries, is it?"

Randy smiled. "I'd rather be inside than out there."

"Quite so. Myself, I'd like to be with a cuppa tea in front of the telly. Broadchurch *or something juicy like that." He shrugged. "Perhaps later if it stays slow. Did anything catch your eye, sir?"*

Gates enthusiastically nodded his approval of Randy's questions about the work in the window. He was small next to Randy's bulk, but he hoisted the large canvas with ease and placed it on gallery hooks against a white wall to allow Randy to study it more closely.

"Lovely brush work, as you can see, Mr., uh..."

"Vaughan."

"Indeed. Mr. Vaughan. I have this on consignment from an estate. The heirs are quite interested in liquidating their grandfather's collection. He apparently referred to it as the Sunrise *painting."*

"It's unsigned," Randy observed. "Do we know who the artist was?"

"My understanding is that we do not. The heirs' best guess is a student of the post-impressionists painted this in imitation of the style of Jean-Pierre Brousseau. The composition is quite different to most of Brousseau's body of work, but the ruin on the hills here appears to be an homage. Perhaps it was even painted by a private student of

his. Are you familiar with Brousseau?"

Randy rolled his eyes and turned his full, heavy stare on the short gallery owner. It wasn't the first time people assumed his muscle couldn't possibly support brains too. In fact he knew quite a bit about art, both from his academic studies before he switched to criminal justice, and from countless trips to museums with his uncle Kevin before he died in the line of duty. In his driest tone, he said, "I'm familiar with the post-impressionists."

Gates blinked rapidly and returned to the Sunrise *painting. "Of course, Mr. Vaughan. You will be aware, then, that Brousseau pioneered a style of heavy impasto that he would use to bring a movement and depth to his canvas that was revolutionary. You see how the artist here attempted to do so, though in a far inferior manner to the elegance of Brousseau's brushwork.*

"As you probably know, van Gogh cited Brousseau as one of his principal inspirations when he began searching for a new style during his years in Arles. Brousseau left detailed descriptions and records of approximately four hundred and fifty oil paintings and many other works he created. Nothing is quite like the subject of this painting, so this isn't a simple copy of an existing work. It's possible that the artist, whoever he or she may have been, was attempting a pastiche of elements of different Brousseau paintings, or rather applying his techniques to attempt an original composition."

Randy considered Gates's words before he said, "Five hundred." Gates blinked at him again, and Randy commented, "Brousseau painted almost five hundred oils, not four-fifty."

"Ah. Yes."

The intense colors of the sky drew Randy in. The rich, velvety texture of the cobalt at the top of the image, where dawn's rays had not yet reached, gradually paled as the viewer's eye trailed down to the horizon. The sun was just out of sight, below the hills, but the artist had captured a warmth in his or her choice of pigments where the sky was obscured by the silhouette of a ruined castle. "What are the consigners asking for this?"

"They have set a price of three thousand, three hundred pounds."

Randy considered the canvas, the condition of the frame, and the shipping costs. He wanted to study the technique at leisure, so he decided to buy Sunrise, *even though the framed canvas was large and shipping it back to the States would be expensive. On the other hand, Gates had let slip that the heirs were interested in a quick liquidation.*

"Twenty-eight hundred pounds," *he offered. That was about thirty-five hundred dollars; it was a little steep for a government worker, but he could afford it. The advantage of no social life, he supposed. Gates sputtered and hemmed a bit but then gave a quick nod of his head.*

"Including shipping," *Randy added. That brought on more sputtering, but Gates eventually took the deal.*

When the letter came from Gates offering to refund the amount paid, Randy ignored it. He had no intention of selling back *Sunrise.* Gates then called him and asked again. When Randy flippantly said he would sell it back for forty thousand dollars, Gates choked and protested but offered to pay six thousand. Randy turned him down and that was that.

But with an additional inquiry from Mr. Fraser of the Kensington Museum, he found he was intrigued.

Maybe not intrigued enough to set up the requested appointment, though. Something about the tone of Fraser's letter got under his skin. The implication that Randy should work with Fraser's *assistant* to schedule a visit. Yeah, no. He had better things to do than coordinate with some guy's assistant. If Fraser cared that much, he could call Randy directly.

He switched off the house lights, set the alarm, and locked the entrance behind himself as he left. The parking lot Mata Hari shared with a club called Pyramid was empty except for his pickup truck, its candy apple red finish gleaming under the harsh light of a streetlamp. Remembering his sense of something off, he scanned the darkness before heading to his truck, but found nothing.

Has to be my imagination.

Chapter Two

SATURDAY ROLLED AROUND, and Randy headed to town early to make sure everything was ready for Mata Hari's busiest evening of the week. Although the bar officially opened at five-thirty, it was rare for anyone to wander in much before seven o'clock. Randy was surprised when the front door opened at six to admit a good-looking man.

The stranger was probably about five foot nine or ten, and wore a three-piece suit that seemed tailored to accentuate a lean build. His dark hair was cut stylishly short on the sides but thick and swept back on the top, and his mustache and full beard were closely trimmed. A brightly colored necktie contrasted with the somber gray of his suit. Randy had trouble assessing the man's age, but he would go with thirty. European, though—Randy would stake the bar on *that* guess.

The newcomer contemplated the walls of Mata Hari, passing almost dismissively over the art on display. He studied each piece for no more than a second before moving to the next, but Randy had a distinct impression the man sought something in particular. As he completed his survey, he kept turning and eventually met Randy's eyes across the bar.

Immediately desire flared in the man's face as his hungry gaze drifted over Randy's tight white shirt and up to his face, lingering on his mouth. Shoulders tightened almost imperceptibly as he drew himself to his full height, yet Randy recognized a softening of hard edges. He lazily ran his own eyes to the stranger's luxurious beard, and he imagined stroking the softness there. He sensed something accommodating. Something potentially submissive, yet more subtle than the wanton displays of obedience and posing he was used to on Mondays at his private club.

Something he would enjoy channeling and rewarding, in the right circumstance.

The man started toward the bar. As he moved, Randy had the odd sense that the suit he wore was ill-fitting, even though it seemed perfectly tailored. A step away from the bar, his face just—closed. That was the only word for it. One instant he was cruising Randy; the next he was stone.

Randy sighed to himself. The guy was probably a closet case on his first night at a gay bar. That usually meant an unsatisfying encounter, even if the newbie didn't rabbit. In any case, it wasn't Randy's thing. He'd had plenty of virgin ass over the years, and preferred his men experienced.

Fine. Nothing for me here. He waited at the bar, vaguely disappointed.

"Sir, good evening." The man's accent was English, his words precise and elegant like his hair and his clothes and his beard. Probably from London. Up close, Randy could see his eyes were a deep shade of brown graced with streaks of gold around the pupils that caught the lights over the bar. "I'm looking for a Mr. Randall Vaughan."

Despite forswearing his immediate attraction to the stranger, that honeyed voice caused Randy to smile slowly and show his teeth. He registered the slight widening of the eyes behind the stranger's mask as he focused on Randy's mouth.

"I'm Randy Vaughan. And you are…?"

The man blinked in surprise. "Oh. The Mr. Vaughan I was seeking is an art collector."

Shit. Just another jerkwad, making assumptions right away. Randy was a big man so he couldn't possibly be knowledgeable about art, could he? *Well, fuck that noise. One more chance.*

"I wouldn't use the term collector, but..." Randy gestured at the walls.

"Quite so," the man said distantly, and turned to sweep his gaze over the works on the nearest wall. "Neither would I."

Randy's back stiffened immediately. The stranger—no, the *asshole*—turned his attention back to Randy and held out a hand. He seemed oblivious to the fact that he'd just royally pissed Randy off. "My name is Jack Fraser. I'm from the Kensington Museum in London." Fraser paused as if waiting for Randy to be impressed. "I sent you a letter recently."

Randy willed himself not to think further about Fraser's whiskey-colored eyes or the luxuriousness of his beard, and he didn't take the offered hand. Instead, he wiped a small spill on the counter before him. "You did," he agreed in a bored tone.

Fraser dropped his hand. "Ah, yes." A pause. "My secretary didn't hear from you to set up an appointment."

"Which was my answer to your request," Randy said, letting some snarl appear as he met Fraser's eyes. They were still guarded and closed off, but Randy could see embers burning deep inside. In the right setting, and with proper motivation, he could imagine making those embers flare and ignite in the slender man before him. For the moment, though, the eyes just narrowed in calculation.

Before Fraser could say anything, Randy turned away. "If you'll excuse me, I have work to do."

"May I buy a pint?" Fraser asked, desperation shading his smooth accent.

Randy considered calling Malcolm over to deal with it, but stopped in front of the beer taps. He was annoyed at his lingering attraction, and he decided to push back on this prick a bit. "Fine. What's your pleasure?"

"Guinness. If you have it."

"Of course you'd drink Guinness." A little scorn curled Randy's lip. "Well, the closest beer I have is a stout from Flying Dog." He let his sneer turn feral. "It's called Pearl Necklace." He dropped his eyes to Fraser's necktie, as if he could picture that very thing replacing the colorful silk.

Fraser blinked nervously. Probably he could picture it too. Maybe he even imagined Randy's hot jizz splattering his chest and neck as his reward. *Well, he shouldn't have been a condescending shit out of the gate then.* Randy waited, one hand on the tap, the other idly scratching his ear to make his bicep flex under his white shirt. Fraser focused on his arm and swallowed audibly.

"That'll be fine," he said. "A, uh, Flying Dog then." Randy drew the pint to set before Fraser on a coaster. He didn't wait for the man to take a sip or comment, but headed to the other end of the bar to check inventory.

He stayed busy but somehow noticed that Fraser lingered at the bar for several minutes, apparently hoping Randy would come back and let him ask again about the piece Randy had purchased from the Gates Gallery. When Randy deliberately kept his distance, Fraser took his beer (which, Randy was pleased to note, was more than half gone) and wandered around the room to examine more carefully each painting displayed. Sometimes he moved on quickly to the next piece of art. Other times, he gave a slight shake of his head.

Randy's ears burned, and he considered throwing the guy out. Since he'd opened Mata Hari *no one* had given him grief about his collection. To be honest, no one had studied it the way Fraser did, but still. Each piece had been acquired because Randy connected to something in it. To have this handsome English stuffed shirt look down his nose offended Randy in a way he couldn't even articulate. He seethed inside the longer Fraser spent on his dismissive tour of the room.

When Fraser reached a landscape that was hung over a small settee, he gave a distinct snort. He set his empty beer glass on a nearby table and Randy swooped over to pick it up, ostentatiously swiping the wood as if it had left a ring. "Another Pearl Necklace?" he snarled.

"Ah, no. Thank you." Fraser seemed surprised to find Randy so near, though his eyes remained closed off and stony. "But it was a quite nice stout after all. Thank you for the recommendation."

Randy gestured at the landscape with his chin. "Is that painting offensive to you for some reason? You're practically laughing at it."

"What? Oh no, it's...fine. Competent. It's the presentation, the arrangement of the art, that I find amusing."

Randy ran his gaze over the pieces arranged on that wall of the bar. He'd decided where to hang each and every work over a long stretch of time as he'd readied Mata Hari for opening. He revisited the collection frequently and rotated different pieces in and out of prominent positions. Most of his customers were oblivious but Randy took great satisfaction in presenting something unique in the atmosphere of his bar.

"What's amusing about it?"

"Well, there's no story, is there?" Fraser answered him.

"What do you mean?"

"Individually each piece is presentable. A few are even intriguing. But see here," he gestured at the landscape, "this is a nicely executed pastoral, yet it's positioned between a Japanese scroll and a watercolor of a monarch butterfly. The pieces say nothing about each other, and have no intrinsic relationship.

"But over there," he indicated the wall opposite, "is a modern landscape. Change the frames to something complementary, place them side by side, and the two landscapes together suggest a conversation in, oh, quite a lot actually. Painting techniques, the subject and tonal changes in works separated by two artistic traditions. You see?"

Randy did see, but he'd be damned if he'd admit it. "Two landscapes here wouldn't fit," he said stubbornly.

"Ah. Art as furniture. Of course," Fraser said with a smirk, and that did it.

"No charge for the Pearl Necklace," Randy barked. "Since you made the trip for nothing."

Fraser whirled to face Randy. He was breathing heavily, and his fists were squeezed tightly. The coals in his eyes were burning now, and the pseudo-aristocratic bearing slipped.

Finally, an honest reaction. The glimpse of the man beneath the façade was intriguing and Randy briefly pondered how to peel back the layers to see more.

"May I ask why you won't let me see the painting?" Fraser choked out in a strained voice.

"I don't even know which one you want to see," Randy lied. Fraser reached into the inner pocket of his slim-fitted suit jacket, revealing a glimpse of a linen shirt stretched taut over a leanly muscled chest. He pulled out a piece of paper, which he unfolded before offering it to Randy.

It was a copy of one of the forms Randy usually had to complete with US customs to import a work of art; this one included a thumbnail image of the specific piece. As Randy'd expected, it was the unsigned oil from the Gates Gallery.

He scowled at the paper. "How did you get that?"

"With a Freedom of Information Act request to your American customs bureau. It took some time to get a response, but there you are."

Huh. Randy would have to think about that one.

When he didn't take the offered paper, Fraser said in an exasperated tone, "Do you at least still own the painting shown here?"

Randy glanced at it and frowned. "I think I still have that one. Somewhere."

Fraser was turning red, but the eagerness and impatience in his eyes were at least more genuine than the stone-cold gaze he'd leveled on Randy before. "Please, Mr. Vaughan. This is highly important to me. I'd be very grateful if you would show me the painting. I can make myself available at your convenience."

Make yourself available. Randy squelched the flirtatious comment that came to mind. "Why do you want to see it?" he asked instead. He had no intention of pursuing anything with Fraser, he told himself. He just wanted to enjoy knocking the self-righteous dickweed off his game.

Fraser's expressive face closed up again, until Randy once more saw only something remote and still as a marble statue. "As I mentioned in my letter, it may be extremely valuable to some research I've undertaken." Randy was about to ask more when Fraser added, "It's nothing you'd be interested in, I'm sure, but it could shed light on the development of Jean-Pierre Brousseau's work. You may have heard of him."

And there it was again. The dismissal of Randy as anything but an acquirer of dreck, a muscle-bound clod who couldn't possibly have real appreciation for art.

"Of course I could have no interest in that, Mr. Fraser. I'm just a, what do you call it in England? A publican. A saloon keeper. As enlightening as your critique of my collection has been, I have to get to work. I'm sure you recall where the door is located."

And Randy stalked away rather than acknowledge the frustration, shock, anger, and, strangely, fear that flooded Fraser's handsome face.

Chapter Three

RANDY WAS AWARE when Fraser left the bar later, but then Mata Hari was slammed, and he had no time to weigh his sense of relief, mixed maybe with some disappointment. Slim-cut suits and dark eyes that hinted at mysteries would have to wait for the rush to end.

Before he knew it, nine-thirty came around and Thomas Scarborough, his best friend, was sliding onto his favorite bar stool. Well, best friend and Randy's financial backer in Mata Hari. Once Randy took a shine to Thomas's idea of opening a bar, he helped things move quickly with a business loan on generous terms plus a twenty-percent equity investment. Thomas had no particular desire to own part of a gay bar, but he was wealthy and had been happy to back the venture.

"Hiya buddy," Randy said as he mixed a drink for a customer. Thomas smirked a hello at him. It would have been irritating on someone else, *someone English*, but with Thomas's model-quality looks, wavy dark hair, and bright blue eyes, he somehow could get away with that shit. "Where's Zachary?"

"Parking the car," Thomas answered in his warm baritone. "The lot was full so he's circling the block. We just saw a movie in Georgetown and thought we'd stop by for a drink before heading home."

"The great player Thomas Scarborough, reduced to domesticity." Randy shook his head in mock despair. "Hearts weep across the land."

Thomas laughed. "It turns out I like being stretched on a couch reading a book on a Saturday night. Who knew?"

Zachary Hall walked in the front door and made his way through the crowd. He was slender, a bit like a certain prick from London, though much taller than Fraser. Randy wondered what Zachary would look like in a fitted suit. Nice, probably, but Zachary was too earnest and open to pull off the European soignée sophistication that Fraser affected.

Zachary tossed a key fob to Thomas as he reached the bar. "You're insured, right?" he asked, and Thomas stiffened as alarm shot across his face—his blue Maserati was his baby. Zachary grinned at him. "Just kidding. Nothing happened to her."

Randy chuckled as he slid their usual drinks across the bar. "Hi, Zachary. Scotch on the rocks for you, Thomas, and a seven and seven for Mario Andretti here."

Thomas snaked his arm around Zachary's waist as they took their glasses, and Zachary leaned in toward his side. Watching them, Randy felt a little jolt of envy. Other than the interlude with Trevor, it had been years since he'd had more than a hookup, and longer still since he'd spent a full night with someone. His house in Arlington felt empty when he finally got home at three or four each morning.

He shoved away the unworthy emotions stirred by his buddy's happiness. Zachary had only been in Thomas's life for a few months, but his friend was settled in his skin in a way Randy had never before seen in the years they'd known each other. The sharp style Thomas had always cultivated when he was pulling man after man was still there, but he'd somehow softened too.

It was in the eyes, Randy realized. Zachary brought out that warm expression, and gave Thomas a quiet place in his heart where love stilled the restless need and doubts left by some terrible experiences in Seattle years earlier and the abandonment by his parents, back when Thomas was called Jason. He left that name behind when he started over in DC, but it took Zachary to heal the damage. Zachary and Thomas fit well, Randy thought. He liked the angle of their heads as they sipped their drinks. They were *together* in a palpable way, without having to be demonstrative. He wished he had his sketch pad and the time to work out the image he was seeing. He considered getting out his phone but then Zachary shifted and the moment was gone.

"Randy? I asked how you've been," Zachary said.

Randy shook his head clear. "Sorry. I was thinking about drawing the two of you."

Thomas was pleased. "Are you painting again? It's been a while since you created anything new, I think."

"Well, I've been dabbling here and there. Mainly at night when I get home from the bar. Nothing I'm excited about really." More customers had approached for drinks. "I'll be back if I can," he said, rapping his knuckles twice on the bar.

. . .

ON SUNDAY RANDY puttered around his house in the Maywood section of Arlington, Virginia, handling the chores he tended to ignore during the week. He stuffed too much laundry in the washer and had to stop what he was doing to mop up suds that spilled over. Clothes left in the dryer the previous week were wrinkled, and even when he cycled them through again with a wet washcloth, everything still ended up looking like shit. Disgusted, he abandoned housework and took himself off to the gym.

As Randy hefted the barbell for his bench presses, he wondered if he'd see Fraser again. The man obviously had something going on in connection with Randy's painting that was deeply important to him. Not that Randy would give in, but he didn't mind the prospect of admiring those expressive brown eyes again.

He breathed rhythmically as he pressed the bar—loaded to two hundred and forty-five pounds—through his warm-up set and wondered what it would be like to paint Fraser. He racked the bar and added another twenty pounds as he thought about the portrait he might attempt.

It would have to be a nude, he realized. Fraser reclining on a sofa, maybe, with one knee raised to hide his genitals and leave some mystery. Holding something back. A secret known only to him. In the imagined canvas, Fraser would probably be peering over the artist's shoulder so those remarkable eyes would be in clear view.

By the time Randy finished his chest presses, he had a fairly clear image in mind of the painting he'd like to attempt. Only when he was putting away the metal plates did he remember that Jack Fraser was an asshole and Randy certainly wouldn't be sitting down to sketch him in any case, let alone nude. A small pang of regret made him wince.

When Randy returned to his bungalow after his workout, though, he decided to do some digging for himself. Maybe see if he could understand Fraser's angle, or his interest in the unsigned painting. He'd take the letter to the bar, and if there was any time before opening, he'd noodle around a bit on the internet. Instead of going right into the house he veered toward the garage at the end of his driveway that he'd converted into a studio; his pickup wouldn't fit in it anyway.

The door was unlocked, which wasn't that surprising since he sometimes crawled out of his studio exhausted and forgetful. He recalled tossing the letter on his workbench the Tuesday night he'd read it in the bar and then ended up sketching in his studio until early in the morning. It wasn't there now, though. He moved some things around, lifted a few sketch pads and a stray art book on post-impressionists, but he couldn't find the letter.

Oh well, he'd probably thrown it away. The bitch of turning fifty-one was that his memory wasn't what it used to be. That and all the extra work he had to do in order to keep his belly flat.

. . .

AT WORK LATER, Randy was grateful for a quiet Sunday evening. Malcolm had the bar traffic covered, so Randy checked in with his piano player. Ethel Jonson was an African-American woman in her sixties who told all the patrons to call her Miss Ethel. She attracted a loyal following for her Nina Simone repertoire and Broadway songbook. Her customary white suit, chunky jewelry, and gray hair, straightened and arranged in waves to her neck, classed up the bar.

"You doing all right tonight, Miss Ethel?" Randy asked as he rested a hand on her shoulder. She just gave him a little wink as she started in on "Don't Let Me Be Misunderstood."

Randy'd felt no more of the odd tension that had plagued him on Tuesday, and there seemed to be nothing that needed his attention, so he sat in his office and keyed awkwardly at his old computer. Since he had misplaced Fraser's letter, he opened a search engine and tried remembering the name of Fraser's employer. When he searched for "Jack Fraser London Museum," he found dozens of names and images but none that seemed right. With "Jack Fraser Brousseau," however, his browser brought up a picture of the correct man. He leaned back in his creaky leather desk chair to begin his investigation.

Several press releases addressed Fraser's promotion to a vice president role at a major auction house, Valcoates, based in London. He had apparently graduated twelve years earlier *magna cum laude* from the University of St. Andrews in Scotland with a graduate diploma in museum and gallery studies. *Huh. So he's probably more like thirty-five.* Three years previously, Fraser left the auction house and joined the Kensington Museum of European Art (*Of course. That was the name from the letter*) as their expert on Brousseau and other post-impressionist artists.

Since then, he'd apparently published a few monographs and several articles. In particular, he seemed interested in a transition period when Brousseau resided near the town of Fontaine-Chaalis in France.

Randy tapped his fingers on the desk, thinking. Nothing in his research suggested why Fraser would have gone to all the trouble of filing a FOIA request to track down a painting in Washington, DC. On the other hand, nothing about his research indicated a particularly sterling or noteworthy career. Fraser apparently had held a modest but not executive position at the auction house, and then at the museum he was still an assistant curator rather than a full curator or director. His writings appeared in standard journals but didn't rate notice on the covers.

Still, Randy couldn't help a twinge of jealousy. The life of an art historian, immersed in the world of famous paintings and important works—that was the path he'd chosen for himself before Uncle Kevin's death, before the Secret Service and everything that had followed.

Randy had no regrets about his career in law enforcement, and he'd done a lot of good over the years. But the luxury of hour upon hour to study the great masters, to ferret out their influences and their mark on further developments, would have satisfied something deep in his soul that protecting political figures could never supply.

Malcolm poked his head through the office door just then. "Uh, boss? There's a guy out front asking if he can talk to you."

"Medium height, dark hair, full beard?" he asked, and Malcolm nodded. *Think of the devil, and the devil, he appears.*

Randy put his hands on his desk and pushed himself up, steeling for another confrontation with Fraser. Perhaps he should bring him back to his office? No, that implied a level of intimacy Randy did not want. Or more accurately, would not *admit* he wanted.

He followed Malcolm out to the front of the house and found Fraser in a side room, facing away from the entrance as he studied one of the paintings. Dressed more casually this time, he almost slouched in his navy blazer and dark jeans. The blazer was tailored to hint at broad shoulders, a narrow waist, and strong arms. The tail of it curved over the seat of his jeans, and Randy couldn't help but appreciate the glimpse of a denim-covered ass and of straight, slim legs that ended in black leather loafers.

"Okay, Mr. Fraser," Randy said in a put-upon tone. "You asked to see me."

Fraser turned away from the small framed portrait of a handsome man with bright blue eyes and dark, wavy hair. The subject wore a white shirt, opened at the throat to reveal a glimpse of lightly haired torso. Thomas had sat for the painting a year earlier; Randy had deliberately left it unsigned to avoid comments from his bar's patrons. The figure of Thomas was stylized enough to prevent casual viewers from recognizing the model. Randy had no illusions that the work was anything but amateurish, but he braced himself nonetheless for a sharp comment.

"This is quite good," Fraser opined. "I don't recognize the artist." Surprisingly, his eyes and expression were bright and friendly, and he made no further remark on the painting. Still, Randy sensed an act. Fraser's need leeched from his skin into the room, and it set Randy on edge.

Fraser stepped toward him and held out his hand. "Mr. Vaughan, thank you for seeing me. I fear I made a poor impression on you yesterday, and I'd like to try again."

Randy ignored the hand a second time, but gestured for Fraser to sit in one of the wingback chairs in the small room. He took the one opposite, leaving a cocktail table between them, and let the silence build rather than help Fraser out.

Fraser eventually leaned forward in his chair. "Look, I realize I was a tactless arse yesterday. You neither requested nor needed my opinion on your collection or its arrangement, and I apologize for insulting both."

Randy tilted his head in acknowledgment of the apology. Acknowledgment, but not acceptance.

"Your collection is intriguing, Mr. Vaughan," Fraser said earnestly. "I won't pretend I care for every work, but that would be true of virtually any assemblage of paintings. You obviously chose pieces that moved you, and a great many of them also speak to me."

Randy grunted. "My ego isn't so fragile that I need your approval. Cut the crap and move on."

Fraser's eyebrows rose and he blinked, but then cleared his throat nervously. He leaned even farther toward Randy and dropped his voice slightly. "Here's the thing. I've invested a great deal of time in researching rumors of a particular work of art. If it even exists, I believe I've narrowed it down to three or four likely possibilities. The painting you imported from England a few years ago is one of those possibilities. Another is in Philadelphia and one in New York. Therefore, I decided to fly over to America to attempt to examine them for myself, in order to narrow down the candidates."

"And what is it you're trying to discover, that you need to see this painting in person?" Randy asked. The friendly eyes immediately shuttered, and once more Randy was presented with a stony glare.

"I'd prefer not to say yet, Mr. Vaughan. You must understand. If my research is validated, there could be a great deal of attention. I simply can't risk someone stealing my work. Not when I'm this close."

"Well, that's very interesting, Mr. Fraser—"

"Jack. Please."

"That's interesting, but I don't particularly want attention. You may have noticed this is a bar that caters to gay men and women." A flicker of need escaped the set of Jack's eyes, and Randy had to fight the urge to smile. Or growl. "I think my business could suffer, in fact, if I got publicity for a painting in my collection."

Fraser clasped his hands as if in prayer. "You obviously have a passion for art, Mr. Vaughan. Doesn't the possibility that something you collected could clarify a mystery about Jean-Pierre Brousseau excite you?"

"Maybe." Fraser's eyes lit up, but Randy continued. "*If* I knew what the mystery was."

At those words, he stiffened and fear crept back into his face. "I can't..." he said feebly.

"Then my answer remains the same. If you can't explain to me, I don't believe we have anything else to discuss."

He stood and turned to leave, but Fraser called out, "Please, Mr. Vaughan. I have to travel to New York tomorrow, and then Philadelphia at the end of the week. My time in this country is short. If you don't let me look at your painting, I... I likely will not have another chance to see it in person."

Though he'd turned away from Fraser, Randy closed his eyes. Of course he would be leaving soon. Randy had been foolish to daydream about painting him, spending time with him, seeing what was behind that glint of desire and the need that leaked through cracks in the polished façade. Despite himself, Randy faced Fraser.

"Whatever you're refusing to tell me is obviously very important to you, but it also makes you desperate and fearful." The dismay and consternation that mingled with disappointment in Fraser's face was almost painful to see. Yet Randy refused to cave. "Trust is a two-way street."

Fraser also stood and approached Randy, holding out a business card between his thumb and forefinger. He met Randy's eyes, swallowed, and took another step closer. Randy could smell his cologne, something like dark fruit, earthy yet tart. In a near whisper, Fraser said, "Please take my card. In case you change your mind. I'm staying at the W Hotel, near Pennsylvania Avenue. I'll be back in Washington Wednesday, and then I'm to take the train to Philadelphia later in the week."

Randy almost forgot he was in his own bar. Seconds ticked by. The handsome face was tipped up toward him, with dark eyes blown wide and sensuous lips slightly parted. Heat came off Fraser—*Jack*—through his expensive clothes. The hair of his beard was glossy and Randy wanted very much to run his hands over that pelt, to feel it under his fingers, to have it brush against his own face. *Christ, when did I develop a fetish for beards?*

He licked his lips, and when Fraser's eyes tracked the tip of his tongue, Randy's rod began to swell down the leg of his pants. Again Jack's shoulders sloped down, and his eyes softened while he watched Randy.

He knew the signs. Jack was hungry for a man like Randy to take charge of him and bring him the joy of submission. All Randy had to do was touch his hair, tighten his fingers in the dark locks, press downward on his shoulder, and Jack would be his. For an hour or so, anyway.

Two men wandered into the room, and the connection between Randy and Jack shattered and fell away. He plucked the business card from Jack's fingers and said, "I'll consider it."

Jack glanced nervously at the newcomers and then hurried away, leaving Randy with his card and regret for a missed chance.

Chapter Four

THE REST OF Sunday evening passed smoothly, with only occasional flurries of customers. Several times Randy's eye was drawn to the landscape that had caused Fraser to shoot off his mouth. He gritted his teeth each time, and once murmured, "asshole." Malcolm was walking by just then and chuckled.

On Mondays Randy kept Mata Hari closed. Usually he reserved that night to go out and seek a little action of his own, but he found to his surprise he wasn't in the mood. Instead he met Thomas and Zachary for dinner at a new restaurant in the Shaw area of DC. The food was fancier than he liked, but he enjoyed the chance to hang out and bullshit with his friends over a nice bottle of red. Thomas had superb taste in wine and he loved to treat Randy and Zachary to fine dinners.

It had bothered Randy at first, when he and Thomas started to spend time together as friends, long before Zachary was in the picture, that Thomas always picked up the bill. Finally Thomas all but ordered him to shut up and enjoy the good food without worrying about the cost. Randy ceased his protests and just said thank you for the meals.

The evening ended early since Thomas and Zachary both worked normal hours instead of a bartender's reverse schedule, and Randy had time to sketch some ideas in his studio. Tuesday was again a slow night and he found himself watching the door too closely when it opened sporadically. He finally realized he was hoping for one particular customer to walk in, but then he recalled Fraser was supposed to be in New York.

He shook his head angrily at himself and took a walk around the bar, chatting up customers and trying to be a good host. Mindful of Malcolm's math that flirting equaled bigger tips for his staff, he smiled more often. Given some of the startled reactions, he must have looked more feral than inviting, so he quickly abandoned the attempt.

After closing up, Randy grabbed the deposit bag with the night's receipts and stepped out the front door into the parking lot. The neighboring dance club Pyramid was dark on Tuesdays and the lot was mostly empty as Randy headed for his truck. Throwing the bag onto the passenger seat first, he climbed into his pickup and gave the engine a minute to warm up. It was only October, but a cold snap had hit the mid-Atlantic, and his patrons had been complaining all week about the low temps.

Randy put his truck in drive and headed toward the O Street exit from the lot. His headlights swept across a flurry of movement, and in a pounding heartbeat he realized what was illuminated: Three men were holding down a kid and kicking him. A knife flashed.

Randy threw the truck into park and charged into the brawl before he even thought about what he was doing. He catalogued and ranked potential threats as he ran. A tall Hispanic-looking man stood closest, a stocky dark-skinned man was holding the kid down, while a Caucasian guy stood close by with a knife displayed.

Randy's breathing was disciplined despite the rage that swept through him at the sight of the boy on the ground, and every muscle in his big body flexed as he hurtled toward the apparent mugging.

The tallest man's face whipped toward the sound of approach. He was probably scared shitless as Randy charged, so it was no surprise when he took off running. That left two attackers.

The glint of a blade caught Randy's eye, and he crashed into the man holding it. Adrenaline pumped, blood rushed and thrummed in his ears, but decades of combat training had Randy's arms and legs working effortlessly as he grabbed the knife hand. The man grunted in pain as Randy twisted hard at the same time his fist connected with the guy's gut. He sagged as Randy twisted harder and the knife fell from his hand. Kicking the blade aside, Randy forced the mugger away in the opposite direction, leaving him sprawled on the pavement. One to go.

The asshole with his hands balled in the kid's sweatshirt recovered from his surprise and shouted, "You're dead, muh'fucker." He dropped the boy, then surged up toward Randy, fist back, ready to swing. Randy gave a savage grin as he sidestepped the lunge and shoved the mugger, driving him right onto the hood of his truck. Grabbing the back of the guy's jacket in both hands, Randy grunted as he hoisted him in the air and threw him like a sack of potatoes toward his cohort sprawled on the ground.

The dickwad who had lost his knife scrambled to his feet as he tugged on his buddy's arm, and the two of them took off into the darkness after their cowardly friend. Randy snatched up the fallen knife as he caught his breath and waited, still tense, to make sure the muggers were really gone. After a moment he was satisfied, so he tucked the blade into the back of his belt before he crouched to help the kid.

His eyes were closed, but he groaned slightly as Randy leaned over him. Age was tough to tell; Randy figured maybe fifteen. He wore a torn and stained purple sweatshirt and dirty jeans. His sneakers showed gaps between the canvas and the rubber soles.

No jacket, despite the cold night air. Under the sodium street-light, his hair seemed to be red. Blood smeared his mouth where he'd clearly been punched in the face so hard it split his lip.

Gently, Randy touched the boy's bony shoulder. There wasn't much flesh there under the sweatshirt. "Kid, can you hear me? It's okay now. They're gone."

The boy opened his eyes and stared up at Randy, his breath coming fast and his hands raised to keep Randy back. A wince of pain washed over his pale, delicate features. "I don't have nothin', mister. Please don't hurt me."

Aching for him, Randy leaned away quickly and released his shoulder. But that look of fear hurt.

In the Secret Service, Randy had never felt more worthy than when he could stand between danger and someone in trouble. He loved being big and strong. The power in his arms and legs, the way his jeans stretched around his thighs, the shadow he cast—all of it made him proud. Yet he'd had women or slight men cross the street rather than pass by him on a sidewalk at night. It always stung.

Randy suppressed a grimace as he held out his hand, palm open. "I'm not gonna hurt you. I just want to see if you're all right."

The boy scooted back on his butt, then pushed himself up awkwardly until he was in a crouch. He winced and closed his eyes as he touched his ribs.

"Easy, easy," Randy murmured. "Your mouth is bleeding a little. Did they get you anywhere else? Did they cut you?"

The boy looked at him in alarm but shook his head slightly. That movement made him groan, and he held his side where they'd kicked him. "I think I'm okay." He paused but then asked in a trembling voice, "They had a knife, didn't they?"

"Yeah. Did they get anything from you?" Randy rested on his

haunches to try to be less intimidating. In the glow from his truck's headlights, he studied the boy's face and what he could tell under the sweatshirt. He didn't see any blood besides the split lip, and nothing seemed to be broken based on how he was moving.

The kid seemed to think about Randy's question for a minute. "Nothin' to get."

"We should call the cops. You live around here?" Randy asked. "I can give you a ride home. Or call someone if you want." He pulled his cell phone from his jacket pocket to dial, but the boy shook his head more energetically.

"Please don't get the police. I'll be okay. Thanks for... Thanks for stopping them."

He got to his feet, swaying a bit. Randy stood up quickly and reached out to help steady him, but stopped when he flinched away.

"I'm not gonna hurt you," Randy said again, and the kid froze.

"I know. Sorry. I just..." He blushed and glanced down at the pavement. He couldn't be more than five-seven, and if he weighed a buck and a quarter, Randy would be surprised.

"Where do you live, kid?"

"Danny. I'm Danny."

"Randy Vaughan. Where do you live, Danny?"

Danny turned in the direction of the nearby park and shrugged. Randy knew a lot of homeless people slept among the trees there, or down at the edge of Rock Creek where it ran through the park.

"You got any family around? Friends?"

He shook his head with his eyes on the pavement.

"You turning tricks, Danny?" Randy asked softly. The kid jerked around in alarm, eyes wide.

"No! I don't do that. I was just..." His eyes flicked to the dumpsters that Mata Hari shared with a few restaurants on P Street. Searching for food. Of course.

Randy's thoughts flew to his friend Joe, who ran a shelter for homeless LGBT youth. He didn't know if Danny were gay, but there was time to worry about that later. "How old are you, Danny?"

"Seventeen."

Randy frowned. "Honestly?" It could be true, he supposed. He was a lousy judge of age, which was why he carded almost any new customer in the bar who didn't have gray hair.

"Really. I'm just small."

Okay, this might work. Joe's shelter, Rainbow Space, took kids until they were seventeen, but after turning eighteen they had to move on because Rainbow Space had too few beds as it was. Randy could give Joe a call, and if Rainbow Space was full, maybe Joe'd have another suggestion. But he wouldn't call at two in the morning.

Randy looked out at the trees that edged the P Street park. Danny might be hurt more than was obvious. Someone should keep an eye on him for a few hours at least, to make sure he had nothing worse than a few bruises coming. *Well, shit.*

"You hungry?" Randy asked. Danny licked his lips nervously and shook his head even as his stomach gave a loud rumble.

"I just closed my bar there," Randy indicated with a shrug of his shoulder, "and I'm planning to grab a burger at the diner over on Eighteenth Street. I'm not looking for sex. You're welcome to come eat with me, and you can clean up in the bathroom there." Danny's stomach rumbled again, and his eyes had a slightly glazed expression that worried Randy. "I mean it, Danny. Just food, and no strings attached."

Danny stared at him so long that Randy was about to give up.

He wished he hadn't given his cash to Malcolm. Suddenly Danny made up his mind and nodded quickly. "Thanks. I'd really appreciate that."

"Are you sure you don't want me to call the police?"

Danny pleaded with his eyes. "Please don't. They didn't get anything anyway. An' I don't know what…" He swallowed hard. "I don't want to get sent to a foster home."

Randy wasn't sure a seventeen-year-old would be put into foster care, but he didn't really know. He could understand Danny's reluctance to come to the attention of the police, and it was true the cops were unlikely to have much time to track down three guys who didn't even manage to rob Danny.

"Okay," Randy said reluctantly. "No cops." He opened the passenger door of his truck and grabbed his deposits bag off the seat to make room for Danny. He helped him up, both because the running board was high and the kid seemed unsteady. As he climbed in the driver's side, he recalled the knife tucked into his belt and quickly stashed it under his seat.

"I just need to swing by my bank for a minute, okay? Then we'll eat." Danny pulled his seat belt over his shoulder and Randy drove slowly away, keeping an eye out for the muggers. He wasn't sure he'd even recognize them because things had happened so fast, but they might be looking for other homeless people to harass. He didn't spot them again, though, before he pulled up at the curb by his bank.

"Hold on a minute." It crossed Randy's mind to turn off the truck and take his keys. He glanced over at Danny; the boy stared back at him trustingly. After a moment, Randy left the engine running and climbed out.

He walked to the night deposit drawer, keeping his eyes straight ahead but straining his ears for the sound of movement, or of the truck being put into gear. He was fast enough he might be able to reach the passenger side door before Danny could pull away.

He made his deposit, tense and ready to launch into motion.

The truck rumbled steadily at the curb.

He withdrew some cash from the ATM before he walked slowly back to the truck and climbed in. "That's done," he said brightly, and Danny gave him a small, shy smile. "Burger next."

Shortly they pulled up in front of Del's Diner, a standby for late-night food after the bars closed. Inside, the overhead lights cast a ghastly glow over the Formica tabletops and orange plastic seats, but the diner was clean and the food was good. Only a few tables were occupied, which was unsurprising for a Tuesday night.

When they walked in, Del greeted Randy by name as he gestured from behind the cash register for them to take any seat. His head was as bald as Randy's on top but fringed in white, and his yellow polyester shirt seemed to glow in the harsh light of the diner. Watery blue eyes lingered questioningly on Danny.

Randy chose a booth by the front window and pointed Danny toward the men's room at the back. "I'll order. Burger, medium rare good for you? Okay, you go clean up. There's still blood on your face."

"Mornin', Randy," his favorite waitress called. Her gray hair was pulled back tightly from her mahogany face, and her sturdy-soled shoes squeaked on the linoleum as she shuffled over with two menus. "Coffee?"

"Hey, Vonda. How's your back?" She grunted but gave a pleased smile that he'd asked. "Yes to the coffee. Let's get two cheeseburgers, medium rare, the works. And would you bring the kid something hot while we wait? Maybe tea and some soup?"

"Sure thing, sugar." She pointed her chin toward the restrooms. "You trying out somethin' new, Randy?"

He frowned. "You know me better 'n that. I'm just helping out."

"You can't stop yourself, can you, sugar? Gotta take care of everyone." Vonda cackled as she turned to walk away. Danny made his way back to the table, eyes on the floor. Randy would guess he'd been run off of places like this before, but Vonda just tapped Danny on the shoulder as he passed. "I'll bring you some hot tea, hon. You like chicken noodle soup? Del's is right tasty." Danny nodded nervously and muttered thanks before slipping into the booth across from Randy.

He'd washed off the blood, but his cheek was a ripening pink where he'd been hit. His chin was scraped raw too, and Randy had another rush of anger at the assholes who'd hurt him. Dark circles smudged under his large amber eyes, giving him a hollow appearance. But his hair was a lively auburn, with brighter copper strands standing out under the fluorescent lights of the diner. There was an androgynous quality to Danny—an unusually wide mouth, eyes almost too big, something Slavic in the planes of his face—that intrigued Randy. Danny reminded him of someone, maybe an actor he'd seen on TV or something. Or maybe he'd seen Danny around the neighborhood without really noticing a starved, homeless boy.

The hunger he saw in Danny's eyes was for more than food, though. It drew him in. He'd like to paint those distinctive features. It would take a light touch of the brush on canvas, and he thought about the pigments he would mix to find just the right shading for the porcelain skin.

"You come here a lot?" Danny asked, interrupting his thoughts.

"What? Oh, yeah. Sometimes after I close Mata Hari, maybe once or twice a week."

"I guess running a bar makes for strange hours."

Randy shrugged. "That's true. I'm there usually from four until closing, so I have to sleep when other people are going about their days. And I eat at odd times."

"You must eat a lot."

"You saying I'm fat?" Randy asked, but with a smile.

Danny's eyes flashed alarm anyway. "No. I just mean you're so big. You must have to eat a lot to stay that way." He sounded panicked, like he was afraid Randy would get mad.

"Easy, kid. You're right, I do eat a lot." Danny blinked at him and gnawed on his bottom lip. "You doing all right? Any headache or dizziness?"

"I'm okay. A little sore where they kicked me, I guess, but that's it."

Vonda returned with his coffee and Danny's tea, plus a big bowl of chicken noodle soup and a handful of saltine crackers in plastic packets. She took a glance at Danny and returned shortly with a bag of ice. Randy smiled up at her in thanks as he doctored his coffee while Danny grabbed his spoon and shoveled in the soup.

The barest moan reached Randy's ears as Danny ate. After three or four big spoonfuls, he stopped long enough to tear open two packages and crumble crackers into the soup. The bowl was empty in less than a minute, and only then did Danny look up at him. He still seemed a little scared, but also defiant. Eyes intent on Randy's, he took his paper napkin and wiped his mouth, careful to dab around the split lip and the scraped chin. The fear that had faded was replaced with something that suggested gratitude.

Randy broke the gaze and sipped at his coffee while Danny pushed his empty bowl slightly to the side and opened another packet of saltines. "You want some more soup?" Randy asked, but Danny shook his head.

He picked up the bag of ice and applied it to his face, closing his eyes. "Thank you...Randy," he said shyly. "I'll wait for the burger."

They sat quietly for a few minutes, and Randy refrained from filling the silence with questions. Danny would talk or not. Eventually Vonda returned with two plates, burgers piled high with lettuce and tomato plus heaping mounds of french fries.

"Here you boys go," she said as she lowered the plates. "Randy, no more fries for you this week after tonight. Else you'll whine about the carbs to no end and who's got time for that?" She retrieved Danny's empty bowl and the torn plastic wrappers. "More tea, sugar?"

"Yes please," Danny answered.

"Polite. I like that. Be right back."

Danny seemed to wait for a cue, so Randy scooped up his burger and ate a third of it in one bite. Danny snatched up his and started in, too fast. "Take it easy, Danny," Randy murmured. "No one's gonna take that away from you. Don't make yourself sick."

Danny made a noise that sounded like a scoff, but he set his burger back down and chewed what was already in his mouth before he picked up a fry. When he bit down, he closed his eyes. "Oh, that's good," he moaned softly. Randy could imagine what the salt and grease tasted like to a hungry boy.

"Del does great french fries. Hand cuts them every day," Randy said as he picked up a few and dipped them in ketchup. Vonda returned with Danny's tea and more coffee for Randy, and they ate in companionable quiet. Finally, though, the food was done, Randy declined another refill, and Danny turned his head to stare out the window of the diner.

Eighteenth Street was dark, and most of the businesses that lined the road were shuttered. A single car rolled up as they watched, and backed into a parking space. A man climbed out and pulled his heavy coat tight around himself as he hurried away. Cold radiated from the glass, and Randy's eyes trailed over Danny's thin purple sweatshirt.

"You sleep on the P Street Beach?" Randy asked quietly, picturing the shoals of Rock Creek, at the foot of a bridge that crossed from Dupont Circle into Georgetown. People froze to death there every winter. Danny didn't turn away from the window, but he nodded. "Why not a shelter?"

Danny's reflection glanced at him in the glass. After a long moment, he said, "I can get away easier if I'm outside."

Of course. A small, pretty boy like Danny would be an easy target for some of the grizzled men who haunted the city-run shelters. That was exactly why Joe started Rainbow Space.

"You got blankets, or a coat?" Randy asked. Danny shook his head again without meeting his eyes. When Randy tapped his fingers on the countertop, Vonda took that as a sign to bring him the check. He glanced at it and pulled some cash out of his pocket to cover the meal plus a generous tip. He pulled another hundred in bills out, and slid them toward Danny. "Buy a coat," he said gruffly.

Danny looked at the money, and then up at him. He didn't reach to take it. He swallowed. "What do you want me to do for that?"

Randy fixed him with a stare. "Nothing. I told you, no strings attached." Danny held his eyes as his fingers crept to the table and he swept away the small stack of twenties. "Hide that carefully," Randy warned, and Danny mouthed thanks before turning back toward the window.

"Do you think they'd let me stay in here a while longer?" Danny asked quietly as he gazed intently at the street.

"Del's is open until four. Vonda won't run you off earlier."

It was already three, and likely to get even colder. This part of town would be risky for Danny to sleep in, even if he found a covered spot or doorway. Randy could offer to drop him at the Beach, where Danny at least would have his routine down, but he cringed at the thought of Danny climbing out of his truck and walking down the slope of P Street Beach into the darkness.

Randy was usually home and in bed by now, unless he needed to paint, in which case he was in his little studio. He was going to want to paint tonight, he thought. Or maybe sketch a scared young man with porcelain skin and wide, amber eyes.

Before he knew what he was doing, Randy heard himself say, "I can give you a safe place to sleep tonight. If you want."

Chapter Five

RANDY PULLED HIS truck into the driveway. "C'mon. I'll show you the bedroom and then I have some work I want to do." Danny climbed down from the passenger side and trailed him to the wraparound porch of his bungalow, where Randy unlocked the kitchen door and ushered Danny inside, snagging his mail from the letterbox next to it as he followed.

The kitchen flooded with light when he flipped the switch, and Danny looked around, blinking. It was a big space because Randy had combined the dining and living rooms with the formerly cramped galley kitchen into one great room that stretched the width of the house.

A big mission-style island anchored the kitchen area, providing a chopping and prep surface within easy reach of the refrigerator, gas stove, and a farmhouse sink with a porcelain apron. Glass-fronted cabinets provided lots of storage. A long dining table, also in the mission style, sat in front of a set of French doors that opened to the fenced backyard. An overstuffed sectional sofa and two coordinating chairs flanked a brick-fronted fireplace, below a large flat-screen TV mounted on the chimney.

Randy flicked quickly through his stack of mail and muttered to Danny, "Give me just a minute here." He set aside two bills to pay before he threw the rest of the flyers and junk mail into the trash. "I'll give you a tour later if you want, but I bet you could use a shower and bed." He led the way up a staircase to the second floor and opened a door off the top of the landing.

"You'll sleep here. The john is right across the hall, and there are towels on the shelf, spare toothbrush and razor in the medicine cabinet." He looked Danny up and down, and shook his head. "I don't have any clothes your size, but I can get you one of my T-shirts if you want to sleep in that."

Danny bit his lip and looked nervously into the bedroom. "This is real nice." He reached out a hand tentatively and rested it on Randy's forearm. "You sure I can't, uh, thank you?"

Randy stepped back. "Don't do that, Danny. I told you no strings and I meant it."

Danny swallowed hard. "What if it's not payment?" Randy tilted his head, puzzled, and Danny said more boldly, "Maybe I just think you're hot." He leaned forward and stretched on his toes to try for a kiss.

Randy held him back with his hands on Danny's thin arms. "Ah, kid. Thanks. I'm flattered but you're, what? More than thirty years younger than me. No offense, but I'm into men closer to my age, not to mention legal. Okay?" He'd tried to be light, but Danny dropped his eyes to the ground and turned red. "Don't look like that. You took a shot and I turned you down. That's all. Nothing ventured, nothing gained, right?"

"I'm not good enough for you," Danny mumbled, and Randy shook his head.

"You're good enough that I brought you into my home. Shit, you're plenty cute but you're way too young for me. When you find the right guy it'll all come together. Besides, you've got the balls to go for what you want. That's good too."

He looked up shyly. "Okay. I'm sorry I made things weird."

"It doesn't have to be weird. Grab a shower and I'll leave a shirt on the bed for you. Toss your clothes outside the bathroom when you strip and I can throw them in the wash."

Danny started to move into the hall bath, then whirled around and blurted, "Why are you being so nice to me, if you don't want sex?"

"It's just how I was raised," Randy said with a shrug. "You see someone you can help, you do it. Maybe someday there will be somebody you can help, and you'll step in. That's enough for me."

"You don't even know me. What if I, dunno, try to rob you while you're sleeping?"

Randy caught him with a gimlet stare. "You planning on doing that?" Danny turned pale and wide-eyed as if Randy had grown bigger without even moving. The boy shook his head quickly. "Didn't think you would. So, shower. Bed. I usually get up by eleven, so if you wake up earlier and you're hungry, help yourself in the kitchen." He turned away toward his own bedroom.

A little later, after throwing Danny's clothes into the washing machine, Randy let himself out of the kitchen and crossed the walkway to his studio. Fingers twitching, he wanted to get down the sadness and fragility in Danny's face. He should be in bed but allowed himself an hour to sketch to see what he could come up with. He unlocked the door and flipped on first the overhead light, then a small lamp. Grabbing a sketchpad and some pencils, he sat in his rocker and began to rough out what he saw in his mind's eye.

Nearly two hours passed before Randy caught sight of the small clock on his workbench and realized it was already five-thirty. "Shit," he muttered. He was going to be exhausted if he didn't get some sleep. One more look at the sketchpad, and he was pleased. He'd done a decent job of suggesting Danny's delicate features and the loneliness and fear in his eyes as he stared through a window and into the night. Behind the pensive figure,

Randy had roughed in the key details of Del's Diner. He'd like to do a few more sketches of Danny from different angles before he committed, but he thought this could make a powerful painting.

. . .

WHEN HE WOKE at eleven, Randy was fuzzy from lack of sleep, but he could smell coffee and bacon. In the quiet of the house, he heard the dryer door open and close again, followed by a few beeps. He tensed for a moment at the unfamiliar scents and sounds before he remembered.

Danny.

Randy wore sweat pants over his gym shorts downstairs. He didn't bother with a shirt, but realized that might have been a mistake when he walked into the kitchen, scratching his hairy chest, and Danny ran his eyes up and down his torso. *Dammit.* He wasn't trying to stir shit up with the kid; he just didn't think. The front of Danny's oversized T-shirt tented out a bit but Randy pretended not to notice.

He remembered what it was like to be a teenager and bone up over every decent-looking guy that passed by. Rather than run awkwardly back upstairs, he ignored the flush on Danny's face and poured himself a cup of coffee. Drank deeply. Muttered, "That's good. Thanks."

Another sip and he woke up enough to ask, "How are you feeling today? Are you having any nausea or trouble with your eyes?"

Danny shook his head. "I don't think so. My face aches a little and my ribs are sore, but it isn't too bad."

"Good. You've got a bruise coming in there on your cheek. Be sure to put some more ice on your face and your side both. That'll help with the swelling."

Danny fidgeted under Randy's gaze before he whirled away

and tugged down the edge of his shirt. "Oh! I cooked up some bacon too. I hope that's okay. You said to help myself."

"It's fine."

"I made extra. It's keeping warm in the oven. Can I make you some eggs to go with it?"

"Uh, sure. Why not?"

Randy sat on a stool at the center kitchen island and watched Danny bustle around. He'd figured out where the basic pans, utensils, and plates were kept, and in a few minutes he placed a platter of scrambled eggs, bacon, and buttered toast before Randy. He was obviously competent at basic cooking, which suggested that at some point he'd enjoyed a normal home life with a caring parent.

"This looks good. Thank you."

Danny'd apparently gotten himself under control, so he poured another coffee and leaned against the counter as Randy ate. He drew himself inward somehow, making him seem even smaller than he had the night before in his thin sweatshirt. Still and quiet, there was an air of eagerness to please. Wary, yes, but not out of his element in a comfortable kitchen. Randy would bet Danny hadn't been on the streets long.

He couldn't help himself—he had to know. He took a bite of eggs and glanced up casually. "So, how'd you end up homeless? Your parents kick you out?"

Danny flushed and turned away, but Randy just waited. Sure he was being nosy, but he had some investment in this kid's well-being. If Danny told him to fuck off, well, that was his prerogative. But maybe he'd want to talk.

"My mother died six months ago," Danny finally answered, his voice soft and thick. "Heart attack. There was no money, and I couldn't find any work except bagging groceries. That wasn't enough to keep the rental house. When the landlord changed the locks, I took what money was left and just got on a bus. I figured anyplace was better than that." He shrugged. "I ran out of money when I got to Washington."

"Father?"

Danny flicked him a glance, and the emotions Randy read there were confusing. Anger. Doubt.

Finally he spoke. "My dad hasn't been in the picture much. I don't really know him. I just saw him a few times a year."

"No other family?" Randy asked, and Danny shook his head.

Shoulders hunched, he clutched the coffee cup to his chest. Abruptly, he asked, "What time do you go back into DC?"

Randy flicked a glance to the wall clock. "Usually I head in around three, three-thirty, to get the bar ready for opening."

"Oh. Can I, um, get a ride with you? Back in." Danny turned red. "To the park."

Randy winced. What the hell was he thinking to bring this boy home? He only wanted to give Danny a warm place to spend a night as a break from the homeless camp under the bridge. Now he had to think about sending this small, thin, bruised-up kid back out into the same scary space, alone. His stomach rebelled at the thought.

"You need a safer place to sleep. The Beach isn't good for you."

Danny flushed deeply. "I'll buy a coat with what you gave me last night." His color faded quickly from red to almost-green. "Unless you want the money back." He swallowed hard. "It's there on the dining room table if you want it."

Randy shook his head. "I don't want the money back. I can take you to buy a coat this morning. Maybe some other clothes."

"No. I mean, thanks but if I'm wearing anything new…"

"You'll have to fight or lose it. Okay." Randy finished his breakfast, and Danny leapt to take his plate and cutlery to wash.

"You don't have to do that."

"I want to. To say thank you." Danny wouldn't look at him as he rinsed the dishes and loaded them into the washer. As he bent over, his skinny pale butt flashed. Embarrassed, Randy scooped up the bills he'd deposited on the counter and started reading through them until a beep signaled that the dryer in the utility closet between the kitchen and study was done. Danny dashed over to pull out his jeans, underwear, and sweatshirt. He clutched them to his chest. "I'll, uh, I'll go put these on upstairs."

While he was gone, Randy tapped the counter and thought hard. Finally, he reached for his cell phone.

"This is Joe Mulholland," he heard. Randy had to smile at the soft words in a slight Boston accent from his favorite customer.

"Hey, Joe. It's Randy. Am I disturbing you?"

"Randall! Of course not. I'm always delighted to hear from you, dear heart. Can I do something for you on this beautiful autumn day?"

"I have a question. I know how full up you are at Rainbow Space, but could you make room for a seventeen-year-old? For a few days?"

"Oh, my dear, I so wish I could." Joe sounded distressed. "Every bed I have is taken, and Child Protective Services keeps sending me more names."

"I get it. Listen, is there another place you'd recommend? Something safe for a gay kid?" Not that he knew for sure, but the way Danny reacted to him made it a safe bet he was either gay or bisexual.

Joe sighed. "If only there was. The city runs several shelters, of course, and they do try. But you know the dangers, especially for a young person on his own. Or is it her own?"

"His. It's a homeless boy I met last night. He's been sleeping on the P Street Beach, but I don't know since when. Not very long, I'd guess."

"Covenant House might be a solution. One or two other places come to mind. I can make some calls for you to see if I could locate a placement."

"Would you do that? It would mean a lot to me."

"Of course, Randall. I'd be delighted to help. It might take some time though. Perhaps even a week."

"I understand. Drinks are on me the next time you come in."

"Careful, dear heart. You know I insist upon top shelf vodka."

Randy chuckled. "You deserve nothing less. Let me know if you find anything. Give Terry my best."

Joe rang off, and when Randy turned, Danny stood in the doorway, dressed again in his purple sweatshirt. He tugged at the end of the strings dangling from the hood. His eyes were on the ground, and Randy's stomach lurched again. He couldn't do it. He couldn't push this boy out of his truck and hope he made it through another night. He'd taken on some kind of responsibility for Danny when he rescued him from the muggers, fed him, gave him a haven. He needed time to think.

"You mind hanging out here for a few hours? I'd like to go to the gym."

Danny looked up at him, shy all over again. "It's okay. I can get back to town on my own."

"No. Just hunker down for a bit. I've got cable, or there're books."

After a long moment, Danny blinked. "Okay. Thank you."

Randy grabbed his workout shirt and his sneakers from his bedroom, but he scowled at the rug as he pulled them on. He climbed into his truck and drove the mile to his gym, frowning the whole way. Normally he ran there as a warm-up, but he wasn't in the mood today. He moved through his lifting routine in a slight fog until he nearly dropped an iron plate on his foot and realized he had to get his head out of his ass.

He focused then on his workout and pushed everything out of his noisy brain. Of course as soon as he got his mind off Danny, thoughts of Jack Fraser returned with a vengeance.

It was ridiculous since he barely knew the man. Hell, he didn't even *like* him. Yet something about Jack tugged at him, and Randy wondered if he was having any luck in New York, tracking down the painting he wanted. If he did, that probably meant Randy would never see him again. Jack would return to London and his mystery. The thought shouldn't have bothered him.

On the off chance Jack *did* come to see him again, maybe Randy should get the *Sunrise* painting back from Thomas's apartment where he currently kept it. That way, if Jack finally gave him the full story, Randy could casually invite him out to Arlington to see it. He'd like to talk to Jack about the post-impressionists in which he specialized, and hear about the life of an art historian.

I want to show him the leather and the ropes in my closet and see if I'm right about what he needs.

Dammit, he had to stop fantasizing about that. Concentrating carefully on each press, each position, allowed him to set aside concerns about Danny and his preoccupation with the annoying Jack for a little while. He even reached a personal best on his front squats, carrying down and back up a barbell loaded to three hundred and eighty-five pounds. By the time he re-racked the barbell at the end of a grueling set, he knew what he had to do about one of his problems.

When Randy pulled up in front of his house again, Danny was sitting on the porch in a shaft of sunlight. A paperback was open on his lap, but he was studying the little garden in Randy's front yard. The day was mild enough to enjoy the sun, though the cold snap had yet to break.

He got out of his truck and walked up two steps to join Danny on the porch. Without preliminaries, he said, "My friend Joe is hunting for a safe place for you. It may take him a few days. Until then I'd like you to stay here with me. Still no strings."

Danny's jaw dropped open and then snapped closed again. He looked up at Randy and his eyes narrowed a bit. "I don't get it. You don't know me."

"I trust my instincts. You need a safe place to get on your feet, and I can give that to you."

Danny was silent, though Randy could see his eyes darting back and forth as he tried to calculate the angles. Apparently he gave up, and he exhaled heavily. "Do you mean it?" he asked softly.

"Yes." Randy gave a small smile. "My only condition is that you don't hit on me again. I don't like awkward. Does that work for you?"

Danny nodded and stood. He rubbed his hands nervously on his jeans. "Can I, uh, do anything to help you around the house? I'd feel better about staying."

"You don't owe me anything. I don't want you to barter."

"It isn't that. I just, uh…" Danny gestured widely, a curious hunger on his face.

He needed to be useful, Randy guessed. So he wasn't just a charity case. A sponge. Randy thought about it and finally said, "Tell you what. I hate doing laundry. And I could use help getting my yard ready for winter."

Danny lit up instantly. "I can do those things for you."

He rapped his knuckles twice on the wooden railing of the porch. "Deal. Bed and board until Joe finds you something, and I'll make up a list of chores."

Chapter Six

THEY SETTLED INTO a fairly easy routine. Danny worked hard, so by Saturday afternoon when Randy left to open the bar, the fallen leaves in both the front and back of the house were raked and bagged, dead annuals were pulled from the garden, the grass was cut, and decorative mums lined the walk of the house. Danny even drained the irrigation system to be ready for the first frost.

His bruises faded fairly quickly, and his lip healed until just a small scab remained. He made meals for them, and had something waiting for Randy each night in the warming drawer of the oven when he got back from Mata Hari. He kept his room clean, the laundry done, and the house picked up. As a roommate, he wasn't bad.

Randy tried to be subtle with checking around the house when he got home from the bar each night, and he was relieved when nothing turned up missing. He believed in the maxim "trust but verify," and Danny didn't disappoint.

Still, Randy had lived alone for most of the last twenty-five years, and it made him itchy to have someone share his space. Other than a few short-term boyfriends in his twenties, and of course the fiasco with Trevor, he'd never had to adjust to the presence of another. Small things grated, like remembering to put on clothes before he went downstairs in the morning, or being mindful of the television volume if he turned it on at three in the morning while he ate the food Danny left for him.

Even when he jacked off, he was careful to keep down the moans, and that really sucked because he tended to be loud when he came. Danny respected Randy's instruction not to hit on him again, but he was a normal teenager beset by hormones, and his eyes tracked Randy through the house when he came back from the gym all pumped up and sweaty. Randy had no idea whether Danny was into bears or daddies or muscle, and that was *not* a conversation he was going to enter into with a seventeen-year-old boy. Regardless, Randy qualified for any of those fetishes, and a few others. It was useful and gratifying when he was around men into his own kinks; not so much when he was sheltering a hero-struck kid too inexperienced to hide his desires.

As the days passed, Randy also found himself watching the door at Mata Hari too often. Fraser had said he planned to return from New York on Wednesday, and Randy half-hoped he'd try again to see the *Sunrise* painting that evening. He never showed up. Thursday also passed without a sign of the elegant English-man, and Randy chalked it all up to a momentary attraction and nothing more. Perhaps Fraser had found the painting he was seeking in New York or Philadelphia.

Or perhaps he was unwilling to face Randy again because of the reaction they apparently produced in one another.

Friday evening he found himself standing with a glass in his hand, daydreaming about how it might have been to take Fraser somewhere private where they could explore that longing to submit that Randy detected. He really wished that he'd been able to stroke that beard. It looked so soft and fine that Randy shivered as he imagined Fraser's cheeks brushing down Randy's chest and over his taut belly as he sought Randy's cock.

Damn, I need to get laid.

Monday was looming, and he predicted Danny was going to

be upset when he headed out in his leather. But dammit, Mondays were Randy's play time, and he was getting horny. He'd skipped the previous week, but he needed to cut loose. Get his nut with a willing stranger. That was his love life these days (well, these *years*), and the private club he liked to frequent had a strict leather dress code.

Maybe Danny would be gone by Monday anyway. Joe had struck out repeatedly but he remained hopeful, so Randy was able to put off concerns about what they'd do if no shelter bed turned up. He also tried not to think about what it would be like to return to a dark, empty house at three o'clock every morning.

Over their eleven a.m. breakfast on Saturday, Randy said, "How about I finally take you to get some clothes today? Truth to tell, I'm getting sick of that purple sweatshirt."

Danny dipped his head and smiled a bit. "I'm pretty tired of it too. Where would we go?"

"I get that you don't want anything new and flashy. There's a thrift store on Route 50, not too far away. You could probably score a warm jacket, maybe some shoes and a few shirts there."

Danny focused on his breakfast. "What do you think of these waffles? They're made mostly from protein powder, not flour."

Randy raised an eyebrow. "No kidding? I couldn't tell that." He took another bite and said with a full mouth, "I like 'em."

"I was going through some of your body building magazines yesterday and I came across the recipe. I figured you probably could use a break from all those protein shakes."

"My magazines, huh?" Randy grinned and caught Danny's eye. "I hope the pages aren't stuck together." Danny blushed crimson and Randy laughed. "Shit, I'm just teasing you. Thanks for doing this."

Danny moved his food around with his fork, then looked up at Randy. "I've been wondering about all the art on the walls.

The pictures are real, right? Not posters, or whatever they call them? Like, from Bed Bath and Beyond?"

"You're probably thinking of prints. You're right, though. Most of what I have are original works, not copies. I collected these when I traveled a lot for my old job, before I opened the bar."

"You're really into art, huh? You have tons of books on it." Danny blushed again. "I wasn't being nosy. I just saw them all on the shelves in the study."

"It's not a problem. Yeah, I really dig fine art. Mainly European masters, but also some Asian works, some contemporary stuff. It's what I studied in college for a while."

"Oh? Why'd you give it up?"

Randy hesitated. He didn't want to get into the real reason. He and Danny were already too cozy and comfortable. It was going to be hard enough—on both of them—when Joe came through and it was time for Danny to leave. Keeping some boundaries was important against that inevitable day. "I decided that a career in art wouldn't pay well enough, I suppose," he deflected.

"There are so many pictures. Maybe you could, uh, tell me about some of them? Some time?"

The request made Randy nervous. It implied a longer term than he was prepared to acknowledge. On the other hand, he couldn't resist the opportunity to share a bit with Danny, like Uncle Kevin and his partner Luc always had with him when he was a kid. What could it hurt, really, to let Danny see a bit of his passion?

"Actually, this is just part of my collection. I have a lot more paintings and other original work that I put up at Mata Hari." And stored with friends, and up in Luc's house in Portland. Yeah, he had too much art. It was an addiction. "Anything here appeal to you in particular?"

Danny considered the room and his gaze landed on a rustic scene painted on wood panels. "I like that one."

"Uh-huh. I found that when I went to an auction in Maine, where I'm from. The artist was active in the 1920s and '30s, and she painted on reclaimed wood before it became a fad."

"It seems, I dunno. Homey."

"It does," Randy agreed. "See that young girl heading into the hen house? Think about the way the fall of her skirt mirrors the lines of the house and also of the trees you see beyond. I believe that was the artist saying that the girl belongs right there. She's part of the *essence* of it all."

Danny chewed his lip. His gaze moved to the next painting on the wall. "What about that one? The colors are really pretty."

Randy smiled. "You caught me. That's one of mine."

Danny quickly turned back. "You paint? Is that what you do in the garage at night?"

He chuckled ruefully. "Yeah, that's my studio. It normally relaxes me, though I'm having trouble getting my current one right."

"Oh? What are you painting?"

"Actually, it's going to be a portrait of you, sitting in Del's Diner. Well, it's still in the sketch stage now, but I'll paint it when I know I've got it right."

"Me?" Danny blushed. "Why would you want to paint me?"

"Your eyes have this interesting expression I want to get down. Would you mind sitting for me for an hour or so? I think I could get the sketch right then."

"If you want. What would I have to do?"

"Oh, just sit still. Maybe later today, or tomorrow morning when the light's good. I'll just have you sit by the window and gaze out. It might be boring for you, but we can play music and stuff to pass the time."

"Sure. Whatever." Ah, the classic teenage response. Randy had to smile.

"C'mon. Let's go get you some clothes."

. . .

RANDY LEFT DANNY with a list of additional chores around the yard and the house. It wasn't much—a few hours' work at most—but Danny seemed happy when he was kept busy. It was a relief to see him in a different shirt, pants, and sneakers. Randy left the house to the image of Danny turning and twisting in the mirror, admiring his new-to-him Fall jacket. It was eggplant-hued, another shade of the purple color he seemed to favor. Randy tried not to think about him having to deal with a bag of belongings when he moved to a shelter. Or back to the Beach, if Joe couldn't score a bed.

For Danny, having something he loved meant something he could lose.

Randy's stomach rolled over unpleasantly as he climbed into his truck. *Not yet. I won't worry about it yet.* His thoughts turned instead to Jack Fraser. He still had the business card in his wallet that Jack had offered the previous Sunday evening. Perhaps he should give a call. *Hey, just wondering if you found what you wanted in New York or Philly.*

No, that sounded pathetic. Never mind. *Think about Monday*, he ordered himself.

But he couldn't deny his surge of excitement when the door to Mata Hari opened at five-thirty and a dark-haired, bearded man in a narrow tailored jacket and slim-cut jeans walked through. There was no mistaking the desire in Fraser's eyes when he found Randy behind the bar, and he quickly crossed the floor. Randy nodded a greeting and tried to keep his own face neutral.

"Jack," he said evenly, but he caught a glimmer of a smile as Jack noted that he'd finally used his first name.

"Hello, Randy. I was strolling the neighborhood and I thought a pint of that Flying Dog would go down well." The casualness Jack affected sounded false, but he drew the beer and placed it on a coaster. Jack took a sip and murmured, "Yes, that's quite nice."

"So you've just been hanging around DC today?" Randy asked, reaching for a mild tone.

"Yes, the weather's been smashing these few days."

"You've been back for a while then." It came out too quickly, with a tinge of hurt, and Randy cursed himself for his eagerness. Jack's lips curved into a real smile as he flicked a glance up at Randy with those eyes.

"Since Wednesday. The New York lead didn't pan out and then my appointment in Philadelphia was rescheduled for next week."

A snarky comment about Jack making another run at him in the interim crossed Randy's mind, but he cut it off. His wariness remained in place, yet he couldn't lie to himself and pretend he wasn't glad to see Jack again. No need to go antagonistic. "What have you been doing with yourself?" he asked instead.

Jack took another sip of his beer, then dabbed some foam from his mustache with a paper napkin. "Mainly I've been enjoying the museums here. The variety is truly impressive."

One of Randy's favorite things to do on a free Sunday was to drag Thomas, and often Zachary, through various museums, so he couldn't help but ask, "Which ones have you hit so far?"

"Since most of the museums I'm familiar with in London feature European art, I've been exploring those here that seem peculiarly American instead." He gave Randy a grin. "The National Museum of the American Indian was fascinating."

"It's kind of eye-opening," Randy agreed. "At least if you were raised in the public school system here on the Founding Fathers. When I was growing up, they never taught us about the Native diplomats who tried to negotiate treaties."

"Try visiting a museum in Mumbai about British colonial rule. That will shake your assumptions as well." Jack drank and leaned forward with his elbows on the bar. "The Air and Space one on your Mall is unlike anything I've seen in Europe. We have the Imperial War Museum with its collection of World War II military aircraft, and there's a nice one in Le Bourget, but I find their collections rather narrow and focused. I can't say I've ever been particularly keen on flying, but a few hours at your Air and Space and I came away with a new appreciation of the breadth of the subject."

Randy found himself nodding. "It's a great museum. There's a companion facility out in Virginia called Udvar-Hazy that houses an even larger collection. I haven't been in a few years but the last time I was there, they had a decommissioned space shuttle and the Spirit of St. Louis."

"That's the one Lindbergh flew solo across the Atlantic, correct?" Jack shuddered. "I'm too claustrophobic to think that would have been a fun trip."

Randy chuckled. "I dunno, a little jaunt over the pond sounds like a good time."

Jack rolled his eyes. "Honestly, no one says 'the pond' except in the films or on telly."

"Noted." He dried a few glasses and stored them for easy reach as he asked, "Have you been to the National Gallery of Art? That's my favorite."

"I went to the east building portion. I'm not particularly a fan of the modernists yet I was captivated by the Villareal light sculpture. By many of the exhibits, in fact."

Randy found himself engrossed in a discussion of a variety of the artists whose works were displayed as he and Jack compared their tastes and attitudes to different media. Their conversation paused periodically as he absent-mindedly served a few customers who came in, but the bar stayed relatively low-key for a Saturday. As soon as Malcolm clocked in, Randy gestured for him to handle some new arrivals gathered around a sofa so he could keep talking with Jack.

Even with Thomas and Zachary, Randy couldn't engage in the kind of in-depth discussion he craved. They were interested enough in the major works and artists that Randy showed them but he was always aware of his tendency to go overboard and held back for fear of sounding like a lecturer. With Jack, though, Randy could speak in the same language and let his passion show.

Yet as much as they shared in relaxed talk, Jack didn't mention the *Sunrise* painting once after he arrived, and Randy began to wonder about that. Was the omission contrived to get Randy to lower his guard? Was Jack just trying to get his friendship as better leverage to renew the request?

A dark suspicion tried to intrude on Randy's enjoyment. He *thought* Jack was attracted to him, but maybe that was an act as well. Like with…

Nope. Not going there. Forget Trevor.

Jack inadvertently gave Randy an opening. He took the last swallow of his beer, and as he returned the glass to the counter, he observed, "We have the Tate Modern in London, of course, but the artists on exhibition here seem to come from an entirely different perspective."

That was just what Randy needed to test his theory about Jack. He commented casually, "I read recently that the Tate is bringing in a show dedicated to queer artists next year."

Sure enough, Jack's face instantly shuttered again. *Dammit.*

Straight, or at least deeply in the closet. He has to be.

"That's, uh, yes, I believe I read about that as well." Jack kept his face angled down toward the bar and pushed nervously at the empty beer glass. Randy couldn't resist poking a little, to see what might slip out.

"Will you go? To the queer artists exhibition?"

"Oh, well, perhaps if I find the time." Jack sounded strangled. He looked left and right as if noticing for the first time that Mata Hari had begun to fill with customers while he and Randy talked. "I can tell you're getting ready for the rush so I'd best not keep you any longer." He reached for his wallet but Randy rapped on the bar counter.

"No charge. I enjoyed talking with you about the museums."

"Oh. Well, thank you. Perhaps…"

Randy waited with his head tilted, wondering if Jack would suggest getting together outside of the bar. He could read the conflict in Jack's eyes, and it irked him. Just like the not-quite-right tailored clothes and the almost-too-precise London accent, Jack seemed unable to deal honestly with a man he apparently desired. Which wouldn't have been a problem normally, except Randy was increasingly aware that he wanted more time with the enigmatic art historian. If Jack walked out, though, Randy had a sense the last opportunity would be gone.

So keep him talking.

Jack apparently cancelled whatever he'd been trying to say and turned away from the bar. *Think, Vaughan.*

"I'm surprised, Jack," he blurted out. "You didn't ask me this time about seeing *Sunrise.*"

Well, that was about as graceful as a herd of elephants, but it did the trick. Jack turned his head back toward the bar, then his whole body. A flush crept up his neck, but whether it was embarrassment or anger, Randy couldn't tell.

"To be honest, I saw no point in raising the subject again." Jack tried to sound nonchalant but there was no hiding the flash in his brown eyes or the hunger that leaked into his face. "You know I want to see it, you have my number, and if you decide to permit access you know I'd be very grateful."

"Still thinking about it," Randy said casually, as if he hadn't deliberately tossed a conversational bomb. He wasn't entirely sure why he refused to just show *Sunrise* to Jack. Randy gained nothing by being an asshole, yet he couldn't seem to help himself. Sure his ego had been bruised when Jack dismissed his curating within Mata Hari. It had stung to have Jack shocked that an ox of a man like Randy considered himself a collector. Was he really that fragile that he would churlishly turn his back on art scholarship because his pride had been hurt?

Except he won't tell me why he wants to see the painting. He doesn't trust me.

Jack held his stare for a moment longer before shaking his head and turning away. "I wish you a successful evening, Randy," he called back. Then he was gone, taking the chance to explore his mysteries with him.

Chapter Seven

FRIDAY EVENING WAS a success in business terms. The stream of customers increased steadily, and Randy barely had time to acknowledge his friends Joe and Terry, so they moved over to the piano to sing with Miss Ethel and her crowd. Thomas and Zachary came in a little later after having had dinner in the neighborhood, but they could tell Randy was in the weeds and didn't try to engage him.

A wave of people kept Randy hustling for another solid forty minutes. When a lull finally hit, his friends were still there and he stopped by their stools to take a breather. "What's up with you two?" he asked.

Zachary turned glowing eyes on Thomas, a question on his face. Thomas grinned at him and said, "Go ahead."

He turned back to Randy. "I'm moving into Thomas's condo."

"No shit?" Randy grabbed three shot glasses and poured a round of tequila. "That needs a toast." They all downed their shots, and Randy slammed his glass on the bar. "I'm really happy for the both of you."

"Thanks, Randy," Thomas said. "Zach stays over most nights anyway, so I'm kind of used to him. He's promised to keep his graphic novels and comic books corralled in the den, though."

Zachary laughed. "Don't think I haven't noticed the bookmark creeping through my *Y the Last Man* editions. Admit it,

Thomas. You're hooked!"

"Well, that one is pretty good. Randy, do you think you'd have some time to help us pack boxes and move a few things next week? There's lunch in it for you at Momofuku afterward."

"I can give you a few hours. No sweat. I'm surprised you aren't just hiring movers."

Thomas turned soft eyes toward Zachary again and smiled sweetly. "We could, I suppose, but it seems more momentous if we do this ourselves." Zachary stroked a hand through Thomas's dark hair. Randy watched his fingers comb and wondered how soft Jack's hair would feel.

Nope. The ship has sailed. "Hey, if you don't mind a tagalong, I might have someone else I can bring to help with the packing and moving."

Zachary whipped his head back and his eyes went wide. "Are you seeing someone? I can't wait to meet him. I've been wondering for *months* about your type!"

Randy snorted. "It's nothing like that." He explained about Danny and how he was helping out around his house until Joe found a placement for him. By the time he finished, Zachary was beaming but Thomas appeared concerned.

Randy rolled his eyes. "Go ahead, buddy. Get it off your chest."

"Are you sure this is a good idea? You bringing in a homeless boy, a stranger. You've never even had a roommate, have you?"

Trevor, sort of. But Randy didn't say that out loud. "I trust my instincts. Danny's a good kid. I've left him alone for several days now and nothing's missing."

Thomas shook his head. "That isn't what I mean. Of course your instincts are good. But I can't see you spending this much time with someone and then cutting him loose to live in a shelter or on the streets again."

"Danny's not a puppy. I'm just helping out for a little while like…" Randy cut off what he was going to say, but Zachary, naturally, couldn't let it go.

"Like your uncle Kevin would have, right?"

Damn his intuition. And damn the barrage of memories evoked by such a simple comment.

Thomas and Zachary headed out soon after, and the rest of the night flew by. It wasn't until Randy locked the door of Mata Hari, set the alarm, and climbed into his pickup truck that he gave into the shit storm that Zachary's innocent words rained down on his heart.

• • •

KEVIN CHAMBERS HAD been Randy's hero. His idol. His mom's brother lived near them in Portland, and worked as a Maine state trooper. Uncle Kevin had seen something in Randy even when he was twelve—a deep love of art—that he wanted to nurture despite what his sister and brother-in-law thought.

Kevin took him to museums every Sunday that he was off-duty and spent hours talking to Randy about painting and sculpture. Kevin and his partner, Luc Simard, brought Randy to New York for his fifteenth birthday, and not only sprang for expensive Broadway tickets but spent a full day with him in the Metropolitan Museum.

His mom occasionally tried to understand, but his dad just sneered. "That queer shit," he muttered, and it wasn't clear if he meant the museums or Kevin himself. "He ever touches you, boy, tell me and I'll shoot his ass."

It was so ridiculous that Randy didn't even bother to respond. Kevin was more a father to him than his own dad, and it was Kevin who taught Randy how to be a man. Kevin was a blond giant, even taller than Randy's eventual six-foot-three, and he loved to lift weights and work on his body. So Randy, gifted from his mother's side with a big frame and muscles that were responsive to hard work, wanted to do that too. Kevin helped him train and grow. When Randy went out for football during high school, Kevin worked with him on running, tackling, and throwing.

Randy loved to have dinner with Kevin and the smaller, black-haired Luc. Although not into body building himself, Luc prepared healthy, protein-rich meals to help his partner and his almost-nephew meet their goals. Kevin always asserted that body building was eighty percent about nutrition, so Luc took it on himself to make sure they got what they needed from food. Randy's mom refused to make the dishes that Luc did because Randy's dad didn't like "all that queer rabbit food," so Luc taught Randy how to cook for himself.

When Randy came out to Kevin and Luc in his junior year of high school, neither seemed surprised. They talked with him late into the night about how to approach his parents, but in the end it made little difference. His mom seemed sad and resigned, and begged Randy to keep quiet about it. "What will I say to everyone?" she moaned.

His dad, though. When his dad raged and accused Kevin of molesting his son, Randy leapt to his feet and used his muscled frame to herd his much smaller father into a corner. It was still the 1980s, when gossip and smears could have devastating consequences. In a low but deadly serious voice, Randy growled to his dad, "Neither Kevin nor Luc ever touched me. You repeat that bullshit to anyone else and your teeth are going." His dad never brought it up again as far as Randy knew.

When it came time for college and Randy wanted to pursue art history, his dad sneered. "It's loans or scholarships, or you ain't going. I ain't spending my money so you can be even more of a homo. You pay for it or just go to work. What the fuck is a degree in art history going to do for you anyway?"

Randy remembered telling Kevin he was probably going to try night school at the community college for a while and work in the grocery store close to his house to save up some money for a university.

Kevin and Luc shared a glance, and Luc nodded. Kevin said to Randy, "No, you aren't. You're going to U of Maine or anywhere else you can get into. You'll get as much in scholarships as you can, and Luc and I are going to pay for whatever else you need."

"No way, Kev. You and Luc need to save for retirement."

Luc reached across the kitchen table and gripped his wrist lightly. His bright hazel eyes drew Randy's gaze, and he said quietly, kindly, "Randy, we think of you as our own son. Please. Let us do this for you."

If Kevin had blustered at him, he would have been every bit as stubborn as his uncle and refused to take the money. But the gentle words from his uncle's partner left Randy defenseless. He scraped his chair back and threw his arms around both men. "Thank you. I'll pay you back somehow."

Kevin hugged him tightly. "Make art. Or at least make the world better. That's all we want from you." Randy was still young enough then that he couldn't keep himself from crying.

Two years after that night, Randy was twenty and crossing campus to get to his class in European history when his roommate jogged up and said Randy's family was trying to reach him urgently. It was before cell phones, so he ran to the nearest pay phone and called his mom. He could tell she was crying as soon as she answered.

"Randy? Oh Randy. I got something terrible to tell you." He swallowed hard. Somehow, he always thought afterward, he'd already known. "Kevin was killed. He was trying to calm down this man who was high on something, and the man shot him. Oh Randy. Can you come home right away?"

The funeral was a blur. Kevin had died in the line of duty, and the police gave him the highest honors. It was only when they were entering the church that Randy realized Luc was stopping to enter a pew several rows behind the area reserved for Kevin's family. Anger building, Randy hesitated next to Luc. This was wrong.

His mom tugged his hand and said, "We talked about this, Randy. Luc and me. This ain't the place."

Luc seemed so lost. So helpless. Dark circles shadowed his eyes, and though his hair was brushed and his black suit was neat, he seemed about to collapse. But he reached out and touched Randy's wrist. In his quiet voice, he said, "Sit with your mother. I'll be okay here."

Randy didn't want to make a scene at his uncle's funeral, so he sat in the pew next to his mom. His dad sat on her other side and muttered that the faggots were out of their lives now and thank god. Randy twisted the funeral program in his hands so tightly it ripped.

The graveside service was worse. Chairs were reserved for Randy's mom and the other immediate family, near the coffin draped with the Maine state flag. Randy searched for Luc, and found him in a small throng, blocked from the open grave by the many strangers who came to show their support for a fallen trooper. When Randy's dad took one of the family chairs, Randy had enough. He stepped into the crowd, grateful for his size as well-wishers parted before the expression on his face. When he reached Luc, he took his arm and gently drew him forward.

His mom glanced up as they approached the grave site. "Oh no, Randy. Please don't. Not today. Not here." Some of the officers nearby muttered and turned their heads away from Luc. Randy's dad sneered until Randy leaned down into his face, letting all of his bulk cast his smaller father in shadow, and said one word.

"Move."

His dad turned red and started to bluster, but he must have seen that Randy wasn't going to back off. He slid sideways out of his chair and away from Randy's reach, stepping around to stand behind Randy's mom. Randy lightly pressed Luc to sit and took the chair next to him. The crowd muttered a bit, the troopers were scandalized, and his mom was crying. But Randy heard Luc say in his ear, "Thank you, son," and that was all he needed.

He attended the trial of Henry Winiarski, the man who had killed Uncle Kevin. Just nineteen at the time and strung out on PCP, he had one prior offense for selling drugs. Winiarski was charged with murder, but convicted of manslaughter. Luc spoke at the sentencing hearing of the loss of his friend of twenty years; the prosecutors had warned him not to go further for fear the judge would give a lighter sentence if he knew the deceased officer was homosexual.

It was left to Randy to tell the judge about the uncle who had meant everything to him, and whose life had been snuffed out by a stupid boy who willingly took drugs and went on a rampage with a gun. Randy called Kevin his true father, and he testified about how Kevin had given him guidance, college tuition, even taught him football. The judge was a rabid supporter of law enforcement and apparently a football fan, and he sentenced Winiarski to life in prison.

Kevin had left Luc everything including his insurance and all his benefits, but the State of Maine refused to provide survivor benefits to Luc, and Luc didn't want to fight. When Randy's mother and father tried to contest the will, though, Randy would not let Luc back down. Randy moved into Luc's house and testified against his parents about Kevin's wishes to provide for Luc. It was a near thing but the will was ultimately upheld.

Luc insisted he keep paying for Randy's college, but Randy's world had been shaken. Art was important, but it wasn't enough anymore. Kevin had lost his life, Luc had lost his partner, and Randy had lost his illusions that the world was a fair and good place.

He understood that the love of two men, no matter how sincere and profound, could never be truly safe. He wanted to change that. It *should* be safe, dammit, and fuck people who hated something pure and sweet and good like Kevin and Luc's love for each other. He switched his major from art history to criminal justice and entered a career in law enforcement.

Every few years after that, Winiarski applied for reconsideration of his sentence, or for commutation. Maine had abolished parole in the 1970s, so Winiarksi's options were limited. But he tried again and again. Randy had registered himself and Luc with the victims notification system in Maine; whenever Winiarski tried another avenue, they received word. Each time Randy got one of those notices, anger flared anew. All he had to do was picture Uncle Kevin standing next to him in a museum in New York, and he'd book a flight to Maine to testify before the sentencing judge. He would always move heaven and earth to make sure the court remembered the value of the life that had been taken.

Winiarski's latest attempt to get out of prison came a little more than two years ago. The original judge who sentenced Winiarski retired and a new judge inherited the case, so Randy made an extra effort. He appeared before Judge Carolyn Rhodes in a black suit. He spoke to Judge Rhodes of Kevin's love of justice, and how that inspired Randy to become a Secret Service agent. He described Kevin's love of art and how he tried to honor his uncle's memory by funding a small scholarship to the Maine College of Art in Portland.

But he did not mention Kevin's love of Luc, or talk about the man who grew older and more frail, alone in a small, creaking house he'd intended to share with the love of his life.

It was enough, though. Judge Rhodes denied Winiarski's application, and the world continued to turn.

The money Kevin left to Luc was starting to run low, and Randy worried about the man he considered his remaining father. Luc was still a tough bird, despite the arthritis that crept into his hands. Randy tried a few times to get Luc to move to Virginia and live with him, but Luc always just patted his arm and refused.

"I feel close to Kevin here, and Maine is where I grew up," Luc told him. "I belong here." Randy sent money to Luc every month, but it wasn't like he was rolling in it either. He hoped Mata Hari would truly take off and put him in a better position to care for Luc when he needed it, but that day remained years away.

. . . .

RANDY WAS SO caught in his reverie that he almost missed his exit. He liked Zachary, and he knew Thomas had a shot at a great life because of that young man's presence in it. But that night—really morning—he cursed Zachary for his carelessness in evoking painful memories.

As he pulled his truck into his driveway, Randy saw the lights in the great room were on. Danny was apparently still awake, probably watching a movie. Zachary's words from the bar reverberated in his skull, and he had to agree with the truth of them.

He wanted to help Danny the way Kevin and Luc had helped

him. If Joe didn't find a good placement, Randy would suck it up and tell Danny to stay with him.

He would not send that scared young man back out into the darkness of P Street Beach alone.

Chapter Eight

AFTER A RESTLESS night thinking of Kevin and Luc, interspersed with moments of irrational anger at a slender, bearded Englishman with whiskey-colored eyes, Randy awoke on Sunday morning with a need to push aside all the crap in his head. When they finished breakfast, he posed Danny near the window that overlooked his front garden. The light was brighter than he would ultimately want for the painting he had in mind, but the illumination in Danny's eyes and on the planes of his face would help Randy's sketches. Randy told him he could talk as long as he kept relatively still, and so Danny made random observations about how his mom had loved Halloween, romance novels, and torch songs.

After an hour or so of sketching, Randy put away his drawing materials and then settled on the sofa, feet sprawled in front of him with his computer on his lap and a cup of coffee in easy reach. He was reviewing an article published by one Jack Fraser of the Kensington Museum when Danny set aside his paperback and got himself some juice. As he returned, he passed behind Randy and paused to read over his shoulder. "What's post-impressionism?"

"It refers to a movement that took place in the art world after the influence of impressionists like Monet began to fade." Danny moved around to a chair and tucked his feet under as he sipped from his glass. He kept his eyes on Randy and appeared to be waiting for more. "Do you really want to hear about this?" Danny nodded.

"Anyway, Brousseau was one of the post-impressionists. That's who I'm reading about."

"I guess I've heard that name. Do you have any paintings of his?"

Randy had to laugh. "Don't I wish? Original Brousseaus sell for tens of millions of dollars. But you must have seen pictures of his stuff, right? *Captured Innocence?* His self-portrait? Here." Randy typed into his laptop and pulled up several images of Brousseau's work. As Danny sat next to him on the couch, he leaned in to see the laptop screen.

Randy enlarged the image of a young woman sitting at a dressing table while she contemplated what appeared to be an engagement ring on her hand. "This is *Captured Innocence.* It's probably Brousseau's most famous work. You know this one, right?" He clicked some more, "And this is called *Madonna of the Castle.*" The image of a wealthy woman in fine clothes holding her infant son on her lap, a castle visible through the window behind her, filled his computer screen. The intentional aping of Botticelli's *Madonna* made Randy smile contentedly. "I love this painting. The original hangs in the Getty Museum. I got to see it on a trip out to California."

"It's really pretty," Danny said, and Randy realized the boy's hand was on his knee. Ostensibly, he was resting it there as he leaned in to share the computer, but his fingers were starting to twitch against Randy's leg.

Shit. He really didn't want to embarrass Danny, but this was so not going to happen. For many reasons. Randy groaned inwardly, but he had no choice other than to address this head on.

He sat back slightly to catch Danny's attention and held the boy's eyes as he reached down to remove the hand from his knee. Danny blushed deeply and scooted away.

"We talked about this," Randy said as kindly as he could. "You're safe here, you're my guest, and we're going to get you fixed up. That's it."

Danny glanced everywhere but at Randy. "I'm sorry," he muttered.

"No, don't be sorry. I'm flattered, but nothing is going to happen between us. Okay?"

"Okay." The kid's restless gaze flew around the room; he was desperate to be away from Randy, at least for a little while.

"Why don't you get dressed?" Randy suggested in a brighter tone. "I'll take us out to lunch." Danny practically ran upstairs.

After lunch, Danny asked Randy to bring him to Mata Hari to help out. "There really isn't anything more for me to do out here, and I'd like to help out." Randy saw no reason not to do it, as long as Danny didn't try to sneak a drink, so he introduced Malcolm to Danny and put him to work. Randy kept one eye on him all evening; he was pleased with how Danny did.

A few hours into the evening, a pair of men standing near the bar made a crude comment as Danny walked by with a tray of glasses; his ears turned red. Randy growled pointedly at the duo. "He's underage and off limits, guys. Chicken isn't on the menu here." He maintained his menacing stare until they apologized before taking their drinks to another part of the bar.

With the extra pair of hands to help Malcolm, Randy had time to wander the bar and chat up customers. Some were regulars whose names he was making an effort to learn, and there were a lot of new faces as well. Miss Ethel was sailing through some of the most popular show tunes on her piano, everything from *Avenue Q* to *Hello Dolly* and even *South Pacific*. Her crowd of fans stood three deep and roared the words as she kept the tempo easy and fun. Randy couldn't sing for shit, but he enjoyed the sheer happiness that filled the bar when Miss Ethel had her boys worked up.

Idly, Randy wished that Jack would wander in for a beer. He'd like the chance to talk about an exhibit he noticed was opening in a few days at the Hirshhorn. Maybe he'd see if Jack would like to go with him…

He sighed as his traitorous brain drew him back to the art historian with his unsolicited advice. The man may have been clueless about hurting Randy's feelings, yet it hadn't stopped Randy from spending far too much time pondering someone who was only in town for a short time. *So why do I keep thinking about him?*

Maybe it was as simple as Jack living the life Randy had once wanted for himself. Or was it the vulnerability he sensed? The fear that showed in Jack's eyes? Maybe it was the same thing that made him help Danny, an urge to step in and protect.

He had no answers for himself.

. . .

LATE ON SUNDAY night after Randy closed the bar, he and Danny were settled in front of the TV with takeout Chinese when Randy's cell phone went off. The ring tone was Joan Jett and the Blackhearts' song "Black Leather," and Randy scrambled out of his chair because he knew what that particular ring signified. The screen of his phone showed three-thirty in the morning.

"Mother fuck," he swore under his breath as he read the display.

Danny sat up straight in the chair across which he'd been sprawled. "What's going on?"

"Someone's trying to break into Mata Hari." Randy's phone

rang again; his alarm company this time. He confirmed that the alarm was real, and asked the company to tell the police he would meet them at the bar. He called to Danny, "I'll be back as soon as I can," before hustling out the door, donning his jacket as he went.

Twenty minutes later, he pulled into the driveway he shared with Pyramid. Two police cruisers were parked near the door to Mata Hari, painting the building and pavement with red and blue light. One officer turned to face him, a hand on her holstered weapon, as he climbed out of his truck. She was a tall black woman in full uniform, and she kept her eyes on Randy as he approached her with his hands visible, his driver's license held between his thumb and forefinger. "I'm Randy Vaughan," he called out. "This is my bar."

"Good morning, sir," the officer said and reached to take his license. A quick scan and she nodded. "The alarm service alerted us you were coming. I'm Officer Chavez. We found a broken window on the side, but we haven't entered the premises yet. We have officers watching the broken window and the rear of the building, but no one has come out."

"Understood. Here's the key to the front door." He handed over his ring and started to follow Chavez, but she looked over her shoulder at him.

"Sir, it's better if you hang back and we go in alone, in case one or more persons are still inside."

Randy grunted in frustration but came to a halt. "Okay. I'll wait. The door opens toward you. Main light switch is immediately to the left of the door as you step in."

The officer signaled her partner and waited at the entrance until he joined her. She turned the key, unholstered her weapon, and waited to make sure her partner was ready. He held a flashlight as well as his gun. As soon as Chavez pulled the door open, he swept his beam across the bar. Apparently nothing caught their attention because Chavez stepped inside and a moment later, the house lights came on. Randy tensed as the two police officers moved out of sight.

He waited, kicking at the pavement with hands clenched in his pockets, hating that he was sidelined as others faced danger. Mata Hari was his bar; he should be the one searching. Not for the first time, he reminded himself that was part of being retired. He was a bartender now, not a law enforcer.

After about ten minutes, Chavez came back to the front door and waved Randy over. He jogged up, and she said, "There's no sign of any intruder still on the premises, Mr. Vaughan. The door to your storage area seems to have been how the person got in. Whoever it was must have gone back out the way he came in when the alarm went off, before we arrived. Or possibly through the broken window we found."

"Anything damaged inside?" Randy asked.

"Nothing other than the window that we can tell on a quick sweep, but you'll want to check carefully." Chavez held the door for him as he stepped into Mata Hari. She indicated her partner. "Officer Gentry will accompany you, just in case."

In case the burglar was still inside and in hiding. Randy got that it made sense to be cautious. Gentry tipped his head in a greeting and gestured for Randy to follow him in. "We've looked in each room including the bathrooms but we've tried to leave doors as we found them in case you notice something unusual," he said.

The main room of the bar had the same abandoned air as that moment after last call, when the ambiance Randy created disappeared under too-bright house lights. The door to the coat room was closed, though he was pretty sure he'd left it that way. He touched Gentry's shoulder to get his attention and pointed with his chin. Gentry said softly, "It's empty," but he aimed his weapon upward while he turned the knob to push the door open. The room was bare except for a few forgotten coats hung on the racks. Gentry pulled the door shut again.

Randy led the way to the bar itself and leaned over the counter to confirm no surprise was waiting before he raised the pass. He checked the register but it didn't appear to have been opened. Not that it would've meant much loss since he'd taken the receipts as usual when he left with Danny a few hours earlier.

Gentry started to speak but clammed up when Randy stiffened. A slight breeze caressed his cheek, one that shouldn't be coming from the hall that led to the restrooms and then to his office. The office door was ajar.

He never left that open.

Gritting his teeth, he started down the hall but Gentry stepped in front of him and held up a hand to signal caution. He said in an undertone, "We looked and found no one, but let's go slow." He led the way again but hesitated as they reached the restroom doors. Randy gestured insistently to his office, and Gentry nodded.

Gun pointed straight ahead in his left hand, Gentry used his right to ease open the door. The handle was bent and hung loose where someone had broken the lock. Randy's heart beat faster and his breath came quickly as he followed Gentry into the room, ready to take a swing at anyone who might still be in his personal space. A window to the alley outside was busted and a chilly breeze poured in, making Randy shiver. Given the office door was forced open from the other side, Randy figured the shattered window was the way out of the bar, not in.

Gentry looked behind the door and in corners, but found no one hiding. Randy narrowed his eyes at his computer, intact on the desk and still powered down. He frowned. If someone was looking for an easy score, why didn't he or she take the computer?

They looked into the unisex restrooms together, even though Gentry said they'd been checked once already. Each was for a single person with no stall to hide in. Each was empty.

Moving more quickly once everyone was satisfied that the burglar was gone already, they completed a walk-through of the side rooms and storage area. Even the bottles of high-end liquor were undisturbed.

Finally, they came to a halt in the middle of the main room, and Randy shook his head. "I'm not seeing that anything was taken."

Gentry didn't seem that troubled. "It was probably someone looking for easy drug money and when the alarm went off, he panicked and ran."

"Makes sense," Randy agreed reluctantly, but then he paused as he focused on one wall, specifically at a landscape situated between two arm chairs. The picture was slightly crooked. It was the same landscape Fraser had critiqued in that high-handed tone of his, only the elegance of his English accent preventing it from being an outright insult.

Fraser.

He'd seemed desperate when they spoke the first two times he came in. Desperate to see *Sunrise*. He might have assumed, incorrectly, that the painting was somewhere in the bar, possibly in Randy's private office. That could explain why nothing seemed to be missing.

Gentry had stepped away and was conferring with Chavez about their report. Randy thought fast. He had Fraser's card in his pocket, and he knew the name of the hotel where he was staying. Should he point the police in Fraser's direction? It seemed incredible the man would break in, no matter how determined or needful he was.

More than that, Randy didn't want to think he was involved, but he shied away from the reason. *I'm thinking with my dick. I don't want to believe Jack's a bad guy because I want to fuck him. Simple as that.*

It wasn't that simple, of course, but the situation had hallmarks of the Trevor fiasco all over it. Randy trusted his instincts in most scenarios, except he knew from painful experience he had a blind spot for men he wanted. And like it or not, he wanted Jack Fraser.

He pulled out his cell and sent a text to a stored contact:

It's Randy Vaughan. Would you give me a call when you can? Not urgent, but I could use your help and insight.

Hah. Torres would see right through his good-natured flattery, but he'd gotten to know her pretty well. Even if she suspected she was being played, she'd call him to find out what he needed. She was good like that.

He'd met Detective Maria Torres months earlier when a monster murdered one of his patrons and then went after Zachary Hall. Working with Torres to stop the crime had been deeply satisfying, not only because they saved Zachary, but because he'd been useful again. All of his law enforcement training, his contacts and his experience had come to bear, and Torres had respected what he had to offer. He missed that sense of being valued. Running a bar was great, but it couldn't compare with the satisfaction of standing between a friend and disaster.

By the time Randy boarded up the broken window, wrapped up things with Chavez and her team, reset the alarm, and drove home, it was almost six in the morning. The remaining Chinese food was in the warming drawer. Randy had just fixed a plate for himself when Danny wandered into the kitchen, sleep-tousled hair and flannel pants under the long-sleeved shirt draped over his beanpole frame making him seem like a boy instead of a young man.

"Everything okay at the bar?" He appeared nervous for some reason.

"Yeah," Randy sighed. "Break-in, but I don't think anything was taken. Probably scared away."

Danny squirmed uncomfortably, though Randy couldn't think why. "Who do you think it was?" Danny asked. "What did they want?"

Randy shrugged. "You got me." He kept his eyes on Danny until the kid flushed slightly and turned away. "Danny? Is there anything you know about this?"

"Umm, well, I don't *know* anything." He looked directly at Randy, all earnest and sincere. "But when we were at the bar this evening, I took a break and went out front of Mata Hari. I thought I saw one of those guys who jumped me, and he may have spotted me too. I ducked back inside right away, but I didn't want to say anything and stir up trouble."

Randy thought about that. "So maybe he saw you too and figured you were staying inside the bar?"

"Maybe." Danny seemed eager now. "Or maybe he knows you're the guy who decked him and he was looking for payback, once he knew I was there?"

It was unlikely. Unlikely, but not impossible. "Could be. If you recognized this guy, do you think you could identify a mug shot? Or pick him out of a lineup?"

Danny's eagerness drained away. He started to tug at the edge of his shirt, twisting it in his fingers. "I don't know. Maybe?"

"Good. Tell you what. Tomorrow, I mean later today, I'll contact the officer who took the call and have you give her a description of the guy. It may come to nothing, but at least they'll be on the lookout."

Danny yawned. "You better eat something. I'm going back to bed, okay?"

"Sure. I'll see you later."

Randy ate before heading to his studio. He was exhausted by the sleepless night but too keyed up at the idea of someone breaking into his bar to settle down and go to bed. Fortunately, it was Monday, the day Mata Hari stayed closed, and so he wouldn't have to face a long shift behind the bar with no sleep.

Plus, it was his night to play, thank God, because he was restless and horny as hell. He promised himself he'd get a good long nap in later so he'd be fresh for the club.

In his studio, he began the process of preparing a canvas. He wasn't ready yet to start the portrait of Danny, but it was good to lay the groundwork. He still wanted to draft out a more complete image before tackling the painting itself. As he moved around his studio, he had trouble finding his gesso. And where was his palette knife? Randy shook his head; the forgetfulness was starting to bug the shit out of him.

Eventually he located his materials and finished a coat of gesso on the medium-sized canvas, then picked up his sketch pad to fill in details on the rough image he liked best. Before he knew it, the sun had risen and his cell phone buzzed in his back pocket with the "La Vida Loca" ring tone.

"Maria!" he exclaimed as he answered. "You're up early. The MPD getting tough on you slacking off?"

"Hey, old man. You're the one who usually sleeps until noon. This is normal for me." Maria's sarcastic tone worked like coffee on Randy, and he chuckled. She said, "I'm disappointed you picked up so quickly. I was hoping I'd get to wake you to share my insights."

"Still up, unfortunately. Listen, Maria, I had a weird night.

Someone broke into Mata Hari early this morning. Beat cops came and I went through the place with them, but there was no sign of anything missing. I don't think they even tried to get into the cash register, and they didn't take my computer."

"That ancient piece of shit? You couldn't pay someone to take that."

"Eh. It does enough for me."

"So what do you need?"

"Here's the thing. I think whoever it was might have been after one of the paintings in my collection. A landscape had been moved. You know how I have them on the walls of the bar? I know it sounds small, but I straighten those pictures every night before I leave. At least one was out of place."

"Could they have been searching for a safe behind a painting? Like in a movie?"

"Yeaaah," Randy drawled as he thought about that idea. "It could be that, but I have a different angle I'd like to talk through with you." He explained about the mysterious contacts with Fraser, his reluctance to explain what he was after, and the desperation and fear he saw in Fraser's eyes. "I don't really have a reason to think Fraser would be the type to break in, but there's something going on I don't understand."

Maria was quiet for a minute, but Randy could hear her pen tapping. "It's odd. I'll give you that." *Tap-tap*. "Do you think this painting is valuable? Enough to explain desperation? Maybe trip a guy over into attempting some B&E?"

"Well, I paid about three and a half grand for it, and I was offered six. That's not nothing, but it's not the kind of piece that would draw an international art thief from the UK."

"What about another painting hidden beneath the obvious canvas?"

Randy chuckled. "You've been watching *Antiques Roadshow*

again, haven't you?"

"That show's the *shit*. Leave me alone."

"You need to get a new boyfriend and off the couch before your brain rots."

"Yeah, yeah, thanks for the advice, Mr. Clean. Where's *your* love life heading, Randy?"

"I get plenty of action, thank you very much."

"That's what your friend Scarborough used to say, and look at him now."

Right. Look at Thomas, all paired up with Zachary. Thomas, who had been a confirmed slut, always bouncing from one man to the next, until a kid from Utah stepped into Mata Hari. Now they were moving in together, and probably were gonna start hosting movie nights or some bullshit.

Years of moving around with the Secret Service had put the kibosh on Randy's own boyhood dreams of finding someone who would see him the way Luc had seen Kevin. Always traveling, frequently facing reassignment as he climbed the ranks until he was head of his own protective detail. All that left time for was hookups and random hotel encounters. Until he met Trevor, and look how that turned out.

No, casual sex was what Randy was good at, and sex was enough. At least one perk of retiring early and owning his business was that he could bank on more regular action. His Monday night sessions gave him plenty of opportunities to scratch his itch without cramping his lifestyle. And while Danny was staying with him, sure, it was nice to come home to a house with lights on and dinner in the oven. But he didn't live in a sitcom from the 1950s.

He pushed away the unwelcome rumination and tried to get himself and Maria both back on track. "Anyway. Fraser. What do you think?"

"Well, how about if I drop by his hotel, or give him a call? Rattle his cage a little, and see if it triggers a response."

Randy rubbed a finger along his forehead as he considered that. If Fraser were as desperate as Randy sensed, the plan could backfire. On the other hand, maybe the urge to demonstrate he had nothing to do with attempted burglary would shake something loose. Help to make sense of the situation.

"I think that's a good idea. It won't get you in any trouble with your captain?"

"It won't take long, and Captain Nelson knows how much you did when we rescued Hall. Read me the number he gave you." Randy recited the UK cell number from Fraser's card and repeated the name of his hotel. "Got it. I'll push him a bit, let you know what I learn."

. . .

RANDY SPENT HIS morning attending to personal shit like bills, but he was surprised when he ran out of chores he needed to do. Having Danny around really freed up his schedule. The kid had finished the laundry and yard work, even vacuumed and dusted.

By early afternoon, Randy was dragging ass from lack of sleep, and he wanted to be fresh to enjoy his night at the club. Danny had made himself scarce since they had lunch, so Randy holed up in his room and stripped nude before crawling into the sheets. He'd just started to doze off when his cell phone buzzed. When Randy glanced at the display and read "Tightass Torres," he picked up the call.

"Hey, Maria," he said around a yawn. "What's shaking?"

"It's the accent, isn't it?" she asked. "I talked to Fraser. It's that English accent that has your boxers in a bunch."

"I don't know what you're talking about," Randy huffed.

She chortled "Okay, have it your way. Mr. Jack Fraser of

London, England, was very cooperative. We met in person, and I'd suggest you get some fashion advice from him. Those fitted clothes he wears. *Muy caliente.* Anyway, he told me the same story he gave you, about wanting to see a painting you bought a few years back. He says he was in his room alone last night, so he doesn't have an alibi for three in the morning, but that isn't unusual in and of itself. I flashed my badge and the hotel clerk pulled up the key card records for me, even though he technically should have waited for a subpoena. The door to Fraser's room was unlocked at eleven fifteen the night before, and not again until nine this morning."

"What was your take on Fraser? Straight up guy, or shifty?"

Maria was silent for a moment. "I'd go with straight up. I saw the edge that you mentioned, the fear, and I agree—there's something more going on than he's saying. But breaking and entering? No."

Randy found himself nodding. "Thanks, Maria. It means a lot to me that you did this."

"*De nada.* I should warn you, though. Fraser was *pissed.* I mean, it was clear you were the one who gave me his name and contact details."

He snorted. "Fine, I'll prepare myself for a tongue lashing from a vindictive curator."

"Yeah, you'd like a tongue lashing from that oh-so-proper guy, would ya?"

"Get back to work, Torres. That's my tax dollars at work for you to yank my chain."

"Heh heh. Yank your chain…"

Randy disconnected while Maria was still teasing him. He returned his phone to the night stand, crossed his arms over his chest, and thought. He was relieved by Maria's assessment of Jack, and that troubled him slightly. He was self-aware enough to know it was more than having Maria second his judgment. That was reassuring, of course, but it didn't tell the whole story. The fact remained that there was something off about the art historian, something that made Randy suspicious despite his desire.

Is that why I don't just show Jack the Sunrise *painting? Because I can't reconcile the secrets with the attraction? Or is it because once I show him the painting he'll have no more reason to come around?*

The problem worried at him until exhaustion finally carried him off to fitful dreams.

Chapter Nine

"RANDY? DO YOU want some dinner?"

Danny's voice through his bedroom door woke Randy with a start. He was disoriented for a moment, but remembered to twitch the comforter over his naked body before calling out, "What was that?"

The door creaked open and Danny leaned his head in. His eyes went wide as he saw Randy stretched out on the bed, and he turned red. "Oh, sorry. I was just checking to see if you want something to eat."

He glanced over at the clock on his table. Already nine in the evening. Geez, he really had been exhausted to sleep so long. "Sure, sounds good. I'll take a shower and be down in twenty minutes or so."

Danny withdrew, and Randy headed for the shower. Once the falling water cleared the cobwebs, he started to get a little turned on. It was Monday night, at last. Time to indulge himself. As water sluiced down his body, he imagined hands stroking his skin. His dick started to get hard, and he gave it a tug as he turned his shoulders left and right to enjoy the warmth cascading down his back and the warmth building in his balls. As tempting as it was to go for an orgasm, he wanted to save it for the club so he finished up his shower quickly.

Once dry, Randy grabbed his clippers and trimmed the fringe of hair around the side and back of his head until it was just fuzz again. The rest of his scalp had been bare since he was in his late twenties, and what was left of his brown hair had turned mostly gray, but he didn't mind the look. He rubbed some moisturizer over his scalp and face. He'd begun doing that early, which might be why people tended to think he was younger than fifty-one. *Or maybe that's just what they say to get into my pants?* Randy snorted at himself in the mirror.

Maybe no one would call him handsome, but he still got noticed. Usually, he figured it was people drawn to his size. When he was young, attention came easily and he took it for granted. Men liked to rub up against his big body, stroke his hairy chest, squeeze his arms and his thighs. Yes, he worked damn hard for his muscle, but a lot of it was lucky genetics too. Any time he was hot for company then, he could just go into a bar, lean against the wall with a beer, and weed through the contenders who approached him until he found whatever he wanted that night.

By the time he was forty, the pickings were slimmer, and he had to work a lot harder to find someone to play with. Oh, plenty of men still wanted the muscle and the experience, but he also had to endure the occasional dismissive looks as some twink in his twenties slid a quick glance over his graying hair and moved on without a pause, or shook his head when Randy tried to strike up a conversation.

These days, even though he was past fifty, plenty of customers at Mata Hari hit on him. Fucking around with someone who came regularly to his place of business seemed unwise. Crude, maybe. Notwithstanding his unusual reaction to Jack, he was determined to keep his sex and work lives distinct. When he went to the D/s clubs or leather bars, though, it was often just the guys seeking a muscle daddy who responded when he offered to buy a beer. That was fine. He still enjoyed the dynamic, even if sometimes he was putting on a performance for a visitor from the Midwest who watched a lot of porn and hoped Randy would show him what the rough stuff was like in real life. He could do that, though he occasionally ended up feeling like an extra in a stranger's dirty fantasy. But who was he to bitch? He still got sex most of the time he went hunting for it.

Out of the bathroom, he hesitated in front of his open closet. Normally he'd go ahead and pull on his leather gear for the night, but Danny's presence made him pause. *Yeah, this is gonna be awkward.* He pulled on sweats for the time being and headed downstairs.

Danny had prepared chili in Randy's crock pot. An opened beer sat at Randy's place on the table, so he took a big swallow while Danny finished up. "Smells really good, kid."

Danny glanced at him and blushed. "It's nothing special, but I think it turned out pretty well," he said as he carried two bowls to the table and placed them next to a variety of toppings already laid out. Randy helped himself to shredded cheese and sour cream while Danny spooned some jalapeños onto his own bowl.

Randy tucked in, then grunted his approval. "This is perfect chili. Thanks for going to so much trouble."

"It's no trouble. Just something I learned from my mom."

They ate in silence for a moment, then Randy decided he had to get it over with. "Listen, Danny. I'm going out tonight, so you'll have the house to yourself. Or if you want to go into Washington for a late movie or something, I can give you a ride."

Danny's head shot up. "I thought the bar was closed on Mondays."

"It is. This is personal."

"A date?" The sullen edge to Danny's tone bothered Randy, but he chose not to comment.

"Not exactly. There's a club I like to go to on my night off."

Danny's big eyes were fixed on him. "It's a leather club. I may be out all night."

Silence filled the room, though Randy could swear he heard Danny's heart pounding. He'd tried to avoid this situation, but Danny's crush on him was painfully obvious. And never more so than at that moment, when Danny looked like a kicked puppy. Finally, he asked, "Will you be okay alone tonight?"

Danny swallowed hard, blinked, and then nodded. He turned back to his bowl of chili and didn't meet Randy's eyes through the rest of the meal. As soon as Randy finished, Danny swept his bowl away and began to clean the kitchen. Randy waited, but he didn't really know what he expected to happen. It wasn't likely that Danny would ask him any questions or make small talk about where Randy was headed. He didn't owe Danny an explanation in any case, and he didn't want to do anything to encourage the crush.

Still, guilt and unease warred with the chili in his stomach. He carried his empty beer bottle to the kitchen and laid a hand on Danny's shoulder. "Are you going to be okay?" he asked again, softly.

Danny flicked a glance at him and said quickly, "I'm fine. You have a good time. I'll..." He choked off, then straightened and tried again. "I'm just going to watch another few episodes of *The Walking Dead* on Netflix and then go to bed."

Randy felt sorry for the kid as he returned upstairs. He'd had his share of crushes when he was Danny's age. He knew how real it could seem, and how much it hurt when the affection wasn't returned. But what was he supposed to do? He'd been consistent from the beginning about turning down Danny's hints and advances. Short of kicking him out, he didn't see anything he could do differently.

Randy took a deep, centering breath to push away the awkward dinner. He opened the closet where his gear was stored and let the scent of leather begin to guide him to the head space he craved. The light came on automatically and illuminated his second, more private hobby.

The sight of his leather did things to him for which he had no explanation. Maybe it was why he endured the occasional sting of rejection and the disappointment of being nothing more than a one-time fantasy. He still had a reason to don the armor and step into the safe spaces where his leather was more than a costume.

Ever since he was a teenager and stumbled across a copy of *Drummer* magazine, he'd been lost to it. The images of muscular men in harnesses and chaps, arm bands and jocks, had stirred something unexpected and primal. He lusted after the football players he saw naked in the showers after practice, sure. But the men he saw pictured in *Drummer*—sometimes hairy, sometimes with bellies, and always *men*—oh he wanted them so much more than any teenager in his high school gym.

He never found a way to talk to Kevin or Luc about it, even though they might have understood. The leather was so important that he couldn't take the risk someone might make fun of him. Over the years, it became his obsession, second only to his love of art. At first he bought just a small armband or a strap. Later, when he made a little more money, he acquired his first vest.

Only when he got older and went into a few leather bars did he discover that some leather men frowned on those like Randy who paid for their gear instead of waiting to be gifted it by a mentor who decided he'd earned it. He went that route for a while with different men who taught him about the leather community and being a top man, but ultimately they wanted a deeper commitment to the culture than he was willing to make. The leather was highly personal for Randy, and following others' expectations of what it should mean dulled his enjoyment.

He'd ultimately amassed a treasure trove of purchased and gifted gear, and it was something he discussed with no one outside of the scene. Well, that wasn't quite true. He and Thomas had talked about it, one drunken night when Randy confessed what the leather meant to him. As close as they were, though, Thomas didn't really understand. He had his own needs and hidden desires and would never judge Randy, but he didn't get the allure of the second skin. Maybe no one ever would.

Randy dropped his sweats to the floor and began to dress again, from the skin out. A strap went around his balls and cock and snapped into place, presenting his set for display should anyone get him naked that night. A black jockstrap with a blue waistband covered the jewels next. He pulled on a pair of silk-lined leather pants that strained around his heavy thighs and his meaty ass, and buttoned up the front. They were slung low to reveal the sharp cut of his groin. With each piece of gear, he grew stronger and more real. Tense with promise and confident as his secret self took over.

He debated for a while over his harnesses before choosing instead a bar vest that barely covered his nips and left his hairy chest and tight stomach exposed. A wide leather band covered his right bicep. A narrower one fitted around his thick left wrist. He opened a drawer and retrieved a silver ring to replace the simple bar threaded through his right nipple, then gave it a tug or two until the delicious pull went straight to his balls.

He stepped into his leather boots. Often he added a motorcycle hat but tonight he liked the shine of his bare scalp. He grabbed a pair of black fingerless gloves. Stroking a hard dick with a leather-covered palm made it that much hotter and intense for both parties.

Randy stepped back to study himself in the full-length mirror. It was a good look for him. His hours at the gym showed in his arms and shoulders, and the gray in his chest hair drew the men hungering for a leather daddy. The vest revealed that he took good care of himself. The leather pants molded and presented his big package just right. Randy flexed his hands in their gloves and let the slight creak of leather crank him up. *Hell yeah, it's going to be a good night.*

He slipped some condoms and small packets of lube into the pocket of his pants. He'd leave his wallet with his jacket. The club owner wisely had a system for regular patrons so they could sign for their drinks or whatever else they ordered; it avoided the need to carry cash or a credit card around the club, simplifying matters greatly. After grabbing a leather motorcycle jacket, Randy hurried down the stairs and called out a farewell to Danny so he wouldn't have to face the kid in his full gear.

Traffic was reasonably light, so just twenty minutes later, he parked his truck near the club on Fourteenth Street in northwest DC. From the road, the building was fairly nondescript. A shop that sold stuffed animals, apparently destined for traveling carnivals, attracted the attention of passers-by, so they rarely noticed the small door to the left of the display window and the brass plaque that read "Cuir." Even if they did, few would recognize the French word for "leather."

Randy rang the buzzer beneath the plaque. "Yes?" came through the intercom. Sounded like Liam.

"It's Randy Vaughan," he said, and the door clicked as Liam unlocked it remotely. The stairs leading up to the second-floor club were black, and the walls of the stairwell were painted a dark blue. It was maybe over the top, but Randy liked that it set a tone.

At the top of the stairs, he brushed through a curtain that newcomers usually failed to register was made of dozens of whips hanging down. Liam greeted him, all dapper and respectful in his neat black leather jacket cut like a sports coat, worn over a crisp gray shirt and patterned blue tie. Liam had short white hair styled forward on top, and a beard that framed his narrow, craggy face elegantly and gave him gravity. His large dark eyes twinkled in welcome.

The anteroom where Liam waited next to a host stand was done in a more welcoming shade of blue than the stairs and was lit pleasantly with a torchiere and small lamp that rested on a mirrored table alongside a chair in black leather and chrome. Liam held out a hand to Randy as he entered the room.

"Good to see you, sir." Liam turned a guest book around, and Randy signed his name. "Can I take your jacket, or will you keep it with you tonight?"

Randy shrugged out of the garment. "Yeah, I'll leave it out here. Thanks." He placed his keys and wallet in the inner pocket before handing it over. Liam opened a cabinet to place the jacket on a padded hanger, then turned back. He ran appraising and approving eyes over Randy.

"If I may say so, sir, that's a very nice look. It's quiet tonight so far, but I don't think you'll have trouble finding someone to keep you amused." He grinned slightly, and Randy returned it. Once upon a time, he'd had Liam keep him company for an evening. Liam knew what he liked, including the "sir."

"Anyone new tonight?" Randy asked.

"A few fresh faces. Have a good time, and please tell Patrick I said your first drink is on me."

Randy clapped Liam on the shoulder and stepped through the door Liam opened for him to the interior of Cuir.

The main room of the club filled most of the second floor. A narrow bar drew the eye, with discrete pinpoint lights making the bottles of liquor shine like jewels. Patrick, the bartender, wore a short-sleeved leather shirt, open at the neck to reveal a thick strip of studded leather wrapped around his throat. He smiled wickedly in greeting to Randy and immediately began to pour a drink for him.

Heavy velvet drapes created a semblance of dark corners for those who wanted to pretend at privacy, while spotlights carefully hit two of the sofas for those who preferred to put on a show. At the moment, a young blond man was on his knees before a rugged guy who sat illuminated in the beam of the spot, stroking a hand over the head bobbing into his lap. Randy's dick stirred in his jock at the display.

There were few chairs or stools, but round, bar-height tables punctuated the space to provide convenient resting places for drinks when the moment warranted. A closed door with an electronic lock was tucked to the rear of the room. Regular patrons could, with Liam or Patrick's permission, step through that door to claim one of the private rooms on the second floor, or—once the proprietors were satisfied no party was impaired—climb the stairs to the third floor with its more creative selection of implements, tools, and toys. Randy was definitely in the mood to take his evening up there, should the right partner catch his attention, so he planned to limit himself to one drink.

Patrick slid a Captain Morgan spiced rum and coke toward Randy when he reached the bar. "Liam said to tell you this one is on him," Randy said, and Patrick nodded.

"Are you meeting anyone here tonight, or playing the lottery?" Patrick asked with a wink.

"I'm here alone. Anyone interesting around?" Randy asked.

Patrick seemed thoughtful. "Well, you've already had some fun with Claude before. Are you up for another session? I happen to know he was most appreciative last time." Randy followed Patrick's gaze to a tall, thin man in a skintight rubber shirt. A memory flickered of Claude sobbing and yet arching back into Randy's hands while he applied cream after an intense session with the flogger. The man was facing away from them, and Randy quickly turned his attention back to the bar.

"Claude wasn't bad, but he needs a lot of after-care," Randy murmured. "I'm not that nurturing this evening."

Patrick laughed. "Nurturing is not a word I'd use for you, ever. Not that I'm criticizing." He winked, and Randy flashed to a very pleasant evening upstairs with Patrick, long before Liam had collared him and given him an ownership interest in Cuir. Patrick was very responsive and vocal, and Randy would gladly have another go at him were he not in a relationship.

That might be an odd line to draw, but Randy never knowingly took on a session with any man already partnered up, even in a threesome. Whatever worked for people—open relationships, cheating, cuckolding—was their business. It simply didn't work for Randy.

What Kevin and Luc had shared was the ideal, even if the two of them sometimes had trouble living up to it. He remembered a time as a senior in high school when he came into their house to find Luc red-faced and crying while Kevin slammed cabinet doors like a wounded bear.

Eventually Randy had gotten the story from Kevin. Luc had been out of town at a work convention, drank too much, and ended up in bed with someone. When he confessed, the news devastated Kevin. Randy had never seen him so broken up, and Luc was beside himself with guilt and remorse. It took a few days for Kevin to forgive Luc, and weeks for things to settle down. For a while, Randy really thought they were going to break up.

It occurred to him then that sex, no matter how good, was common and easy, but a real relationship was rare and precious. He never wanted to be the cause of pain like he'd seen on Kevin's face. So Patrick was off limits.

"Why don't you take on a submissive?" Patrick asked. "Really get to know someone so you can push his limits, and he can push yours?"

Randy shook his head. "That isn't me. I get off on this scene part-time, but I don't think I could live it full-time the way some of these Doms do. I compartmentalize too much, you know?"

"I do know. And you're not the only one. Many of these guys have intense jobs. Some of them need D/s all the time to help them manage the stress of their public lives. But a lot are like you. They want to do this for an evening, but then go back to something more vanilla where they don't have to think about the power-exchange constantly."

"Exactly," Randy agreed. "If I ever found myself in something longer term, it would be where the two of us are, I guess, friends in our daily lives more than top man and sub, and the power-exchange happens only when we want it or need it."

Patrick gave him a sly smile. "That's more like my relation-ship with Liam than you'd probably expect."

Time to change the subject to something less esoteric and unlikely than Randy's love life and back to the reason for his visit. "Speaking of, Liam mentioned a few new faces, but I'm only seeing the same players."

Patrick glanced up from the drink he was pouring. "There. Against the pillar on the left, talking to Jorge. He's new tonight; came in as a guest." With a wink, he added, "*Just* as a guest. He's not together with Jorge."

Randy found his friend Jorge Castillo in the small crowd before he shifted his attention to the man with him. His back was to the bar, but what Randy saw made his dick pay attention. The man was slender and wore a harness over bare skin, and the sleekly muscled body on display made Randy's hands itch to touch. Tight leather pants accentuated narrow hips and a beautifully high ass. The man had thick hair, but it was hard to see the color in the dim light of the bar. Maybe dark brown?

Randy tensed. It couldn't be…

Then the man tilted his head back and laughed at something Jorge said. Even the laugh sounded English.

It was Jack Fraser.

Chapter Ten

JORGE SPOTTED RANDY gazing in their direction and gave a friendly nod. Jack turned, still laughing, but when his eyes met Randy's he froze. Even at a distance Randy saw a riot of emotions race across that handsome face. Shock was utmost, but quickly gave way to desire. Heat.

And all that was swept away by rage.

As Jack stalked across the room toward the bar, Randy sipped his drink before shoving it aside. Although Jack stopped a foot away, Randy could see blown pupils, flared nostrils, and a tight mouth. His chest, heaving under his harness, was lightly covered in soft dark hair. He was sex on two legs and Randy couldn't recall the last time he'd wanted someone so much.

Not that it seemed likely he and Jack would be getting intimate.

"You sent the police to interview me," Jack hurled at him, barely louder than a hiss.

Randy stood up straight and let the six-inch difference in their heights register. He waited a beat, then shrugged. "I did. My bar was broken into, and I thought it was important to investigate anything out of the ordinary." Jack started to sputter a response but Randy cut him off. "And you are definitely out of the ordinary."

Jack snapped his mouth shut on whatever he'd been about to say. Confusion clouded his expression, though his jaw and fists remained tense, and he nearly shook with the warring emotions in his body. His eyes narrowed and he tilted his head, clearly trying to decide if Randy was mocking him. "What does that mean?" he finally got out.

Randy met his gaze steadily. "Are you sure you want to have this conversation standing here?" Jack glanced around and suddenly seemed to realize Patrick was in earshot, Jorge had followed him over to Randy, and other men were interested in their confrontation. The fury in Jack's eyes gave way to dismay and the same fear he'd let show at Mata Hari.

Randy took his elbow and crooked his head. "Follow me." He gave a calming gesture of his hand to Jorge, then led Jack to a corner. The arm he could feel through his glove was strong and wiry; Jack could have resisted but he went along with being led. Nevertheless, tension rolled off his skin. Randy positioned him with his back to the velvet curtains in a semi-alcove for some privacy, dropped his elbow, and crossed his own arms. "Now, what do you want to say to me?"

Jack's face reddened and his eyes blazed but he kept his voice down when he spat out, "Listen 'ere, Randy. Who the *fuck* do you think you are, sending the police onto me?" As he ranted, the posh London accent slipped and something rougher, less refined crept into his words. That accent had no business turning Randy on. "I eksed nice like several times, which you chose to ignore like an arsehole. Fine, that's your prerogative. You said no an' I walked away. What fact in that story makes me seem a sodding *burglar?*"

Randy's own temper flared. "I turned you down three times and you kept coming back. You are so intent on seeing the *Sunrise* painting that it's painful to watch, yet you refused to give me the barest explanation of why you need to see it. You apparently even followed me to this club—"

"Now hold on right there, you tosser," Jack sputtered at him. "I'd no idea you'd be here. I had no notion I'd know anyone here other than Jorge." He turned pale. He almost whispered, "I dinna think anyone would see me." Anger apparently returned to mingle with the fear, and he spat, "I suppose you'll tell your bird in the police about this as well, right? Give her more reason to come after me?"

"Fuck off, limey," Randy responded with narrowed eyes. "I don't know what your problem is but I have no desire to out anyone for getting his kink on."

"His *kink*?" Jack was incredulous. "You don't know me, yet you treat me like I'm nowt." His eyes widened again. "It's 'cause I insulted your art collection. That's why you're so hard with me, innit?"

Randy couldn't stop himself. "I built my collection piece by piece as I traveled the world. Every fucking work of art I own means something to me. I couldn't give a shit what a phony git masquerading as an historian thinks of what I hang in my bar."

"*Phony*? You effing…" Jack sputtered himself into near apoplexy. "What are you implying? I am highly credentialed—"

"Yeah, yeah, I know you have the university degree. But c'mon. That accent you affect? I can hear the country burr, especially now that you're angry. Somewhere in the north of England, is it?"

All the things Randy had been observing came together in his head and he found himself making an indictment he hadn't consciously assembled.

"You wear your fancy clothes like a costume. I see how uncomfortable you are in them. You're worried someone will snatch your discovery out from under you, whatever it is, which maybe explains your desperation. My guess is you'll lose your position at the Kensington if you don't produce an original piece of scholarship. And now this? Coming to not only a gay bar, but to an exclusive *leather* bar in a city far from home, obviously terrified someone will tell on you? You live at least one lie, maybe more."

Jack stared at him with his mouth hanging open. After a long moment, he groaned. "How...?"

Randy wasn't ready to let up. He dropped the timbre of his voice to a low register that would be a caress. "I'll tell you what else I see, Jack Fraser. I see through the veneer. I see a man who came here hoping to be set free, if just for one night." Jack snapped his mouth shut, but his eyes opened even wider. Randy saw the truth of his own words in his slumping shoulders, the quiver of his lip. The urge to surrender before Randy's anger.

"I could give you that," Randy murmured. Desire bloomed in Jack's face as he seemed to imagine himself in Randy's hands, until Randy took a step closer and leaned down to whisper in his ear. "But I won't. Because you don't trust me. And until you trust, you can't fly free."

Then he turned to walk away, ridiculously satisfied with himself and ready to leave the mess that was Jack alone in a dark corner.

He made it two steps before he heard the words.

"Randy. Wait. I'll... I'll tell you."

He froze. *Shit.* He hadn't acknowledged to himself how much he wanted that until it was offered. As Randy slowly turned back, he realized it wasn't even the actual secret Jack was keeping. It was the *trust* he craved. That was his greatest weakness.

Jack stood rigidly, elbows slightly bent and arms across his belly as if he were protecting himself from a blow. His face was a picture of fear and desire. The lean muscles under his harness were tense; he quivered, almost like a race horse about to run. Randy's mind leapt ahead and he could already imagine that warm, taut skin under his fingers. He knew what it would be like to strip off his glove and put his palm right up to Jack's rippling stomach. He wanted to stroke the soft beard, and have it brush over his own belly on Jack's way south.

His eyes on Randy's burned with his need and Randy thought irrationally that he could lose himself in their gold-flecked depths. But if Jack were going to do this—really give his trust to Randy—then it shouldn't be in the open where curious men could hear. Randy wanted this gift too much to treat it casually, and even though he was using his voice and presence to draw out the truth, he owed it to Jack to help him keep his secrets from others.

He gestured for him to wait, then found Liam for a quick conversation. Liam looked over Randy's shoulder to satisfy himself that Jack wasn't impaired, then nodded. Randy returned and said in the steady, assured manner that had led teams of Secret Service agents into and then out of danger, "Follow me."

He didn't even glance behind as he walked to the door leading to the private rooms. A click sounded as Liam unlocked the door remotely, and Randy guided Jack through it and down a short hallway to where he selected a smaller room. He held the door until Jack brushed past him, then flipped a discreet sign to "occupied."

Jack studied the room, facing away from Randy. It was on the small side, perhaps ten by fifteen feet. A bed took up more than half the space. A deep couch stood against one wall, facing two straight-backed chairs, and a short cabinet lined the third wall. Randy was aware of the various items it contained; maybe not for that night, though. Every instinct told him that touch and taste were the only tools they would want.

On top of the cabinet were decanters of different kinds of liquor. He poured two small measures of bourbon into tumblers, breathed in the aroma from one glass, then offered Jack the other.

Jack turned to look up at him as he accepted the drink, still a-quiver, his cheeks flushed. Randy could almost feel the ache in his bones. He was ready to ease the ache and give him exactly what he needed, as long as he got what he wanted first.

He held Jack's gaze as he tossed down his bourbon, and Jack sipped at his. When he grunted in appreciation, Randy had to smile. "Liam stocks good stuff in these rooms, but he makes us pay for it. No liquor upstairs, though."

Jack had a quizzical light in his eyes, but Randy waved it away. "I'll explain some other time. Now, I believe you have something to tell me, and then we'll see where the evening goes from there." He set his glass back on the cabinet, strolled to the couch, and seated himself. Jack started to do the same but Randy held out his hand, palm up. "No. Finish your drink, then stand there and wait." Jack gave the slightest noise, something between a protest and a groan, but he obeyed.

Randy kept him standing there for a full minute. The tension in the room grew as he ran his gaze over Jack's body appreciative-ly and rested a palm on his own full crotch. Jack tracked his hand, so Randy stroked it over his covered dick. There was no mistaking the sound of desire he made this time, or the growing bulge in his own tight pants. Perhaps he thought Randy would let him off the hook on his truth-telling, and they would move right to the physical portion of the night. *Wrong. First I get what I need.*

"On your knees." Randy broke the silence in an even tone that was nonetheless an order, and Jack jerked his eyes from Randy's dick to his face. He hesitated, but then placed his glass on the cabinet before carefully lowering himself to the carpet.

"Hands behind your back. Clasp your wrist."

Jack did so, allowing Randy to admire the stretch of the har-ness over his hair-dusted chest. His eyes had dropped to the ground, so Randy ordered, "Look at me." Jack raised his gaze again, and Randy was vindicated at what he found. As he'd expected, Jack was responding to the dominance in Randy's voice and manner, and it gave him freedom to drift away from his own doubts and fears.

Where earlier his chest had heaved with anxiety, under Randy's directions his breathing was calm and deep. The jaw that had tensed in anger hung slack. His shoulders had relaxed too, making him seem more natural and elegant in the harness than he did in his tailored suits and jackets. His face was lightly flushed, his eyes shone, but there was a subtle glow about him as he settled and found his center. He was sinking into obeisance and paradoxically coming alive.

Randy stood and let Jack's eyes wander over him too, then he removed his vest and draped it across one of the chairs. "You know what I'm offering, Jack. The battle I see going on behind your eyes tells me you're always on edge. Always struggling." He studied the upturned face. "You're careful. Rigid." And in a softer tone, he added, "Afraid."

Jack hesitated, then gave a short nod. He began to say something, but Randy held up a finger. He slowly approached, subtly flexing and tightening the muscles of his chest and arms to draw attention as he said, "It's exhausting, isn't it? Holding everything together that way. I'll take that burden from you. I'll keep you safe in here, so that you can just *be*." Relief and desire melted into gratitude in his eyes. His need was palpable in the small room, but Randy asked anyway. "Do you want that? Do you want to hand over your control to me? No words. Just show me."

He blinked at him for a moment, then bent carefully from the waist and rested his lips on Randy's boot. "Good man," Randy praised, and heard a pleased sound rise from Jack's taut body. He brushed his face and beard against the side of Randy's boot as he levered himself back into a kneeling position and turned his face up to meet Randy's again.

"Eyes closed," Randy directed. He walked over to Jack and moved behind him. He was quiescent now; no more tremors showed. *Perfect.* Randy rested a gloved hand on his head, then combed his fingers through the beautiful richly brown hair. He'd longed to do that for days, and the hair was as fine as he'd imagined. Jack made a rumbling, happy noise in his throat, and he didn't shy away. Randy stroked his other hand over his shoulder, and the sound of leather skimming over skin was a whisper. Jack tipped his head so it rested against Randy's forearm. He was still.

He was ready.

Randy returned to sit on the couch and crossed one leg over his knee. "Eyes open and on me," he growled, and Jack slowly focused. Randy crossed his big arms and flexed to hold concentration as he said, "Now. Tell me."

Jack blinked, and Randy watched as the struggle surfaced again in his eyes. It had to be his decision. The moment stretched, and he licked his lips as he fought a final skirmish within himself.

When he spoke at last, it was in a rasp. "The painting I want to see... I've done a lot of research, and I think I can prove..." He stopped again and swallowed hard.

Randy took slow, deep breaths that Jack mimicked unconsciously until the turmoil in his warm eyes gradually cleared. Finally, *finally*, he let his secret out in a rush.

"I think it's an original Brousseau."

Chapter Eleven

"AN ORIGINAL BROUSSEAU." At Randy's flat, unbelieving tone, Jack jerked his head back defiantly.

"Yes. *If* I'm right about you having the correct painting."

"Brousseau's work was extensively catalogued and studied," Randy said with a frown. "How is that remotely possible?"

A gleam appeared in Jack's eye, revealing the excitement of a scholar on the trail of a mystery. "I made a study of Jean-Pierre's letters to François Brousseau. François was—"

"I know who François was," Randy said drily. "Jean-Pierre's brother, and his close confidant. Many of Jean-Pierre's most important paintings were ultimately sold from François's private collection."

Jack flushed. "Yes, of course. I didn't intend to insult you again, merely to place my research in context. I became interested in the transition of Brousseau's style during the period he spent in the town of Fontaine, in the Oise department of France. It was in Oise, of course, that he created many of his most famous works. *River to Ermenonville. Madonna of the Castle.*"

Randy wouldn't be surprised if Jack had forgotten where they were, so excited he seemed now that he'd broken through his reluctance. Perhaps like anyone who has discovered something great, and with fear overcome, at the moment Jack couldn't wait to share.

"In Jean-Pierre's correspondence to François from the summer of 1878," he continued eagerly, "I found a reference to a landscape that he'd undertaken, in which the ruins of the abbey at Chaalis were to figure prominently. The abbey was to be silhouetted by the sunrise. He wrote again to François as the painting progressed that summer, but he was deeply dissatisfied with the work. That was true of many of his paintings, of course. Brousseau's depression—"

"Jack."

"Ah. I beg your pardon for the school master tone." Randy nodded, and Jack continued. "From the letters, it seems clear that Jean-Pierre did in fact complete the canvas, yet no reference to a painting of the sunrise at Chaalis exists in the official catalogues. Nevertheless, I identified in François's papers a reference to a sale in 1901 of a work whose description corresponds to that of the canvas in Jean-Pierre's letter. I'll spare you the gory details, but I have painstakingly assembled a compelling paper trail to demonstrate that the landscape Jean-Pierre described to François was the same one sold in 1901, and thence, quite possibly, ultimately to you four years ago."

"Or to someone in Philadelphia," Randy observed.

"Ye-e-s," Jack agreed reluctantly as he shifted a little on his knees. "There remain a few candidates besides your painting. The images I have been able to assemble are sufficiently ambiguous and of such low quality that I cannot be entirely certain without studying the work itself."

Jack's eyes were almost closed, and something like a religious fervor shone on his face. "I've been to the location in Fontaine that Jean-Pierre described, and I've seen the ruined monastery at Chaalis. I believe I stood on the very ground where Brousseau rested his easel to paint the sunrise."

If Randy had thought Jack handsome before, now he found him transcendent. The yearning he displayed, the glow of scholarship, the deep feeling with which he was finally sharing his hard-won secrets, all put Randy under his spell.

Jack continued in a reverential tone apropos to his position on his knees. "I took photos from the spot. I hope that by connecting the landscape with the physical details of Brousseau's setting, and by performing certain tests, I can prove that your *Sunrise* painting, *if* it's the right one, is indeed the work Jean-Pierre wrote about to François and called *Sunrise at the Abbey of Chaalis*."

The triumphant note in Jack's pronouncement resonated in Randy's chest. He was quiet but expectant, apparently longing for a response. Randy could only stare at him intently. His own breath sounded hoarse as his desire swelled. He wanted to know more, certainly, but there would be time.

Ideas and fantasies flickered through Randy's head as he drew on his experience, to be what Jack needed. To be worthy of the trust gifted to him. That yearning had less to do with the possibility that he might own a valuable painting than with the man who knelt before him. At the moment, he was more drawn to Jack than anyone in years. His passion for his work, for art, for making connections, touched that place inside Randy that Uncle Kevin had noticed and nurtured.

He longed for *his* painting to be the one Jack sought, because he wanted to be there for the man's triumph. Jack would glisten when he proved beyond a doubt that he'd found an unknown work by the master Jean-Pierre Brousseau. He would shine with an inner fire, and Randy needed to see that moment.

"What do you want tonight? What did you come here for?" Randy played with all the colors of his voice, reaching for that low throb that would take Jack deeper.

Jack licked his lips slowly, then met Randy's eyes. "I came here for you, though I didn't know it." Randy waited him out until he said, "Please. Help me fly."

Randy said, "Come here" in a gruff tone edged by his own excitement. Jack's eyes widened as his body responded to the command. He unfolded himself until he was on his feet again, then crossed to stand before Randy. His arms hung at his sides, but his shoulders squared proudly as he waited. Randy rose from the couch to tower above Jack, registering with satisfaction the way his mouth slackened and the lids of his eyes drooped. Not only was Randy a half-foot taller, but his wide shoulders and thick body made Jack's slender form seem delicate. Not feminine, but perfectly in contrast to Randy's own.

Randy's pulse raced, and the hair on his arms and chest felt charged with static electricity. He knew he was flushed as his blood pounded to mirror the excitement in Jack. Randy grew more determined to protect and guide, to shelter him from the world long enough to explore who he really was.

He grasped the strap of the harness where it lay across Jack's sternum, tugging him forward. He wove his other hand through Jack's richly colored hair, then leaned down to claim his mouth. Jack's lips were relaxed and inviting, and he opened quickly to allow Randy's tongue to explore. Heat arced through him like a comet from his toes to the top of his head. He had never felt so powerful, and as he tightened his grip in Jack's hair, he heard an answering moan. Jack rubbed his leather-covered erection against Randy's hip as they kissed, but he made no move to put his own arms around Randy. He just waited, loose and willing, for Randy to do anything to him that he wanted.

And Randy found he wanted to do a great many things, both to and *for* Jack. Breaking the kiss, he leaned back and stared until Jack opened his eyes as if from a daze. He finally allowed himself to stroke that soft, thick beard, and it felt like mink under his fingers.

"You trust me," Randy said seriously. It wasn't a question but Jack nodded. "Keep trusting me. I won't abuse it. Give me your safe words."

Jack seemingly had to drag himself back to be present. "Wha...? Oh. Rothko to slow. Pollack to stop."

Randy laughed softly. "Not a fan of the abstractionists, are you?" He couldn't help himself; he ran his fingers again along the soft beard at his jaw and confessed, "I think I'm going to adore you."

He didn't even wait for an answer, but stroked the leather harness before wrapping his fingers around the straps that framed the pectorals. He began to alternately push and pull with the harness until Jack swayed, slack and pliant. When Randy was satisfied, he unsnapped the top button of Jack's pants and stroked his gloved hand down the concealed shaft before grasping his balls firmly.

"Take these off, fold them neatly, and face the door," Randy rumbled, smiling at the speed with which he was obeyed. Jack set aside his shoes, socks, and folded pants—no underwear, Randy noted with pleasure—before returning to stand at attention as directed, with his feet slightly spread for balance.

Naked other than the harness, Jack was alabaster pale and wiry, but his body needed an additional touch of leather to underscore its natural beauty. Randy removed the band from his own thick wrist and snapped it in place just above Jack's right bicep. *Perfect.*

"This is yours to keep," he said, then wrapped his big arms around Jack and held him tightly through another blistering kiss. His lips were still soft and pliant but his grip on Randy's back was greedy.

"Fold your hands behind your head," Randy ordered when he stepped back from the kiss. Jack obeyed and quivered as Randy circled his body to examine it minutely.

His dick was long and thin, flushed red and with a slight downward curve in the last inch. The head glistened with precome, and the hair around it seemed as silky as Jack's beard. His sac hung full and loose.

Randy surveyed his prize, running one hand along a lean and lightly haired chest, then over tight arms. Jack was toned from, at a guess, many hours of yoga or Pilates. The muscles of his back rippled down to meet the high curve of his ass. Below the pale, firm globes were the ropey legs of a runner.

Randy stopped behind him, then brushed his fingertips down the indentation along his right ass cheek. He repeated the move with the palm of his leather glove, gauging the shiver that ran through Jack's flanks as he stroked. He paused until Jack tensed, then pulled back his hand to give him a swift spank. The crack echoed in the room as he gasped. Randy did the same with the other cheek and watched in satisfaction as the pale skin took on a slight pink color. "Beautiful," he murmured.

He wrapped fingers through the harness strap on the shoulder and snaked the other hand forward around his waist to pull Jack back against his own body until he sagged against Randy's erection and heavy muscles. He lowered his hands from behind his head to clasp Randy's forearm at his waist. His spare body felt tight and solid in Randy's arms.

Randy bent his head and breathed into Jack's ear, "Tonight, this is yours." He crouched so he could rub his still-covered cock up and down the crease of his bare ass. In answer, Jack groaned and pressed back against him. Randy grabbed his dick roughly. "And this is mine." He spun Jack around by the harness, then pressed on his shoulder until he sank to his knees once more. Randy spread his stance slightly, then put his fists on his hips. "Suck my cock."

Jack reached up with shaking hands to undo his pants and peel the leather down his thighs to below his knees. Randy's heavy package stretched the mesh pouch of his jockstrap, and Jack leaned forward to rub his cheek against the black fabric. He inhaled deeply. Randy slipped the pouch to one side so his thick cock and big balls were exposed, then again wove his hand into Jack's hair.

He tightened the grip slightly as he pulled Jack forward and rubbed his erection against the soft beard that graced his cheeks. The silky hair against the fevered skin of his dick was tantalizing, and sliding against it did strange things to Randy's stomach. A curl of something deep and wonderful tickled and spread warmth through his belly and built to an ache in his chest.

Randy angled his hips differently to brush the head across the seam of his lips until Jack opened his mouth and stuck out his flattened tongue He rested the head of his cock on it and stayed still as Jack licked and loved the glans. He tugged forward until Jack brought his lips into play as well, mouthing and cleaning the plum-sized head as he peered up to meet Randy's eyes.

When he tried to take more into his mouth, Randy held him back with his hair. He made shallow thrusts, then dragged his frenulum across the lower lip, pleasantly torturing both of them. Jack's eyes glinted as he lightly grasped the head by closing his teeth wickedly behind the flared ridge.

He didn't scrape, but pressed just enough to make Randy freeze. He worked his clever tongue against the captured head, stroking the underside and teasing the slit until Randy growled his frustration.

Jack chuffed slightly in amusement as he resheathed his teeth and opened wide. The next time, Randy let him tilt forward and slowly bring more cock into his mouth. Jack moaned around him, sending a shiver up Randy's spine. Spit leaked out of the corners of his mouth as he sucked harder and deeper, acting desperate to bring Randy off. Only about half of his length went in, though, so Randy grabbed his hair again and tugged slightly, encouraging Jack to push past his barriers.

"Let me in your throat," he urged. "Swallow around the head of my dick." He pressed forward again but relented at the first sign of gagging. "Good man. Try again. You can do it." Jack renewed his efforts with determination, bobbing his head, swallowing audibly as he tried to get Randy deeper. Drool dripped from the corner of his mouth as he manfully ate more and more of Randy's dick.

Vibration mixing with the noises of excitement coming from below drew Randy's attention down the length of the body before him, to where Jack tugged and jerked on his cock. Randy barked, "No. You come when I say, not before."

Jack moaned, but released his rigid dick and grabbed handfuls of Randy's ass to leverage himself farther onto his erection. His eyes were open and focused on Randy's, seeming to beg for his approval. His red lips stretched around the wet and shiny dick as it slid in and out of his mouth.

Finally, Jack took it all: the strap around the base of Randy's shaft met his lips, and the muscles in his throat contracted and massaged the head until Randy knew he was likely to come. If he were still thirty—hell, even forty—he'd spill in Jack's mouth and then again in his ass twenty minutes later. Sadly, even as turned on as he was, that kind of performance was in his past.

Reluctantly, he grabbed Jack by the ears and stilled his head. Jack protested with a moan, but let Randy pull back and draw out of his mouth slowly, trails of spit glistening in the low light of the club room. His dick pulsed threateningly as he let it bob in the air before the slack mouth.

"Jack." This time it was a command, not a warning, and eyes

snapped up to Randy's face. He dropped his hands to clasp them behind his own back. Randy grunted approvingly; it was a nice display of submission. "Strip me."

Still on his knees, Jack raised Randy's left leg to remove a boot, then the right. He finished peeling down Randy's leather pants, folded those neatly, and set them aside. He slid his hands up the sides of Randy's thighs until his fingers slipped under the leg straps of his jock, then the waist band. Carefully so as not to get the mesh caught on Randy's equipment, he lowered the jock and waited until Randy stepped out of it.

He remained on his knees, eyes on the prominently displayed meat before his face. Randy was left with just his gloves, his arm band, and his cockstrap as the emblems of his role. Normally he needed more gear to help him meet his partner's desires and expectations for an evening. With Jack, what he still wore was enough because the role was more real than ever before.

Jack waited on his knees with his spine erect, but his eyes were glazed with desire. "You're doing well," Randy purred and ran a hand over that soft beard again and along his jaw. Given the opportunity, he'd prefer to take him to the brink again and again with hands and mouth before moving to other pleasures, but he was vaguely aware their time together was limited. That being the case, he wanted inside Jack at least once so he rumbled out, "Get me ready to fuck you."

He saw a flash of concern as Jack contemplated Randy's thick cock leaking just inches from his face. Nervously, he spoke up. "I've, uh, rarely… And never one this size."

Randy crooked a finger under his chin and tilted up his head. He bent over until he was inches from Jack's face. "I have you. When I tell you you're ready for my dick, you *will* take it. Because I want to fuck your perfect ass. Is that understood?"

Jack nodded, and Randy watched his concern give way to lust

and a determination to please. Again he climbed gracefully to his feet and looked around until Randy indicated his folded pants with a nod. He reached into the pocket to find lubricant and a few condoms, selected one, opened the foil packet, added a single drop of lube to the inside, and then unrolled the latex down Randy's length. When Randy was suited up, Jack poured more lube into his hand and stroked up and down to get him slick. Then he waited nervously.

Randy grasped his harness and tugged him slightly off balance and into his arms. "Give me your weight. Good. Now, press two fingers against the rim of your ass." Jack put one arm around Randy's waist and reached the other back behind himself and began to stroke. "That's right. Rub in small circles. It's good, isn't it?"

"Yes, sir," he muttered, his words heavy and thick like molasses. His face rubbed against Randy's muscled and hairy chest like a cat marking its scent.

"Now, press them inside." Jack groaned as he obeyed. "Hold still for a minute. Enjoy your own warmth."

"It's… I'm throbbing. My arsehole is pulsing."

"Good. Now begin to move them around inside." Randy wrapped a hand around the back of Jack's neck and brought their heads together to meet in another blistering kiss. He thrust his tongue in and out of his mouth in a fucking rhythm and Jack caught on. He began moving the fingers in his ass in time to Randy's demands, in and out, in and out. When Randy was satisfied with the noises tumbling from his throat, he wrapped his other arm around his waist to immobilize him, dragging him tightly against his body.

The lean muscle against his own chest and stomach was cool and firm and he swelled with pride. Never had Randy been so strong and capable as a top man. All of his years and all of his partners, good and bad, glimmered in his memory because they let him be what Jack needed that night. He stood as a sentinel, sheltering Jack's body and his fears and his mystery from the judgmental world outside the room and beyond the club.

Randy kept rein on the energy and control Jack had gifted to him, using kisses and a tight grip as he gradually sagged and gave himself to Randy. Jack's drop to sub space on their first and possibly only time together was unprecedented in Randy's experience, but he rolled with it, allowing him to drift downward like a leaf.

When it seemed Randy was the only thing holding Jack up, he used his grip on the harness to turn his body around and guide him toward the chair on which his vest was draped. "Bend over and grab the rungs," Randy ordered. "Spread your legs."

Jack complied, and Randy ran a hand down his back, then over the swell of his ass. "I can't wait to be inside here," he murmured as he pressed a thumb to his opening. It was spongy and relaxed. Well, as relaxed as it could be given what was about to happen, but Randy sensed no doubt, only slight apprehension.

"You're ready," he said, and Jack nodded slowly, as if mesmerized. "Breathe with me. Smell the leather from my vest. Let it anchor you. This is going to hurt for just a little while, but then it will be good, I promise. Better than good."

Randy gripped Jack's hips, lined up his dick and applied just enough pressure that Jack would know he was there at his entrance. He took a loud, deliberate breath in through his nose and let it flow out of his mouth. Jack mirrored his breathing. After three deep breaths, Randy pressed forward.

Jack was tight and he was thick, but suddenly he was through the ring of muscle and the head of his cock was encased in warmth. Jack hissed slightly and his head drooped. Randy paused and said, "Embrace the burn. Feel me inside you." His breath was ragged at first, then grew steadier.

He gave a slight nod, and when Randy felt him relax a little more, he slid deep in one long thrust. Jack's ass fitted against his pelvis perfectly like they were calibrated to be together. Words like *there you are* and *home* drifted through Randy's head. The warm, velvet core pulsed around him and he thought *this this this.*

Jack sighed out "Randy" like a prayer and dropped his torso farther to give better access to his ass. "I didn't know," he moaned.

Randy wished there were no condom between them. It had been many years since he'd taken a man raw but he wanted that with Jack. He moved his hips, at first slowly until he was sure what Jack could handle, then faster when it became clear he was going to take whatever Randy wanted to throw at him.

Fears and reluctance apparently banished, he began to slam back with each stroke, accepting Randy deep in his body. Randy grunted and wrapped an arm around his chest to pull him into a standing position. He held that smooth, cool back against his own fevered skin as he bucked and twisted and jabbed with his cock. He knew he couldn't last long at that pace but he didn't care. He badly needed to get off.

He clamped his teeth on the muscle of Jack's traps and took one hand off his hip so he could stroke his beautiful dick. "You may come," Randy said. Jack arced his arm up and over his head to pull Randy down to bite even harder, then shouted as he exploded across the back of the chair and the floor and Randy's hand.

"Don't stop," he begged as he convulsed in Randy's grip. "Please, sir. Please keep fucking me."

Randy was almost there and he pounded deep. *Home home home.* Jack pulled Randy's spunk-covered hand to his mouth and licked come off his knuckles. That did it. Randy roared, holding

Jack motionless as he let a wondrous orgasm surge from his toes, up through his legs and then erupt from his body.

Jack pulsed around his cock, and Randy trembled with the effort of keeping still. He fought the urge to thrust and rut, and instead let the beauty of a warm and soft body finish the job their fuck had begun. He threw his head back and gasped as the pleasure soared and his come filled the rubber buried in Jack's ass. The orgasm ached in his teeth, it was so good. He shook and groaned as sensation carried him away.

Finally, finally, it ebbed, and Randy returned to himself, panting. He was on his feet still, holding Jack tightly in a bear hug. Jack was almost sobbing against him, his chest heaving with exertion. Reluctantly, Randy loosened his arms to let him go. He slid out carefully, pressed lips to his shoulder for a long moment, then dealt with the condom.

Jack turned to face him. His cheeks were flushed and his eyes shone with tears, but his hands flexed mindlessly. He was shattered, Randy saw. He didn't know what he was supposed to do next.

Randy had this. He crossed to the bed, stretched out, and opened his arms. "Come here, Jack."

And Jack did.

. . .

RANDY WOKE FROM a doze a few minutes or a few hours later, he didn't know which. He was spooned around Jack's warm body, with one arm possessively, protectively, holding Jack against his chest. The muscles of his smooth back against Randy's front shifted slightly.

"You're awake," Jack said softly without turning to him. "Well, more of you is awake. *Something* got up previously." He twitched his hips slightly, and Randy realized his dick lay hard and hot up the crease of Jack's ass.

Randy huffed a soft laugh. "It knows what it likes."

Jack rolled his head slightly back toward Randy and showed a small smile. "I'd be happy to give him more, but you wrecked me. I don't think I've ever been so used and wrung out." Randy stiffened and started to pull free but Jack clutched the arm entwined with his. "I mean that in the best way, Randy. You were wonderful."

He relaxed and dropped back down, then pulled Jack to him tightly again. He hadn't woken up with another man in God only knew how long, and he permitted himself to lie there, indolent and peaceful. He soaked up the warmth of Jack's body, heard the rustle of his hair against the pillow, smelled the lingering traces of leather, sweat, semen and something more artful. Not quite floral, but earthy.

Eventually, Randy asked, "What's that cologne you wear?"

Jack murmured back, "Jo Malone's Pomegranate Noir."

It was curious, Randy thought. Normally, colognes were unwelcome in the scene because their scents interfered with the smell of leather the players craved and responded to, top and bottom alike. Randy had never before appreciated that some scents worked *with* the leather instead of masking it. Something new was in the air, the blend of Jack's cologne and Randy's gear. He breathed in the earthy and tart scent. It was delicious and yet dark, and he let it fill his imagination and turn the scent into colors. Deep red, of course, with jewel tones to highlight.

He could see a painting take shape in his mind, of Jack lying on his side, a pomegranate-colored sheet tugged just over the curve of his ivory hip. Perhaps the vague suggestion of a St. Andrew's Cross in the background. That might be better than the nude he'd imagined painting before.

"Should we leave?" Jack asked, shaking Randy out of his half-dream.

"What? Oh. Yes, probably." Randy hesitated. "Maybe. What time is it?"

"No idea."

"Liam will charge me for the night either way. Do you need to get back to your hotel?"

Jack twisted around until he was facing Randy. His eyes burned intently even in the dim light of the room. "Not necessarily. My train to Philadelphia isn't until Wednesday morning."

Randy weighed the purpose of that comment. Was Jack obliquely reminding him of the issues with *Sunrise*? Or simply letting Randy know that his schedule was open but had an outside limit?

Perhaps Jack sensed the conflict he'd created because he slid his hand down Randy's chest to his hip. "What I mean to say is that I would enjoy more time here with you, if that's all right." His hand moved lower, dragging across Randy's taut stomach, combing through his pubic hair, wrapping around his rock-hard dick.

Randy tried to keep his happiness under control at the thought of more time in bed with Jack. Reasserting his dominant persona for both of their sakes, he let out a rumble of pleasure. He was gratified at the way Jack responded with glassy eyes and a slack jaw as he gripped the erection in his hand more tightly.

Randy rolled onto his back and kicked off the cover sheet. He folded his hands beneath his head and let Jack run hungry eyes up and down the length of his body. The admiration fed fuel to his own yearning for the lean, pale man who had a desire to please— a desire that perfectly suited his own.

He fixed Jack with a heated gaze. "We have all night. If your ass is too sore to take care of me, then I expect you to come up with another solution."

Chapter Twelve

A POLITE KNOCK woke them again a few hours later.

"Randy?" Liam called softly through the door. "It's eight o'clock. I had Patrick deal with the parking meter for your truck so you're good for another hour. The bathroom is available now, and I can have breakfast brought in unless you want to go elsewhere."

Randy glanced at Jack, who gave him a smile and an indifferent shrug. Randy called out, "Thanks, Liam. Breakfast for two sounds good. Surprise us." Liam knocked once to show he heard, then Randy leaned down to kiss Jack. It was safe and peaceful in the bed, and Jack was pliant beneath him. He wrapped his arms around Randy's neck as they kissed, but when it started to deepen into something more he broke away with a laugh.

"Christ, no, you grizzly bear. My arsehole is shredded, my throat is raw, my cock is sore, and I couldn't squeeze out one more drop of jizm at gun point."

"That sounds like a challenge," Randy said before he swiped his tongue up Jack's neck and behind his ear. He inhaled Jack's morning smell, all warm body and the remains of his cologne. Jack laughed again and jumped out of bed.

"Stay!" Jack held out his hands, palms up. "I'm going to shower. Alone," he chuckled.

Randy let him go and took the minutes by himself to arrange his clothes. He wished he had something other than leather to wear home. Late in the evening, heading into a club, his gear was sexy as hell. The morning after, when the leather was cold and stiff—not so much. He should give some thought to leaving a change of clothes at Cuir. Not that an overnight stay happened often.

Or really, ever. Liam had never before had to wake him up and give him the bum's rush.

Jack returned shortly with a towel around his waist and a plastic bag in his hand. "That was kind," he said as he hoisted the bag. "The doorman brought up my street clothes from the coat check, and your leather jacket."

"Doorman? Oh, Liam. He owns the place. Well, along with Patrick." Jack pulled a nice pair of pants and a sweater out of the bag, and Randy was instantly jealous of the casual clothes. "Crap. I'm going to feel ridiculous leaving this place in my leathers."

Jack paused in his dressing with his head just poking through the neck of the sweater. "You, walking the street in your jacket and those boots." He hummed delightedly and his eyes sparkled. "That won't be a walk of shame. It's going to be a strut."

Randy swatted Jack's ass as he left to take his own shower. He hated to admit it, but his body was every bit as sore and used up as Jack described. He hadn't had a marathon fuck session like that in a long, long time, and it turned out his workout routine inadequately prepared him for the specific muscles he'd employed. The hot water helped soothe his body, and Liam fortunately left thick, soft towels for his patrons. He charged them through the nose, but that was all right.

Randy had spent years visiting the standard leather and denim bars. The dark corners and back rooms had been decadent and exciting when he was younger, but as he matured, he tended to notice the sticky floors and the faded Tom of Finland posters more than whatever man had hold of his dick.

Or he'd leave with someone, only to find during the cab ride that his trick had nothing interesting to say. When an old friend invited him to Cuir for the first time, he noticed the difference right away. The lush decor of the place didn't soften the decadence that Randy sought; rather, it worked like a jeweler's tray. The sparkly edge of a man who needed what Randy could give shone brighter against the blue velvet of the club.

Once in a while, Randy went back to the old leather-and-denim hangouts, but he was spoiled by the world Liam and Patrick created at Cuir.

Randy was human again by the time he returned to the room. Food had been delivered in his absence; a tray sat on the low cabinet, and Jack was pouring two coffees as he entered. Dressed, Jack was as elegant and pristine as when he walked into Mata Hari the first time. As if Randy had not spent the night violating him in every way he could imagine.

"Do you take cream or sugar?" Jack asked. Randy muttered "both" as he contemplated the bed, where Jack had arranged his leathers neatly for him to put back on.

"There was a bit of spunk on the vest," Jack observed as he handed a cup to Randy. "I think I got it all off, but you might want to have it professionally cleaned."

"Thank you." He opted to eat breakfast in his towel so he could delay dressing and then looking like a tool. Jack gestured for him to sit on the sofa, and brought him a plate loaded with a toasted bagel and lots of scrambled eggs. He fixed himself just a bowl of fresh fruit and a small helping of eggs, then sat next to Randy.

"I couldn't eat like that and live," Randy teased, with a nod to Jack's breakfast.

"Yes, well, you've got quite a bit more bulk to maintain than I."

"Y'know, that's twice I've been called fat in less than a week."

"Ridiculous." Jack snorted. "You're a solid mountain of a man and there isn't an ounce of fat to be found. I checked. Now eat."

"Hmm. Someone seems more prickly and less deferential in the morning light." Randy said it with a smile to make sure Jack knew he was teasing.

Jack gave him a sly grin in return. "Well, perhaps I am overstepping my bounds. I might deserve to be corrected."

"I'll bear that in mind." He kept to himself the question he really wanted to ask: *When?*

They ate in silence for a few minutes before Randy asked, "You came here as a guest of Jorge Castillo, right? How do you know him?"

Jack smiled demurely. "I met him in New York at a, um, party about a year ago." Randy grunted. He could imagine exactly what kind of party they'd been to. "Jorge took charge of me for the evening and we became friendly afterward. Occasional texts, that sort of thing. Well, I recalled that he lived in Washington, so I contacted him when I knew I was going to be here. He invited me along to Cuir."

Randy knew he was glowering, but he couldn't help it. A surge of jealousy coursed through his body. He and Jorge often attracted the same type of man, and they'd been in more than one semi-friendly alpha male pissing contest over who would claim the hottest guy on a random evening. Normally it was a simple game to keep the scene interesting, but Randy found he hated the thought of Jorge putting his hands on Jack's slender body.

Jack was watching him carefully with those warm brown eyes, and he looked away until a hand on his chin turned his face back. Jack leaned closer and said firmly, "It was one time, quite a while ago. We came here just as friends. Besides, you are ten times the man Jorge could ever hope to be."

Randy turned red, both at the flattery and at how easily Jack saw through him. Resting a hand on Jack's thigh, he admitted, "Last night was one for the record books. You brought out something in me I haven't felt in a long time. Something good." *Ah, be honest with the guy.* Randy cleared his throat. "Lately, it's just an act. You know? I play a role. With you, though, it was natural and real. I wanted to make the decisions so that you could just *be.*"

It was Jack's turn to seem embarrassed. He studied his bowl of fruit but flicked a warm glance back up at Randy. "It was, um, remarkable for me too. I've never been so free. That was a real gift." Silence stretched as they both ate a little more, tense with the mixture of desire and self-disclosure in the room.

Clearly trying to change the mood, Jack said, "Tell me how you began collecting art."

"Oh. Well, my uncle Kevin was the inspiration. My mother's brother. He was a state trooper in Maine." At Jack's puzzled expression, he clarified, "A policeman. Kevin and his partner Luc took me to museums and galleries and got me interested. I studied art history for a while in college, but then Kevin was killed in the line of duty and I decided to go into law enforcement instead. But I already had the collecting bug, so when I traveled I bought pieces that appealed to me."

"Your uncle sounds like an interesting bloke."

"He was. He really taught me about being a man."

"What about your parents?" Jack asked cautiously. "Were they supportive of you?"

Randy snorted. "No, not at all. My father always tried to get me to say Kevin was molesting me, and my mother just wanted me to get along with my father. She probably loved Kevin in her own way, but she was deeply concerned with appearances. She hated that Kevin lived openly with Luc, and she couldn't understand why I would want to spend time with the two of them. When I came out to her, she was only worried about what to tell the priest and neighbors."

Jack murmured quietly, "I know something about the desire to preserve appearances." He offered nothing more, however, and the quiet between them was risky. As if they were both on the verge of baring souls.

Before either of them could say something too revealing, Randy decided it was time to address one of the other elephants in the room. "So. Brousseau."

Jack shot up his head, and the eagerness in his gaze moved Randy. Jack badly wanted to see *Sunrise*, but the nerves he displayed had to be there because he wasn't sure whether he would finally be allowed. Fair enough. Randy hadn't exactly been accommodating before, but it was time to ease Jack's fears. "I don't currently keep that painting at my house. I'll have to call to see when we can go by."

Disappointment and hope warred together on Jack's expressive face. He scrubbed his hands on his thighs, shook his arms, and blew out a deep breath. He rolled his shoulders. "Thank you, Randy. This means a great deal to me. You can't know the years I've invested in this project. What it would mean for my career."

"I can tell it's important to you. I hope you're right."

"If I am, you'll be a wealthy man should you choose to sell."

"That isn't why I hope you're right."

Jack gave him a puzzled frown. He pondered Randy's words, and the moment lingered like the tart scent of spice and earth in the dark. Finally, he asked, "Then why?"

Randy met Jack's gaze and admitted softly, "You want this so much. I'd like to see you prove yourself." He wanted to say, but didn't, that he'd like to be the one to help Jack claim the victory.

He could imagine the joy that would transform Jack's handsome face into something glorious, and he wanted to be there to witness that moment.

Perhaps Jack understood anyway. He leaned toward Randy. "I'm very grateful. I mean it. Sophie told me I should have been more open from the beginning, but I was terrified my research would be stolen."

"Sophie?"

"My fiancée. She told me before I came that I would need to be honest, but I find it very difficult."

Randy stopped chewing. "Your fiancée." He set his plate down carefully, then swallowed the suddenly-unpalatable mouthful of eggs.

"My world is extremely cut-throat. If a colleague angling to make his own name knew what I was on to—" Jack ceased chattering as he became aware that something in the atmosphere had changed. Randy was still. Tight. Controlled.

Jack quirked his head, and alarm shot through his eyes. "Is there a problem?" he asked.

Randy shook his head, finished his coffee, and stood. "No problem." He went to the bed and began to dress. He felt stupid as he pulled on his jock strap and tugged up his leather pants. What a fuckup he was, not bringing a change of clothes in case he stayed. *Idiot.*

Jack was behind him. He touched Randy's shoulder lightly, but Randy shook it off and bent to grab his vest.

"What is it? That I have a fiancée?" Taking the vest out of Randy's hands, Jack helped him situate it properly. He settled it on Randy's shoulders as he waited for an answer. He took a step back, still waiting.

Randy turned at last and his shield dropped into place. It gave him needed distance, enough to be able to say, "I won't fuck with anyone in a relationship. Not knowingly."

Frowning, Jack tilted his head to the side. "But you don't understand about Sophie. She knows about me and what I do when I'm out of the country. Out of England I mean. She doesn't mind."

"Maybe she doesn't mind, but I do."

Jack's voice took on a tinge of anger. "But why? What does it have to do with you?"

Randy didn't bother to answer. He pulled on his jacket and checked for his phone and keys. Jack exhaled in frustration. "Will you still let me see your *Sunrise* then?"

Disappointment made Randy cruel, and he turned slowly to sneer at Jack. His upper lip curled. "I guess that's all this was. A way to make sure you could see the canvas." Jack made a sound of protest but Randy stuffed his gloves into a pocket and crossed the room to the door.

Without glancing back, he said, "The room is already taken care of. I'll contact you at the hotel when I'm able to arrange for you to see *Sunrise*."

He left without another word.

Chapter Thirteen

AS HE DROVE toward Virginia, Randy tried to quell his disappointment and reframe the night with Jack in a way that didn't leave him so raw. He'd gotten laid. That was what he went to Cuir for on Monday nights, and that's what he got. It was enough.

At a stoplight, he dialed his phone and put it on hands-free. He had a promise to keep, even if the one he made it to wasn't worthy.

Stop with the bitter bullshit. Randy rolled his eyes at himself, acting like a butt-hurt teenager.

"Good morning. Thomas Scarborough's office," he heard over the speaker.

"Morning, Anne. This is Randy Vaughan. Is Thomas available for a few minutes?"

"Oh hello, Randy. Let me check." Anne put him on hold, but a few second later Thomas picked up.

"Hey, Randy. How are you today?"

"Fair to middlin'. By any chance are you and Zachary planning to be home tonight?"

"I have a meeting that's scheduled to run late but I think Zach said something about sticking around to study his music for the gay men's chorus. Their Christmas concert is coming up soon. What's up?"

"You remember that painting I convinced you to hang in

your bedroom?"

"Oh, sure. The sunrise one."

"Right. Well, I promised an art historian I'd let him take a look at it for some project he's doing. I was hoping we could get it out of the way this evening because he's leaving town tomorrow."

"Tell you what. I'll give Zach a quick call to check, and then one of us will let you know. What's the historian researching?"

Randy debated whether to tell Thomas that he might be in possession of a genuine, unknown Brousseau, just to hear his reaction. No, fuck that noise. Thomas would freak out and call in a security company or something to make sure the picture was safe. After the events with the stalker who had targeted Thomas and Zachary, security in his condo building had been significantly upgraded. The odds of Fraser being right were astronomically low, so he wouldn't lay this on Thomas at the beginning of his work day. He'd save it for later, over a drink at Mata Hari where they could laugh about it properly.

"I think he's just eliminating some possibilities from a wild goose chase," he told Thomas. "Catch you later, brother."

Randy spent the rest of the drive home anticipating how Danny would react when he pulled in after being out all night. Hurt looks, sulking, a sigh from a moody teenager with a crush—he could only imagine. At the same time, he wondered why he'd gotten himself all twisted up over a stranger from England, someone who would be leaving town anyway in a matter of days.

Sure, he avoided screwing men in relationships, but it wasn't like he quizzed every sexual partner for proof he was single. If Randy didn't know and the guy didn't volunteer, then he normally was content to turn a blind eye. Don't ask don't tell worked just fine for him most of the time. So why should he care that Jack—no, *Fraser*—was engaged to a woman?

Because I wanted to see him again before he leaves.

Fuck it, he thought savagely. They'd had a good roll in the hay, Fraser would return to England, and Randy would find someone new next Monday looking to scratch an itch. If he had to, he'd scratch several times to make sure the memory of Fraser's body under his hands went away.

Somebody single, unlike Fraser. Unlike—
Nope, not going there.

He tried to direct his thoughts elsewhere, and then encountered a slight pang as he worried about the following week. Would Danny still be around, or would Joe find him a safe placement? He was getting used to Danny's calm, quiet presence. But if Danny were still around, would Randy have to go through teenage angst every time?

Well, if Danny wanted to stay with Randy, he'd just have to make his peace with the fact that Randy liked to play with other men. With *lots* of other men, week after week. There was always someone new at Cuir, and if they were interchangeable and disposable, so much the better. He had a bad track record the few times he'd tried anything other than a simple fuck-buddy arrangement.

Look at Trevor.

Shit, he swore he wasn't going to go there. Randy banged his hands on his steering wheel as his thoughts brought him full circle to Fraser. By the time he pulled into his driveway, he was practically spoiling for an argument. He was surprised to find the house empty because Danny had always been there when he arrived before.

He glanced around the kitchen for a note and found nothing, but the kitchen itself was spotless and the dishwasher was running. Randy looked over the great room, tapping his fingers on the island as he wondered. The house seemed still. Empty.

Dammit! He bolted up the stairs and skidded to a stop in front of Danny's room. The door was closed, so Randy rapped the back of his knuckles on it twice.

No answer.

He hesitated with a hand on the knob. *Should I go in, or respect Danny's privacy? Well, it's still my house.* He opened the door carefully. "Danny?" he called.

Still nothing.

He pushed open the door to see the bed was made. There was no visible sign of anyone using the room, in fact. *Surely he didn't leave?*

Guilt washed through Randy as he imagined Danny pacing the empty house until he got fed up and hit the road. Where would he go if he left? Back to the P Street Beach?

He took a deep breath, then opened the closet door. It was full of Danny's clothes still. Randy released the tension in his arms. Well, thank God. Wherever Danny was at the moment, it didn't seem like he'd run away.

Although that was a ridiculous thought. Randy's house was a haven for Danny, but it wasn't his home, so he couldn't run away. All he could do was move on.

Randy shut the closet, then pulled the bedroom door shut behind him. No need to make it obvious he'd been snooping. In his own room, he decided he needed to take out his frustration and break the loop that had hold of his mind by heading to the gym, so he peeled out of his leathers.

He left a note for Danny, then jogged the mile to the gym for a grueling chest workout. The session went well, and with a spot from one of his workout buddies he managed to beat his personal best on the bench press by ten pounds. Even that accomplishment wasn't enough to burn off his bad mood, so he hit the rowing machine for a good long spell. As he slid back and forth on the seat, focusing on his form and the smooth pull of the rope in his hands, he began to find his center. The sweat that poured out of him seemed to take his consternation with it, and thirty minutes later he was both drained and calm.

When he jogged up his driveway again, he saw Danny moving around inside and didn't bother pretending to himself that he wasn't relieved. He came through the kitchen door, all sweaty and mail in hand, as the boy called out a friendly, "Hey, Randy."

"Hi. What've you been up to?"

"I walked down to the grocery store to pick up some stuff we needed. You go through, like, a dozen eggs every other day."

"Oh. Well, thanks for doing that."

"I put the receipt and the change in the petty cash envelope you left me." Randy would have thought everything was fine, except for the fact that Danny wouldn't meet his eye. "Do you want some lunch before you head into Mata Hari? I was going to make some tuna fish for myself." Danny opened a cabinet and started mixing a protein shake for Randy.

He threw the powder, some kale, and an apple into the Vit-aMix blender as he talked. "I was thinking I'd go over to Clarendon and catch a movie this evening. Can I borrow your bicycle? There's a new movie I haven't seen yet." He poured the shake into a glass and passed it to Randy, still without looking directly at him.

Randy decided avoidance worked for him too, so he just accepted the glass as a sign things were okay between the two of them. "This is great, Danny. I really appreciate it. Sure, take my bike, but you'll probably need to adjust the seat. And dress warm. Do you need any money?"

That got him a quick side-eye, but then Danny grinned shyly. "Nah. I haven't spent all that cash you gave me at Del's Diner."

"Well, let me know if you run low. Hell, with all the cooking you've been doing, you're saving me a fortune at Del's. Vonda's gonna think I'm sweet on another girl now." Randy was grateful for Danny's slight chuckle. "We ought to go there for dinner one of these nights so you don't always have to cook for me. Maybe tomorrow you can come to the bar before closing and we'll grab a burger." Danny smiled eagerly. "Okay, I'm gonna take this shake upstairs and grab a shower. And yeah, a sandwich before I go to work would be perfect."

Randy climbed to his bedroom, relieved that they'd dodged a conversational bullet. Best thing about being men, he chuckled to himself. He was probably a coward, but he didn't want to explain anything to Danny. It was almost funny though. He was giving Danny a roof, letting him take his bike, avoiding sex talks, and all but offering him an allowance. It was like having a son of his own. He grinned as he finished his shake and set down the empty glass before checking messages on his phone.

Zachary had left a message while he was at the gym. "Hiya, Randy. Thomas said you'd like to swing by the condo this evening. I'll probably be home from work by six and I'm not going anywhere except maybe the pool. Unless you say differently, I'll look for you around seven-ish."

That time should work. Since it was a Tuesday, Mata Hari would be slow and he could leave Malcolm in charge for an hour. He'd need to let Jack—*Fraser*—know, so he tapped the screen of his phone a few times as he tried to think what to say. He wanted to make it clear this was a one-and-done favor, but he didn't necessarily want to be an asshole. He'd let Fraser see the painting, then Fraser would head off to Philadelphia or return to England or whatever the fuck he needed to do, and he'd be out of Randy's life. Okay, he could do this.

He took a deep breath, then looked up the number for the W Hotel. When the receptionist put him through, the room rang four times before the system clicked over to voice mail. Randy exhaled in relief. Leaving a message was much better.

At the beep, he said, "Jack, this is Randy Vaughan. I was able to make arrangements for you to see the *Sunrise* painting this evening at seven o'clock. I suggest you come by Mata Hari around six-thirty and we can drive over together. Please leave a message with me at the bar if you can't make it. Otherwise I'll see you then."

And done.

He disconnected the call, glad he didn't actually have to speak to Fraser. He'd work a few hours, take a break to get to and from Thomas's condo, then go back to running his bar.

Don't wanna talk to Danny. Don't wanna talk to Jack. Don't wanna think about—

Shit.

In the shower, Randy's restless mind kept bringing him back to the night in Cuir. Fraser was a good fuck, and his body was hot as hell, but that was all. Yes, he was interested in art and no doubt that was part of the reason Randy found him attractive, but it was One. Fucking. Night. *One*, like so many, many before that Randy had spent in Cuir or in other leather bars.

Why was he so pissed?

He trudged naked back out to his bedroom, still toweling off, then dropped heavily onto a leather arm chair in one corner to look out over his small garden. Danny had done a thorough job of cleaning everything up for the winter, but now the bare trees and the severely trimmed hedges seemed bleak. Randy dropped his head back and closed his eyes.

Two years earlier

"HAPPY 'VERSARY, TEDDY bear!"

Randy turned at the lilting words. A handsome, tall man stood in the door of Randy's studio with a Santa hat perched jauntily over his blond hair. He still wore his airline uniform, and its tailored lines showed his long, lean build to perfection. Sparkling blue eyes flashed his merriment.

Randy gave him a huge, silly grin as he set down his palette. "Trevor! I thought you weren't scheduled back through DC for two more days." He wiped his hands, then reached out to pull him into a hug.

Against his neck, Trevor murmured, "I managed to switch some routes around so I could be here for this. Six months together! That should be celebrated." He nipped at Randy's neck and rubbed a hip against Randy's crotch.

Randy growled. "Oh yeah. We can do that. Get your sweet ass back in the house."

"I'm gonna start calling you bossy bear instead of teddy bear," Trevor said, but he turned and scurried away. Randy followed him more slowly to close up, and as he pulled the studio door shut, he noticed a black car parked across the street. He couldn't recall seeing that in the neighborhood before, and it looked official. Ah well, it was probably nothing.

Trevor left a trail of clothes across the kitchen and up the stairs to the bedroom. Randy laughed as he gathered the uniform jacket, tie, white shirt, shoes, belt, and suit pants. By the time he got to the bedroom, Trevor was on his hands and knees, wearing just the Santa hat, white jockey shorts and black socks. He looked back at Randy over his shoulder. "Bet you can't guess what I want for Christmas," he purred.

Twenty minutes later, Randy collapsed onto his back. The sheets were tangled, the Santa hat was on the floor with the comforter, and at least one pillowcase was stained with lube and come. Randy pulled off the used condom and tied a knot in the end.

Trevor lay face down, seemingly boneless. "Whew," he murmured into his pillow. "Now that was a celebration." He flopped over to flounce and wriggle until his cheek rested on Randy's chest and his hand lay on Randy's spent dick. "Can we stay in bed all weekend, teddy bear?"

Randy kissed the top of his blond head and grinned. "What about food?"

"Oh, we'll find someone to deliver. I don't want to move until Monday morning."

"I'd love that, Trev, but I'm going out of town tomorrow. Remember? That's why we said we were going to celebrate *after* I got back and you finished your run to Italy."

"I couldn't wait that long to get me some teddy bear lovin'. Where are you going? Maybe I can change routes again and meet up with you somewhere."

Randy shook his head. "I don't think your airline flies to Oman."

"True. Oh well. I'm scheduled through DC from Milan on Thursday. You back by then?"

"Yeah, I should be home Wednesday night, so let's plan on dinner."

"Mmm, dinner. Now you've done it. I'm hungry. How about you?"

"I could eat."

"You *did* eat. Oh, wait, I thought you were talking about my ass." Randy snorted and Trevor gave him a sweet kiss in response. "I taste good on you. Okay, here's my survival plan. How about I order us some food while you take a shower?"

Randy asked, "You don't want to get in the shower with me?"

"Aw, sweet thing. Course I do! Let me get the food ordered and then I'll be in to scrub your back."

They were downstairs twenty minutes later, eating Chinese takeout, when the knock came on the front door. Well, it wasn't so much a knock as a pound.

Insistent. Official.

Trevor turned extremely pale, his blue eyes widening as Randy went to open the door, where he froze at the sight of two people in black suits. More suits stood farther down the front path, and easily six black cars were parked at the curb and blocked the street. The man closest to the door held an FBI badge in his face. The woman with him had her hand on her weapon.

"Mr. Vaughan? We have a warrant for the arrest of Trevor Mackenzie."

Randy turned in time to see him running toward the door to the back garden. "Trevor, stop!" he called. Trevor no sooner had the door opened than two more men in black suits materialized and grabbed him. The agents at his front door pushed their way past, and Randy stood down, hands visible and at his side, as more FBI poured into his house. Trevor was hauled off, and the way he avoided Randy's gaze stunned him into compliance with whatever the FBI wanted to do.

The next hour was a blur. The agents had a warrant to search his house, and then they asked Randy to come with them. He didn't seem to be under arrest, but as he had no idea what was going on, he went. In an interview room, a young agent brought him coffee. Two more agents came in, the ones who knocked at his door, and laid a stack of paper on the table.

"Agent Vaughan, my name is Agent Dannels," the woman said, then gestured at her partner. "This is Agent Kennedy. Thank you for your cooperation."

"What's happening?" Randy asked. "Why was Trevor taken out in handcuffs?"

Kennedy took a seat. "How long have you known Trevor

Mackenzie?"

"Six months," Randy answered. "Almost exactly."

"And how did you meet?"

"He was an attendant on an international flight I took. We started chatting and ended up friends."

"By friends, you mean lovers?" Kennedy asked.

Randy knew that was coming. Obviously, the FBI had his house under surveillance for some reason. If they were after Trevor, then they probably knew how many nights he'd spent with Randy. He sighed. "Yes. We're lovers."

Dannels adjusted the stack of pages before her slightly, then picked up the top page. She studied the words for a moment, then said, "Mr. Mackenzie sent a text just twenty minutes before we arrested him. You're to accompany Senator Gibson to Oman tomorrow until Wednesday."

Randy opened his mouth to ask how she knew, but suddenly, he didn't have to. Grace Gibson might not be an obvious subject for espionage, but that was beside the point. When someone in her position went abroad or met world leaders domestically, it generated intelligence that could be fit together with other puzzle pieces and, collectively, reveal too much.

"Oh no," he said, and his head sagged. Disaster gaped before him.

He was aware of Kennedy lifting another page from the stack. "Last month you accompanied the senator to Moscow." Kennedy set that one aside, and picked up another. "Two weeks earlier, it was an unscheduled trip to Miami."

"Trevor is a spy?" Randy asked, but he could hear the resignation in his own voice. He would swear after that he never saw it coming, yet the moment he was confronted with the facts, he accepted it as absolute truth.

"Yes, Agent Vaughan. He's been reporting on the movements

of Senator Gibson based upon your own travel."

All of the questions from Trevor about where he was going, when he'd be back, had seemed so innocent. Those little flirtatious comments about planning his own schedule so he could meet Randy in whatever city he was visiting—they took on a mocking tone in memory.

Six months. Trevor had been playing him for *six months*.

Randy was interviewed for hours, and recounted every detail he could recall from the moment Trevor began flirting with him on the flight from Rome back to Washington. Shame threatened to choke him. When the questions seemed to be over, Randy couldn't help himself. His throat was dry, but he croaked out, "How did you identify him? I mean, what drew your attention to Trevor?"

Kennedy shared a look with Dannels before responding. "His wife gave us his name, among others, as part of a deal."

Randy slumped lower in his chair. "His *wife?*"

Dannels looked sympathetic. "Yes. According to her, they've worked essentially the same routine numerous times over the last four years."

Trevor was married.

And Randy never sensed a thing.

He was placed on administrative leave pending further investigation into his involvement with Trevor. The FBI and then the Secret Service's Internal Affairs division ultimately cleared him of complicity, but the damage was done. Randy had carelessly allowed a foreign government to monitor the movements of the Senate majority leader.

After the catastrophe, his superiors couldn't leave him in charge of a security detail. His team had never even known he was gay, and to find out that way eroded the trust they needed to work together efficiently. Randy's career was done.

• • •

RANDY OPENED HIS eyes again and sighed. He was aware that Trevor had been sentenced to twenty years for espionage, but they'd never spoken again after the day of the FBI raid. Randy never got the chance to ask his questions. Was any of it real? How did Trevor know who he was, and how did he move so effortlessly past Randy's usually sharp defenses?

Was Trevor even gay, or had he hated every moment he spent in Randy's bed?

A glance at the clock surprised him. "Get your ass in gear, Vaughan," he grunted, then surged to his feet. He dragged his towel across his hairy chest again but he was dry so he tossed it aside and got dressed.

Randy had eaten his sandwich and driven halfway to DC before he acknowledged why those painful memories had surfaced again after so long. Trevor had a wife. Jack had a fiancée. Was any of it real, or was Jack just playing him to get at the painting, the way Trevor played him to get Grace Gibson's travel schedule?

He needed to get through the evening, and then shut the door on Jack Fraser.

Chapter Fourteen

RANDY DIDN'T LOOK up when the door to Mata Hari opened at six-thirty. He didn't have to. It was as if Jack resonated someplace inside him. He kept his head down as he finished restocking Grey Goose vodka while Jack crossed the room and came to a halt at the bar.

"Hello, Randy," he heard, and then finally glanced up.

Jack was dressed in a black polo shirt under a gray wool blazer. His intense eyes burned with excitement and a touch of nervousness as he gazed at Randy, and his hands resting on the counter trembled slightly. Randy tried hard to think of him as Fraser but it just didn't work. He steeled himself to indifference and nodded. "Jack." He said nothing more but completed his task. Jack had every right to be anxious, and Randy was okay with letting that build.

After a minute or so of silence, Jack cleared his throat. "You said we'd need to leave to make it by seven, I believe?"

Randy beckoned Malcolm over. "Mal, I'm going to be gone for an hour or so. You keep an eye on the place."

Malcolm glanced back and forth between Jack and Randy, and curiosity burned on his face. He knew better than to ask, so he just said, "Sure, Randy. It'll probably be quiet."

Randy gestured for Jack to wait as he retrieved and his truck keys and a thick jacket from his office. He shrugged into its sleeves as he returned to the bar, then jerked his head to indicate

Jack should follow him out to the parking lot.

"I'll drive," Randy said. "Traffic sucks but this way I can come right back when we're done." Jack had an amused expression on his face as he climbed up into the truck and settled in the passenger seat. "What?"

Jack smirked. "This truck. It's so American."

Randy grunted as he started the engine. Before he could pull out of the lot, Jack rested a hand on his arm.

"Are we going to discuss it?"

Randy expected that, and he had his answer ready. "There's nothing we need to talk about. It was a pleasant night, and we both got off. That's it." He pulled onto the street a little fast, hoping to forestall any further conversation.

It didn't work. "You know, I didn't intentionally keep Sophie from you. It just never occurred to me that you'd care."

"I don't care."

Jack snorted. "Of course. That's why you left the way you did."

Randy shot him an angry glance. "I left because we were done."

"Then may I explain about Sophie?"

"Look, Jack. There's really no point. You were just visiting town, you'll be gone tomorrow, and you don't owe me an explanation."

"Ah."

Randy hated the way Jack said that. *Ah*. Like he knew something about Randy. He tightened his grip on the steering wheel. "Tell me how you started researching the painting."

Jack was quiet for a minute, and Randy watched him out of the corner of his eye. A struggle was going on in Jack's face and Randy expected him to refuse. Abruptly, Jack sat up straighter and ran his hands through his hair.

"All right. I told you I was reading through François Brousseau's correspondence. This started about two, no, two and a half years ago now, in preparation for a major exhibit the museum had planned. We intended to showcase Jean-Pierre's time in Oise and specifically in the town of Fontaine-Chaalis by juxtaposing his works with his own descriptions of the creative process. I was assigned to find the most illuminating excerpts from his letters to François and match them to works we had in our possession at the Kensington or that we could negotiate to borrow from other museums.

"Well, it was during that project I noticed the gap in Brousseau's oeuvre. Jean-Pierre wrote to François on the fifth of July 1878 that he had undertaken the painting of an abbey in Chaalis, as I said last night. I recall he wrote that he worked 'beside a group of boulders that looked as if they had bubbled up from the mantle of the Earth, where travelers left the ashes of their fire.' He said 'in the distance was a desolate ruin on a hill and fields of flowers ranged down the valley.' In a later letter, he said he wanted to 'capture the sunrise as it spread across the field like a spill of honey.' He was quite explicit that he had completed the work just the day before, but he was disappointed in it. In fact, he wrote it was 'not at all what I'd hoped to accomplish.'

"I became curious to see this painting, but as I studied the official catalogues, I realized no such work had been described or photographed. In François's personal records of his brother's paintings, however, there was a notation for a work, number 260, that he listed as *Lever de soleil à l'abbaye de Chaalis*. That is, *Sunrise at the Abbey of Chaalis*. Even the title intrigued me, but I could discover no further information about that particular piece except that it had been sold in 1901."

Jack had shifted in his seat to face Randy. "Although records showed the sale, there were no indications of the purchaser's identity. I would have given up the hunt as a mere curiosity, except for the oddest thought." Jack stopped talking, and Randy darted his eyes from traffic to glance over.

He took the bait. "And what was that?"

Jack smiled. "It occurred to me that, sooner or later, someone might have looked at a disappointing old canvas of a ruin on a hill and fields of flowers in a valley, and thought to himself, hmm, that looks suspiciously like a Brousseau. So I wondered, what would you do if you had found such a work, perhaps in the drawing room of a deceased relative as you were settling an estate?"

"You'd find an expert and have it examined, I suppose."

"Precisely," Jack said with satisfaction. "And there really aren't many experts in Jean-Pierre Brousseau's work qualified to tell one if a work were original. So I compiled a short list of possible resources. The Kensington museum where I was employed, of course. A few other notable museums with significant collections of Brousseaus or other post-impressionists. And the big auction houses."

Randy nodded slowly. "Clever. An auction house—I wouldn't have thought of that."

Jack looked pleased. "It took some time, but I had a, um, connection with the biggest house of all, Valcoates, and she was able to pull some strings to get me access to their records. I was armed only with a few details—the approximate date of original sale, the bare description in Jean-Pierre's letters to François—but after months of searching I came across a record of a Norwegian gentleman who had asked whether a painting in his possession mightn't be a work by Brousseau. The description was sufficiently similar that I grew confident I had found what I was seeking. And what do you think?" Randy realized he was leaning slightly toward Jack, drawn in by his excitement. "The noted auction house told the Norwegian collector that his painting was *not* a Brousseau."

"Oh." Randy sagged back into his own seat, unreasonably disappointed.

"No, that was fascinating to me, do you see?" Randy shook his head. "Well, I could tell from the report in the Valcoates archives that they had never made the connection to the letters Jean-Pierre wrote to François. The examination was conducted in the early 1970s, well before certain tests that have been developed in the ensuing decades. The auction house report described the sources consulted, and its conclusion stemmed principally from the fact that the work was unsigned and that the style was different to Jean-Pierre's works both before his time in Fontaine-Chaalis and after. But that was precisely the point. I knew from the letters that this was a *transitional* work. Jean-Pierre painted the abbey and the fields when he was developing his new style. You understand?"

"I do," Randy said with a nod. "They were looking for a fully-realized work of genius by a master, and failed to recognize the fledgling steps he had to take and perhaps abandon in order to develop that genius."

Jack smiled happily. "Precisely. Of course you grasp it." Randy tried to ignore the pride in Jack's tone, or the warmth it spread through his chest.

"So," Jack continued. "I had the letters from Jean-Pierre and an appraisal given to a disappointed collector. I set out to track the owner down, only to learn that he had died at a quite respectable age and left his estate to grandchildren in England. It wasn't easy, but eventually I located one of the heirs, living in Whitechapel. She disclosed that most of her grandfather's art collection had been sold to pay estate taxes. She particularly remembered a canvas that they found in an attic, and how her grandfather had told them many times in disgust that the painting was rubbish, which was why he stored it away up there. She was able to find for me the name of the gallery, and of course that was my next stop."

Randy could imagine Jack taking up the scent of a mystery, and his own heart beat faster at the idea of the hunt. He saw Jack poring over reports in a mahogany-lined library as he looked for clues. Flipping frantically through catalogues to see where the trail might lead. Randy almost had to slam on the brakes as a car in front of him decided at the last second not to run a yellow light. Whitechapel, Jack had said. "Wait a minute. You contacted the gallery owner to ask about the painting?"

"Yes."

"Was this Bernard Gates, in Whitechapel? What did you tell him?"

"Very little, of course. You must see. If I'm right, this discovery will make my professional reputation. I couldn't risk having my work stolen, but once it became known what I was looking for—"

"Anyone would be able to recreate the trail." Randy's mind was whirling. He remembered the letter coming out of the blue from Gates a few months back, offering to repurchase the painting from him. "How long ago did you contact the gallery?"

Jack thought about it. "Probably three or four months back. But realize. It would be feasible to retrace my guesswork yet it would be very difficult to assemble the paper trail that I did. I have the original bill of sale from François Brousseau, the appraisal from the auction house, a handwritten letter from the Norwegian collector to his son describing his disgust with the painting and therefore his decision to not display it any longer, the correspondence from the heirs authorizing the sale by the auction house…"

"Provenance." Randy nodded. "You can demonstrate the provenance of the work."

"Exactly," Jack said proudly. "You know that provenance is key to any sale to a reputable collector or display in a museum. I'm reasonably confident that no one could recreate the records I have assembled."

"There seems to be a major flaw in your thesis, though." Randy took a quick glance at Jack. "An auction house says the painting's *not* an authentic Brousseau. Even with letters from Jean-Pierre to François that describes it, how do you overcome that?"

Jack's face shuttered closed. "I, uh, I have some thoughts on that. First things first, hmm?" he said in a clipped tone. "Let's see if the painting you own is the correct one."

Randy was shocked at the abrupt change. Then he began to get annoyed. For most of the drive, he'd been sucked in by Jack's openness. He'd shared a thrill of discovery that reminded him of the trip to the Metropolitan in New York with Uncle Kevin and Luc, when the world had begun to open before his curious eyes. But Jack had only woven an illusion. He told Randy just enough to get his cooperation, then shut him out again. He still didn't trust Randy, not fully.

Fine. Randy didn't entirely trust Jack either.

They finished the drive in awkward silence. When Randy pulled into the parking garage below Thomas's condo building and said, "We're here," Jack twitched with his growing excitement. They rode the elevator from the garage to the ground floor without exchanging a further word but Jack's eyes shone and he kept wiping his palms against his trousers.

"Randy Vaughan for Zachary and Thomas," he told the concierge. She buzzed upstairs, got approval, then told Randy to go ahead to the penthouse.

Zachary was waiting for them at the open door to the condo. "Hey, Randy. C'mon in," he called as they approached. His hair was damp, so Randy guessed he'd gone for a swim in the building's pool when he got home from work. He had been a swimmer in college and still kept it up.

Zachary was not quite as tall as Randy, but he had a steadiness that hadn't been there when he first walked through the door of Mata Hari six months earlier. The things he'd been through since had destroyed much of his naïveté, but not his essential spirit. Randy admired that, and he was happy Thomas had been able to pull his head out of his ass long enough to see that Zachary was perfect for him.

"Hiya, kid. Zachary Hall, this is Jack Fraser," he said with a gesture. Jack shook hands with Zachary, who then ushered them into the living room.

The condo was stark and furnished in a minimalist style Randy knew dated to a time when Thomas was rebuilding his life and couldn't be bothered to think about comfort. That was one of the reasons Randy had persuaded Thomas to hang some of his art collection there a few years earlier, to add life to what would otherwise have felt like a stark white cell.

Already, though, he could see Zachary was softening the hard edges Thomas had lived with for a long time. Books filled a lot of the shelves, throws had appeared on the backs of chairs, and the space was more lived-in than when Thomas had been alone. "This is the big weekend, huh?" Randy asked.

Zachary glowed. "Yes, and I can't wait." To Jack, he explained, "I'm moving in here with my partner this weekend."

"How do your parents feel about it?" Randy wanted to know.

Zachary held out his hand and wiggled it back and forth. "Pretty mixed, I'd say. They've been trying hard to accept the gay thing, and they liked Thomas when they met him. But their son shacking up with another man? That's a tough one for them."

Jack spoke up. "So you're out to your family then?"

"I am, just recently. It's a long story, but Randy was a big part of it. He saved my life." Jack didn't seem at all surprised at the dramatic statement, and Randy narrowed his eyes.

Jack shrugged. "I did some simple research after I found you at Mata Hari and you all but kicked me out. The story of the stalker and your role was all over the internet. 'Hero Bartender Stops Serial Killer' was the first story I found."

Randy was annoyed but Zachary laughed. "It was a crazy few weeks, with all that publicity. But that's how my parents found out I was gay. I had to tell them before the details hit the news. When my parents flew to New York from Utah and met Randy for our big television interview, they thought he was the best thing since sliced bread."

Jack gazed at Randy with surprising warmth in his eyes again. The coldness of the last few minutes in the truck and then the elevator seemed to be gone. "I can definitely see the hero."

"Hardly," Randy said with a snort. "The story got pretty exaggerated by the end."

Zachary dared to throw an arm over Randy's shoulder. "Not to me. Hero." Randy huffed, but Zachary just chuckled at him. "So. Thomas said you want to see a painting?"

"I had Thomas hang it in the master bedroom a while back, if you haven't moved it since."

"Nope, we haven't started rearranging anything like that. We figured we'd wait until I get my furniture in, not that I have much. And I don't think Thomas is going to let me replace an oil painting with my vintage *Star Wars* poster, even if it *is* signed by Mark Hamill. C'mon," he said, and drew Jack and Randy down the hall to the bedroom.

They stepped into a large, white room, dominated by a window that overlooked the United States Capitol building. The autumn sky was dark already, so the Capitol dome glowed in its uplights. Jack grunted appreciatively, but then he turned slightly and saw the painting under a small portrait light.

His jaw dropped, and it seemed for a moment he might collapse.

Randy had positioned *Sunrise* to the right of the king-size bed. The large canvas was embedded in a rich gilt frame that gleamed under the small light. The painting itself was as unremarkable as Randy recalled, but he tried to look at it with new eyes. Could this really be what Jack was seeking? He checked to see what he thought.

Reverence. That was the word for the expression on Jack's face. His eyes were wide and shiny, lips parted. A sigh escaped from him into the room. One hand moved slightly, inches from the surface, as if he were tracing the image in the air.

So quietly that Randy almost couldn't hear, Jack said, "I've stood where he painted this." A shiver ran down Randy's back.

Zachary looked back and forth between the two of them. "What's going on? Is this painting something special?"

"That's what we're trying to find out, kid," Randy said. Even though he knew the answer, he had to ask. "What do you think, Jack? Is this what you've been looking for?"

Jack licked his lips, then darted a look at Randy. A grin stretched the corners of his mouth into a smile. His eyes shone with joy. "I believe it is."

"Well, son of a bitch." Randy put his hands in his back pockets and studied the work, head slightly tilted. Now that he knew what he was looking for, he could almost see it. The brush work for the sky and clouds. The arrangement of the elements. The abbey itself reminded him of the building in the background of *Madonna of the Castle.*

Zachary was swiveling his head back and forth between Jack and Randy. He was sharp, and he'd spent many a Sunday afternoon with Randy and Thomas strolling through art museums, and any second now…

"Holy *shit*, Randy. Is this an original Brousseau?"

Yep, there it was. "I don't know yet. Jack thinks it might be."

Zachary sank onto the bed. "I almost knocked it off the wall a few days ago when Thomas and I were, um, roughhousing." He looked stunned. "What if we'd damaged it? Oh my god. You have to put it someplace safer."

Jack spoke up quickly. "I absolutely agree. This work is potentially a major link in the development of one of the world's most revered artists."

Randy snorted. "You said it was stored away in an attic for years."

"In ignorance," Jack protested as he whirled on him. His tone vibrated with excitement and urgency. "Randy, this is it. This is the painting Jean-Pierre wrote to his brother about. I can feel it in my bones."

Zachary stood up again. "I have to tell Thomas. He'll know what to do."

"Hold on a minute," Randy begged. "This is what I was afraid of, a big mess. The condo building is safe and secure. I think the painting is good here for now. What am I going to do, hang it in Mata Hari?"

Jack gasped. "What? Of course you can't do that."

"I was making a point," Randy said sarcastically. "Besides, Mata Hari may not be safe anyway." To Zachary, he explained, "Someone broke in recently. They didn't take anything, but the cops came out."

"And you sent them after me," Jack said levelly.

Randy shrugged it away. He refused to be embarrassed over a

reasonable precaution. "Call Thomas if you want, and we can talk more about it but I'd prefer leaving the painting where it is for now." Zachary excused himself to go call his boyfriend, and a heaviness settled in the room between Jack and Randy.

Jack stepped close to the painting and studied it in minute detail. "May I take it off the wall?" Randy helped Jack lift the large frame carefully from its hooks. Jack looked at the back of the painting and huffed disappointedly. "The frame covers the key area of the canvas. I can't see whether it bears the number François would have placed on it." They rehung the work gingerly and then stepped back to look at it side by side.

Finally Randy asked, "I'm glad you're sure, but that won't count for much in an auction house. So when will you tell me what you would need to do to authenticate it?"

Jack sucked in a breath nervously. "I would like your permission to have the painting moved to my museum in London."

"What?"

"There are tests we can run there, in an absolutely sterile and protected environment." Jack's earlier reticence vanished in the excitement of the moment. "We would remove the canvas from the frame to look for François's numbering on the back. We would check the materials used by the artist to look for correspondence with known works by Brousseau from the same time period. We can chemically examine the actual paint used without any damage to the work. Brousseau favored very specific compounds, you see, particularly cobalt, and we can tell if the compounds appear in this work. In a matter of weeks, I can complete the analysis and present my findings to the experts."

Randy's dismay flared into anger as Jack went on. These tests, these ideas… Jack had known all along what he was going to ask Randy for when they came here, and he had refused to disclose it. Jack was playing Randy. Maybe even the night at Cuir was part of a plan, just like fucking Trevor had pulled on him.

Oblivious to Randy's rising fury, Jack continued to talk through his vision. "Once I persuade the experts of the painting's origins, well, there will be plenty of time for you to decide the next steps. It's the validation I need, I mean, *we* need. If we can establish a consensus—"

"No."

Jack stopped speaking at the harsh interruption, and stared aghast at Randy. "No? No what?"

"No," Randy repeated in a slow, deadly serious tone. "You may *not* take the painting."

Jack turned white. A noise came out of his throat that sounded like desperation. He licked his lips, then said in a softer, pleading voice, "You must understand, Randy. These tests are crucial to proving my thesis but there is simply no way I can perform them here."

Randy shook his head sharply, trying to keep hold of his reaction even as he tightened hands into fists and clenched his jaw. "You expect me to hand over a painting that is potentially worth millions of dollars to a stranger, and let him whisk it away to England on a promise? Not going to happen."

"Randy, I'm begging you. You must know you can trust me."

"Trust you? I don't know you at all," he exploded. "You've done nothing to establish your credentials. You try to bully me into compliance and when that doesn't work you say what you need to say to get at the painting. Your manner of speech is affected and an act. You conveniently leave out the fact that you're engaged—"

"Is that what this is about?" Jack shouted right back at him, his burr prominent. "That you fucked me without knowing I was engaged? I told you, that's nowt to do with you."

"Well, how noble of you," Randy sneered. "That surely sets

my mind at ease, that a man who wants to carry off a potential masterpiece has no qualms about fucking around on his fiancée and making me a party to it."

"What?" Jack was stunned, and frankly, so was Randy. He didn't know where the vitriol was coming from but he couldn't stop it.

"So convenient you were in Cuir the same night I was. Was that a setup too, Jack? You said you researched me. Did you figure out I was in the leather community, and then buy yourself a little harness and show up to see if I'd bite? Is that any more real than the clothes you wear like a costume?"

Jack swung his head side to side, whether in denial or shock Randy couldn't tell. "I swear to you, that wasn't a setup. I had no idea you'd be at Cuir." He spread his hands helplessly, but Randy was in no mood to listen.

"It's time to go," he snarled. "I have to get back to my bar." He gestured for Jack to precede him, and after giving one long look at the painting, Jack complied. Randy followed him down the hallway to find Zachary standing in the living room. His phone was still in his hand, and he was pale.

He'd obviously heard the fight, but he tried in true Zachary fashion to keep the mood friendly. "So, Randy. Thomas agrees to whatever you're comfortable with regarding the painting. But he asked you to talk to a lawyer he knows before you make any decisions about releasing it to anyone."

Jack was clearly struggling to control his disappointment, but he expressed his agreement at Zachary's words. "That's a good idea. I should have suggested that. Please, Randy. Talk to someone who works with consignments and auctions. There are industry standards and agreements. We can make you comfortable with this."

A touch of shame crept into Randy's head. He was taking out

his own frustrations, possibly on the wrong person. He looked at Jack steadily for a moment, then away. But he said, "I'll think about it."

"Thank you," Jack sighed. He turned to Zachary and held out his hand. "And thank you for letting us in this evening. I apologize for any drama we created."

Zachary was gracious. "It was fascinating. I know I can't tell anybody about this, but come on. How many people can say they sleep with a Brousseau in their bedroom?" He laughed, and it lightened the mood.

Randy and Jack rode the elevator to the ground floor in silence but less animosity. "Do you want a ride somewhere?" Randy asked somewhat stiffly, but Jack shook his head.

"My hotel is actually not far. I'll walk to save you time getting back to the bar."

Randy started to head for the parking garage, but Jack put a hand on his arm. "Please believe me. I have never intentionally lied to you, or tricked you in any way. Last night at Cuir meant a great deal to me."

Randy faced Jack for a long moment. What should he say? It had meant a lot to him too. More than he cared to admit. The silence stretched and Jack dropped his hand to move away. Randy cleared his throat. "I'll, uh, talk to a lawyer soon, and I'll let you know what I decide."

Jack nodded sadly. "Of course. There's no point in my going to Philadelphia now, so I'll be in Washington through the end of the week." He paused and searched Randy's face. The longing in Jack's eyes was surely just about the painting, Randy told himself. What else could it be?

Jack said softly, "I hope to hear from you soon, whatever you decide." And then he walked out of the lobby and into the October night.

Chapter Fifteen

WHEN RANDY GOT back to Mata Hari, he was surprised to find Danny there helping out. Malcolm tended bar for the few customers as Danny dumped a bucket of ice into the service bin. "Hi, Randy," he called.

"What are you doing here?" Randy asked. "I thought you were going to a movie."

"I did, but when it ended I was bored, so I took the Metro in. I just got here a little while ago."

"Well, thanks. Glad for the help." Randy dropped his jacket in his office, then reclaimed his space behind the bar. "Mal, go grab food or something if you want a break."

Malcolm pulled off his apron and grabbed his own down jacket. "Want me to bring back anything?"

Danny commented to Randy, too loudly, "I left a roast in the slow cooker."

"I guess not, Mal." He could see the question on Malcolm's face. Even though he'd brought Danny into Mata Hari before, he hadn't really explained about their living situation. Danny was letting it be known they were sharing meals, which implied something a little closer than Randy just giving him a place to stay. It was clearly intentional, and Randy sighed. He and Danny were going to have to talk more about this.

A few more customers came in, but it remained slow like most Tuesdays and there were only so many times Randy could wipe down the bar or bus glasses. He started to run out of busy work to keep Danny occupied too. After serving two men and chatting with them a few moments, Randy glanced at his phone and noticed Joe had called. He sent Danny to get beer to restock the bar fridge, then listened to the message.

"Randall, my dear, it's Joe Mulholland." That made Randy smile. As if anyone else spoke in that raspy Bostonian accent. "I've finally heard back from one of my colleagues and she has a bed available in her shelter for your young friend. Her facility is located in Baltimore, but that's the nearest location I've been able to find. It really isn't that far away, if he should decide to come visit you. This shelter has career counselors on staff as well. Please let me know this evening if your friend will be taking the bed, because you know how intense the demand is for these placements. Thank you, dear heart. I'll speak to you soon."

Randy stared at his phone, then disconnected and pushed it back into his pocket. *Baltimore? Well, fuck.* He hadn't thought about this enough. With all the crap going on with Jack and the painting, somehow he'd managed to forget that Danny wasn't really his housemate. Or his project. Or his son.

But dammit, he liked Danny. He liked having him around when he got home at the end of a long day. Danny seemed to enjoy the time they spent together watching TV or talking about art. It was companionable and easy. The house was cleaner than it had been in a long time, and there was always a meal on the table. But was he being fair to Danny? He couldn't be what Danny seemed to want.

It had to be the kid's decision. When Danny finished loading the beers, the bar was still fairly empty and no one waited for a drink. "Danny, we need to talk for a minute," Randy said softly. Danny jerked his head up, surprise and worry flashing across his face.

"Did I do something wrong?"

"What? No, not at all. Listen, I just got a message from my friend Joe. There's a bed available in a youth shelter in Baltimore. I know that's kind of far, but it's a safe place and you'd probably be able to get training and job placement help. The thing is, they need to know tonight if you want to go there."

Danny looked at Randy in shock as his big, expressive eyes took on a shimmer. Randy's heart seized up.

"Oh shit. Look, kid, I'm not kicking you out. Okay?"

Danny stood up straight and squared his narrow, thin shoulders. He sounded hoarse when he spoke. "I get it, Randy. You've been great. But you live alone and you probably want your house back to yourself."

He put a hand on Danny's arm. "This isn't about me. I want to know what *you* want to do. It was weird at first, sharing my house, but I'm used to it now. I like it. If you want to stay, then stay." He dropped his voice lower. "You just need to think about whether that's best for you. I'm not going to become your boyfriend."

Danny flushed and his eyes glistened. "If it's the age thing, I don't care," he said fiercely.

"But I do. It isn't going to happen. I can give you a safe place to stay while you start working on your life. You're good company, I like you, but that's all. So if you want to keep living with me, you need to make sure that works for you."

Danny blinked a few times at that, and a tear spilled over to run down his cheek. Finally he asked tremulously, "You aren't kicking me out?"

"No. This is your choice," Randy told him emphatically.

"I want to stay." Danny ran the back of his hand over his face to wipe away the moisture there. "You make me feel useful. Wanted. Not, like, sexually. I get it. But like you want me there."

"C'mere," Randy said and pulled him into a hug. "I'm your friend, Danny. I do want you there, for as long as you're comfortable."

Danny clutched him hard, then pulled back with his face turned away. He couldn't meet Randy's gaze, though Randy could see tears coursing again. "I'll be right back." Danny ran down the hall toward the restrooms, and Randy let him go with a sigh. He hoped he was doing the right thing all the way around.

When he turned back, Jack stood at the bar. The compassion Randy saw in his eyes surprised him. For some reason, Randy found he was explaining, "Danny's just a kid I'm giving a safe place to stay for a while. Until he finds his feet."

"I heard." Jack sounded husky when he added, "Hero."

Randy shook his head. "It's nothing like that. He was in trouble, and I have room to spare." Jack continued to look at him steadily, and Randy dropped his gaze first. "Do you want a drink?"

"Yes. I do, in fact, want a drink. Badly. Plymouth martini, please. Very dry, with a twist."

Randy iced a glass, then began to assemble the cocktail. He glanced up as he let a few drops of vermouth into the shaker. "What are you doing here, Jack? I haven't had time to deal with anything."

"I know that, but I was walking to my hotel when I understood something." He waited as Randy poured his martini into the chilled glass, added a twist of lemon peel, and slid the drink toward him. When Randy met his eye again, Jack said, "I didn't give you what you really need to make a decision. Trust."

Randy frowned. "I don't understand."

"I think you do. You told me already trust is important to you, but I failed to grasp your meaning fully." His gaze was steady until Randy recalled the moment at Cuir. Jack nodded at the understanding on Randy's face. "You said to me just last night, if I gave you my trust, you wouldn't abuse it. And you didn't. Now I would like to make you that gift again."

Malcolm returned from his dinner break and looked back and forth between Randy and Jack. The questions just had to be piling up in his assistant's head but Randy ignored that. "Mal, can you cover?" Randy gestured with his head for Jack to accompany him to one of the side rooms off the main bar.

They sat down in neighboring wing chairs, and Jack took a sip of his martini. "That's a bit of all right, that," he said before resting it on a cocktail table. He leaned forward and clasped his hands together as they dangled between his knees. "Randy, I'm not trying to flatter you when I say that you see things I'd prefer to keep hidden. Things I thought I'd actually defeated in myself. But I understand that what I conceal out of shame may be perceived as duplicitous. May I trust you again?"

Randy dipped his chin in agreement.

"You are quite right about my clothes and my accent. This inna... well, this isn't me. Not really. I grew up in a blue collar town far from London. About three hours northwest in fact, in a place called Stoke-on-Trent. It dunna sound like much distance, but believe me, the difference between the London art world and the factory where my dad worked—it's vast. Practically uncrossable." As Jack spoke, the London tones relaxed and revealed more of the burr Randy had detected previously.

"I'm the middle child of five, all boys. My mum was a school teacher and my dad worked shifts when he could get 'em. It's a fine place for many, but I felt trapped. I dreamed of getting away to somewhere I could feel free. Somewhere more refined, like. My mates at school, my brothers, even my dad kicked my bum for putting on airs, as they said. Said I was soft. Called me a monstink." Jack gave Randy a small grin. "It means a conceited young 'un. Anyway, my mum understood. She probably knew I couldn't stay in Stoke.

"I went to uni—that is, to university—to study art. Do you know a film called *Little Man Tate*?" Randy did. "There's a part when the boy genius looks at a print of van Gogh's *Irises*. He sees one white iris amidst the purple, and he says, 'Maybe it's lonely.' Well, that was a revelation for me. I was frankly shocked. I had probably seen dozens of posters and brollies an' all with *Irises*, but until that film, it never occurred to me to wonder what the artist meant to convey. It was a sublime touch, this little observation of what van Gogh may have intended. I started looking up things in the library to see what records there were, and came across some of Vincent's correspondence. That was the start of my passion."

Randy got it. What Kevin had done for him was different, but somehow the same. He had kindled something with his questions to Randy, until the curiosity grew into a flame. "I understand."

"My mum saw the change, and she did everything she could to help. She even told off my dad and brothers, to make 'em leave me alone. She was brilliant, really. She spent hours with me to help get me ready for my A Levels in history and in art. I couldna have accomplished nowt else. When I was accepted to university, she was as proud of that as anything."

Randy could only imagine what that kind of support from his mother would have been like. Her near-shame in her own brother and her son had never made sense to him. She'd been so concerned with keeping up appearances in her everyday world, her narrow-minded view of what was appropriate, that she couldn't understand or accept that at least some of the men in her life wanted a world bigger than Portland, Maine.

Jack's words brought him back. "At uni, I came to see the art community had little room for a working class lad. Many of the students in my program had grown up attending museum openings and galas. They were posh themselves, maybe not bright enough for Oxford or Cambridge but better able to move through the academic games than I could. I applied myself in my studies, but even favorite professors treated me as, I don't know." Jack grimaced painfully. "As a mascot. I could write essays as well as anyone. I knew my history, the styles, artistic movements. But when I spoke Potteries dialect, I could see the eye rolls. Perhaps it's different in the States, but in London, at least, a lot of the art world is all polish and sophistication. Veneer. My manner was a tremendous liability. I had to find a way to fit in, and so I changed the manner of my speech and my dress. I was my own *Pygmalion*."

"You learned to pass," Randy said with a slow nod. "You became what they wanted to see, in order to thrive."

"I did." Jack paused, then hung his head sheepishly. His burr was under control again when he spoke. "I suppose you condemn me for that. I doubt you've had to pass as anything but yourself a day in your life."

Randy felt his cheeks burn. "You're wrong about me there. I hid that I was gay all through my career in the Secret Service. I had the best of intentions to make changes from the inside when I rose in the ranks, but somewhere along the way, I suppose I just forgot to be who I was." He could sense Jack's compassion still, and he hoped Jack felt the same from him. "I don't condemn you for doing what you had to do in order to fit in. I guess I just hope there was someone who knew the real Jack Fraser."

Jack grinned shyly. "There was. I met Sophie Valcoates while we were still at uni in Scotland. We were in a seminar together on Egyptian art history, and we became fast friends. She was from that posh world but she understood instantly why I was cultivating this false front. She helped me perfect it and carry it off, in fact."

"Valcoates?" Randy asked. "As in Valcoates Auction House?" He was shocked—that was one of the largest in the world.

"Yes, exactly. It was the family business. Her father was a senior vice president so she grew up with cocktail conversation an' all. It was a lovely game to her, pulling the wool over the eyes of the monstinks that inevitably showed up at galleries and openings just to be seen. When we moved to London, she helped get my start. New manner of speaking, new style I suppose. She even bought me new clothes."

"Did she know about you? That you..." Randy trailed off. In fact, *he* didn't know about Jack. Was he gay? Bi? Hardcore kinkster, or merely a tourist?

Jack turned red. "Yes, she knew I was gay. *Am* gay. And that I like sex rougher than might be acceptable in the art gallery circles. Of course it's mostly theoretical. I don't dare go into any of the gay places, or seek company in London. The gossip would ruin any hope I have of a career. Sophie, though. She loves me anyway, and I love her."

Randy felt his shoulders stiffen and tried to cover his reaction by reaching for his drink until he remembered he didn't have one. His disappointment made him awkward again. He couldn't understand why he had even begun to go down this path with Jack, and why he'd let himself indulge in ridiculous daydreams.

So many men over the years had tried to get Randy to give a relationship a shot. Nice, handsome, sexy men. Through whatever perversity of his own nature, Randy had turned nearly all of them away until Trevor. And even if Randy had finally let himself have something beyond just a steady roll in the hay, that had been a lie from the beginning on Trevor's side. Proof that Randy had no judgment worth speaking of, and no business with anything more than a fuck buddy.

So why was he practically grieving for what could have been?

"You don't have to tell me about this," Randy said, more to protect himself than Jack. "I follow. You're engaged to someone you love, and she lets you get some on the side."

"Randy, I want you to understand." Jack leaned forward and waited until Randy met his eyes. "I do love Sophie, but we're like brother and sister. We've never had sex, not even a real kiss. Sophie simply doesn't have sexual desire for anyone, man or woman. And she doesn't get jealous about me. I think these days people might say she's asexual. Labels don't concern Sophie. But we're the best of friends.

"For years we simply posed as a couple but her father started to apply immense pressure once she turned thirty-five, so we quickly reached an agreement. We announced our engagement last year. She needs a man to keep her father from dragging her to one potential suitor after another, and I need the status and security of a well-connected wife to be taken seriously in our circles. I would never do nowt to embarrass her, of course, so we agreed long ago that it was best if I quell my desires whilst in England, but anything was fair game when I'm abroad."

A flare of desire surged through Randy. *Fair game, huh. I could show you a fair game.*

But almost immediately, the flicker died out. He didn't want to be a part of what Jack described. He was shaking his head before Jack even finished speaking.

"I hear you. And I'm glad you have a situation that works well for the two of you. But if you told me this so I'd take you to bed again, the answer is no."

Disappointment showed in Jack's face. "But why not? Inna this perfect? You know now that it's more of a mutual convenience. I'm not hurting Sophie because I'm not giving away anything she wants."

"You gave away what *I* want."

It just slipped out and revealed hurt Randy meant to hide. When Jack's face registered an O of surprise, he jumped out of his chair, scooping up the empty martini glass as he rose. He spoke fast to cover up his admission. "I appreciate you trusting me. I'm sure that was difficult. It changes nothing, but you're right about me. Honesty is important. I've really got to get back to the bar."

"Randy." Jack reached up and put a hand on his arm. The weight and warmth soaked through Randy's white shirt and to the skin below. He wanted to pull away, but he couldn't quite make himself do it. "You see it as a betrayal, don't you? My relationship with Sophie."

A betrayal? The word brought Randy to a full stop. Jack stroked his thumb back and forth along Randy's forearm as he waited for some kind of response. He opened his mouth to make a smartassed reply, then closed it again.

Betrayal. Even if Sophie and Jack had a bargain, it *was* a betrayal, to Randy. They held themselves out to their world one way, but the reality was different. Perhaps no one had the right to make assumptions or lay expectations at their feet. Jack and Sophie, though—they apparently not only wanted to play the expectations game, they wanted to win. If Randy let himself be drawn in, then he would be complicit in that game.

Randy was on the edge of understanding something about himself. He squatted on his heels and looked up at Jack's face.

"I'd say that your deal with Sophie is none of my business, but you brought this to me so I think you want to make it my business. You've apparently decided my opinion matters, and I wish I could give you the pass. I wish I could take you home and put you in leather and wrap you in chains and take all the noise away. I wish I could fuck you again to make you come apart the way you did last night, and then put you back together. I'm not a moralist, Jack. I don't go out of my way to judge relationships. But you want something with me. Maybe an evening, maybe more. I can't give that to you. I'm sorry."

"Canst thee explain it to me, Randy?" Jack asked softly. "Please try."

Randy hesitated, then held to Jack's gaze. "My uncle and his partner were together for twenty years until Kevin was killed in the line of duty. They were proud of each other and their relationship, even when being out and open cost them. They weren't perfect. They had their fights and problems. Even made a mistake with a stranger a time or two. But from what I saw, it was the honesty that mattered to them. The public commitment. It was who they were.

"I believe in that, Jack. I'm fifty-one years old now, and I probably missed my chance at that kind of relationship some time when I was failing to live up to my own expectations. But even if I can't have that, it doesn't mean I'll settle for being a secret or a second choice or a fool."

Jack's eyes darted back and forth across Randy's face and his mouth opened in surprise. "Oh my god. I just got it."

"Got what?"

"It's right there on the sign above your door, Randy. You've already been badly betrayed, haven't you?"

Randy looked away sharply at the connection Jack drew and tried to laugh it off. "I don't know what you're talking about."

"Mata Hari. The famous French singer who used sex to learn secrets and then passed them along to her spymasters. Greta Garbo was in the film from the early 1930s."

"It's just a name—" Randy tried, but Jack shook his head. He had a vacant look in his eye as he focused inward.

"Let me see. Mata Hari got information from a man who was

in love with her, even though he knew she was a spy. Then, yes, then she was ordered to get information from a pilot about missions he was flying over Germany. But she fell in love with the pilot. The first man then turned her in to the French police."

Randy stood from his squat and winced as his knees cracked. He looked at Jack a moment, then said, "'A spy in love is a tool that has outlived its usefulness.' That's the best line in the movie."

"Randy, what happened to you?" Jack pleaded. He rose to his feet, and Randy let him wind an arm around his waist even though he resented how good it felt to have a warm hand pull him close. He could smell that damn cologne rising from Jack's neck, all dark and mysterious and wonderful.

He closed his eyes, unwilling to meet Jack's. But Jack trusted him even though Randy had been an asshole to him, so he fought down his pride and decided to return the gift.

"It wasn't exactly like the movie. A man named Trevor Mackenzie. For six months, I thought we were in a relationship. He said he loved me and I, well, I thought I loved him. He worked for an airline so we didn't get together that often, but he would fly in to meet me when I was traveling for the Secret Service, or drop in to see me in DC."

For the second time that evening, Randy's face reddened. The shame he usually kept at bay was near that night. Perhaps it was Jack's attempts at honesty, or Randy's own ridiculous disappointment, but he was useless and idiotic and, goddammit, *lonely*. Maybe that was why he made himself finish the story.

"It turned out Trevor was just using me to get information about the senator I was responsible for protecting. He was married to a woman the entire time, and I was just a mark. I was investigated and exonerated of any complicity, but the scandal was an end to my career. Trevor went to jail, and I never saw him again."

Jack made a noise in his throat—sympathy? Pain? Anger? Randy couldn't tell, but he made himself say it all. Just once, to a man who would leave the country soon, he would tell all of it.

"I failed in so many ways. I didn't see what was right in front of me about Trevor's game. I became a piece on the side to a married man. Grace Gibson was a friend as well as my responsibility, and I failed her. I let down the memory of my uncle. I never had the balls to come out as gay, so I let down my team again when they found out what I had done." He closed his eyes tightly to seal in the pain and the guilt that threatened to pour out of him. "I let down my country by my own foolishness. That's why I don't like being called a hero. I'm just a man trying to make up for his mistakes."

Randy opened his eyes again when Jack pressed a kiss to his cheek and to his lips. It was closed-mouth, and Jack didn't try for more, but he was grateful for the contact. For a moment, at least, he felt less of a fool. When Jack broke the kiss but pulled at the back of his head, Randy relaxed and let his forehead down to rest on Jack's shoulder.

"I think a true painting of you would show you standing caught between two men," Jack murmured. "Kevin on one side, showing you what was necessary in a good life. Love, honor, duty. This Trevor bloke on t'other side, using you, betraying your trust, taking advantage of your need to protect. I wish I had the skill to create that canvas for you." Randy jerked away sharply at Jack's words, but he stopped his retreat at the gentle, kind smile he saw. "I'm not taking the mick, Randy. I think I understand. You want to do good, but you're afraid of being used. You're full of hope, but you've been hurt. You want to love, but that requires trust."

Randy pulled back. His throat hurt and his eyes burned, but he blinked that away. He didn't know why it should hurt to be seen so clearly by a man who could at best remain a casual acquaintance. While he straightened his clothes self-consciously, Jack similarly put himself together. Enough had been said, and even though it left them in the same position, they understood each other a little better.

Jack touched Randy lightly, then squeezed his forearm. "Thank you for the gift. I promise you, I won't talk to anyone else about this. Not even Sophie. I willna abuse your trust." They shared a sad smile at the reminder of their night in Cuir.

Jack said, "I'll wait to hear what you decide about the painting," and then he left.

As he did, he brushed past Danny, who was standing in the door to the side room. Randy was startled. "How long have you been there?"

Danny just looked at him for a moment, then said, "Not long." He turned to leave, then came into the room instead and took the empty martini glass from Randy. "I'll wash this."

"Danny..."

"Not now. Okay?" Danny spared him a glance before leaving, and the anguish in those wide, expressive eyes hurt to see. Dammit, the day just kept getting worse.

Chapter Sixteen

WEDNESDAY MORNING, RANDY called the number Thomas had given him for a lawyer to discuss handing over the painting. On the second ring, a woman answered. "Good morning. O'Sullivan Harris, this is David James's office. May I help you?"

"Yes. My name is Randy Vaughan. Thomas Scarborough gave me Mr. James's number. I'd like to see if he has some time available to speak with me about a legal question involving a piece of art."

"Please hold a moment." The woman was back shortly and said, "Mr. Vaughan? Mr. James has a client with him right now but he says Mr. Scarborough let him know you would be calling. He can meet with you at eleven today if that's convenient."

"Oh, that's great. Yes, I can be there."

"Fine, I'll schedule you in." The woman gave Randy the address for the law firm.

Danny handed him a cup of coffee when he came downstairs, but immediately slipped out of the room as he apparently was trying to avoid Randy. Whatever he had heard or seen between Randy and Jack clearly bothered him, and Randy didn't know what to do about it. Should he just wait for Danny to talk to him? Bring it up himself? It wasn't like Jack was going to be in the picture for much longer, so maybe avoidance was in every-one's best interest.

Bingo, Randy decided. Unless Danny brought it up, he was just going to ignore the Jack/jealousy thing.

Danny buzzed through with some laundry, his head still turned away, and Randy decided they at least needed to address the living situation. "Danny, you got a minute?" Danny stopped loading the whites and came back into the kitchen. His head hung down slightly, and his shoulders were stooped.

"Sure. What do you need?"

Randy waited until Danny looked up at him. "I talked to Joe last night and let him know that you wouldn't be going to the shelter in Baltimore." Danny's eyes brightened, and he stood a little straighter. *God, even after our conversation he thought I was going to send him away.* "I meant what I said. You can stay here as long as you want, but if it's going to be long term, I'd just like to know there's a plan to get you set and on your feet."

Danny poked his tongue into his cheek, then asked, "What do you mean?"

"Look, let's sit down and talk a little." Danny moved slowly through the kitchen until he was leaning against the center island. Randy poured himself a second cup of coffee, and put one in front of Danny as well. Almost blindly, Danny picked up the cup in two hands and sipped at it, but he said nothing. Fine. Randy would be the one to push this.

"Well, college, for example. Do you have a high school diploma?"

Danny shook his head. "I never went back when my senior year started. I was trying so hard to make some money."

"Okay. So we could start there. I think you should consider taking some courses to get your high school equivalency. There are good community schools here in Virginia and I bet one of them has a program to get you ready. With your GED you can think about college." He sipped his coffee and evaluated the deerin-the-headlights expression dawning in Danny's face. "We can figure all that out together. If you want."

Danny blinked at him slowly, seeming stunned. "You think I should go back to school? Go to college?"

Randy crooked his head. "I do. Is that a problem for you?"

Danny shook his head carefully but his eyes remained wide. "No. It's just, I never really thought about it. There was no money even when my mom was alive, so I always figured college was for other people." He looked away. "For better people."

"Hey," Randy growled and waited until Danny looked at him. "You are 'better people.' You're bright and a hard worker. Responsible. You like to read. You're a good cook, and you seem interested in art. How were your grades in high school so far?"

"Nothing special. I had a solid 'B' GPA, I guess."

"Don't sneer at that. It means you're above average. Is there anything you know you'd like to do with your life? Any career you've thought about?"

Danny's eyes went even wider than Randy would have thought possible. "A *career*? Randy, I have no idea. How would I even...? Where would I start?" He began to breathe hard, then repeated weakly, "A career?"

"Hey, kid. Relax. It isn't something you have to figure out right away. I didn't bring it up to put pressure on you. I just want you to start thinking about it." Randy poured more coffee as he waited for Danny to calm. "Look, do me a favor. Run a few internet searches about local training courses for the GED. I'll pay for them, and that's it for now. The rest will take care of itself at the right time. If you're up for it, you can maybe do some searches on things you like to do and see if that sparks any ideas for later."

"That...that makes sense." Danny was breathing easier by then as the panicked look faded, but then he flushed again. "You know, in my high school, I never bothered to go to the guidance counselor. There didn't seem to be any point."

"There *is* a point. You're capable, and you can do great things if you believe in yourself."

Danny set down his cup and walked over to Randy. He put his arms around him and pressed his face to Randy's chest. Randy tensed, but there was nothing sexual in Danny's grip, so he breathed out and put his arms around Danny as well. They stood there for a minute and Randy tried to ignore the small shudders and sniffles he heard. He rubbed a hand awkwardly on the boy's sweatshirt and said quietly, "You got this, Danny. You can do this."

Finally Danny broke away, but he wouldn't look at Randy. "Thanks. I'll start trying to come up with some ideas, and then maybe we can talk about it." There was a sadness in his tone that Randy didn't understand. Maybe it was the years of thinking he wasn't good enough to even imagine college? Maybe it was a reminder his own parents couldn't help him figure life out? Whatever the case, Danny practically ran upstairs.

Well, that could have gone better, but it's a start.

    • • •

JUST BEFORE ELEVEN a.m., Randy pulled his truck into the parking garage at the address for David James's law firm. The elevator brought him to the main floor and he pushed through glass doors to enter the marbled reception area of O'Sullivan Harris. A polished young woman in a tweed suit greeted him.

"Good morning," Randy said. "I'm here to meet David James."

"Of course," the receptionist answered. "Please have a seat and I'll let him know you've arrived."

A few minutes later, the receptionist brought him to a conference room, where a man with chestnut hair and green eyes stood to greet him. The man was almost the same height as Randy, and wore a tailored suit that hinted at a body nearly as developed. Another man, younger, Asian, and with a completely shaved head, also stood.

"Thank you, Carole," said the man with green eyes. "Randy, I'm David James. It's nice to meet you."

They shook hands as Randy said, "Thomas sends his greetings."

David gestured. "This is my colleague Christian Fong. Thomas said you have some questions about fine art and that's outside my area of expertise, but Christian here works with many galleries and auction houses."

After Christian shook his hand too, all three sat down at the conference table. Randy said, "Thomas hired lawyers for us when we were getting my bar Mata Hari set up, but I don't really know how this works. I mean, engaging a lawyer for a specific question like this."

"Let's just talk about it for a while," David suggested. "Thomas has been able to help me with some of my pro bono work, so I'm happy to do something to help a friend of his. Also, I believe Thomas said you're friends with Joe Mulholland? Well, there's nothing I wouldn't do for Joe, and I'm sure he'd ask me to help you if I can." Randy chuckled at that.

Christian added, "Why don't we chat about your question in general terms, and then I'll tell you if it's something I'm able to help you with and give you an idea of the time it would take? If it's more than a few hours of work, we can do an engagement letter and we'll talk about hourly rates."

"Okay." Randy relaxed back in his conference chair. "Well, I can't quite believe this myself, but a piece of artwork I bought a few years ago turns out to be potentially quite valuable. I've been approached by an art historian from the Kensington Museum of European Art in London. He wants to take the painting to England to run some tests on it to determine its authenticity. I, uh, don't know this man personally. Or at least, not for long. When I mentioned all this to Thomas, he was concerned about the risks and asked me to make sure I got legal advice before releasing the painting."

David leaned forward. "As I said, this isn't my area but let me ask something. Is there a reason these tests can't be performed at the Smithsonian or one of the other museums here in Washington?"

Randy scratched his head at that. "I don't know a reason, but it isn't something I discussed with Jack." He reached for a pad of paper from the middle of the table, and Christian passed him a pen. Randy began to scribble some notes.

"Jack?" Christian asked.

"Jack Fraser is the historian who approached me. He initially sent me a request on his museum letterhead, and when I didn't respond he came to DC to persuade me to let him examine the painting."

David whistled. "This must be some painting." He apparently sensed Randy's reticence about disclosing too much, because he said earnestly, "You should understand, Randy. We haven't signed an engagement letter, but even a consultation like this is protected by the attorney client privilege. Don't say anything that makes you uncomfortable, but you can be assured it goes no further."

Christian asked, "Other than the letterhead you received, do you have any proof that Mr. Fraser is who he claims to be?"

"I have his business card and the logo matches the Kensington website. After he approached me, I did some internet searches and found several scholarly articles that Jack wrote. The bio attached to the most recent three articles all mention he works for the Kensington. Also, Jack is listed as an assistant curator on the Kensington's website."

David chuckled. "That's very thorough. Thomas mentioned you were formerly in law enforcement."

Christian smiled too and added, "He also suggested you get legal counsel? All of that hits the right note of integrity and professionalism."

"So, assuming for a minute that I do release the painting to his custody, how would that work?" Randy asked.

Christian leaned back in his chair. "Let's consider this in terms of *lending* the artwork, rather than consigning it for sale. That's the closest analogy to what we're talking about here, I would say. Typically, if you were going to entrust a valuable work of art to a museum for inclusion in an exhibit, you would negotiate an agreement with the museum first. A contract. You want to address insurance, of course, in the event of damage or theft. The threat of a terrorist attack is particularly tricky with many insurers.

"Then of course you want to understand the museum's security protocols to prevent damage or theft in the first place. It's quite common to insist upon seeing detailed security plans. You'll want to talk to your own insurance company for its input. If you agree to send the painting outside the United States, there's a program called International Indemnity that might be very useful for additional protection."

Randy scribbled notes as fast as Christian talked. He'd never remember this much detail later. Christian had grown intense while he spoke, and he continued. "Before you ever release the painting, the museum should send a conservator to review the condition of the work, to make sure it's safe to package and transport, and to agree with you on the condition before it ever leaves your custody." He smiled and gave a short chuckle. "I'll pause there, because it looks like you're overwhelmed."

Overwhelmed didn't cover it. Randy could only imagine how ignorant he must look. He'd given no thought to how complicated these issues could be, or what safeguards he should consider. David poured him some water, which Randy sipped gratefully.

He cleared his throat. "I'm kind of in over my head here, to be honest. I'm used to buying and shipping individual works of no great monetary worth. I have insurance, but the limits of coverage are far below what this piece could potentially be worth if it's authenticated."

David frowned. "Are you willing to give us a ballpark of what we're talking about here, in terms of value?"

Randy took a deep breath and let it out. "It could be in the millions of dollars. Maybe as much as ten million."

David's eyes widened, and Christian leaned in gleefully. "This seems like an interesting project. Our law firm's rates are high, but it wouldn't be unusual to insist that the museum pay our legal fee as a condition of negotiations over an exhibit. Even if you ultimately fail to reach an agreement."

That was a relief. Randy hadn't been looking forward to the thought of going into his savings to hire a law firm of O'Sullivan Harris's caliber but it had become clear to him in the last few minutes that he couldn't possibly wing a transaction as important as this.

He recalled Danny's consternation that morning when Randy suggested he think about a career, and how much trouble Danny had wrapping his head around the concept. He understood exactly how lost Danny felt, and he was grateful Thomas had pressed him to come seek advice instead of trying to handle it on his own.

The three men spent another hour discussing the issues

Randy would need to consider and came up with some possible strategies. Then they drafted a list of specific requests that Randy could provide to Jack to pass along to his museum to test how serious it was about a deal. When they were done, Christian shook hands with Randy and excused himself to another meeting. David lingered.

As Randy relaxed in the expensive leather conference chair and contemplated the list before him, David interrupted his thoughts. "Randy, I don't know you, so this question may be out of line. Is there a relationship between you and Mr. Fraser?"

The chair creaked as Randy leaned forward and contemplated David's question. If he was friends with Thomas and Joe, they probably had at least certain tastes and interests in common. His eyes lingered on a gold band on David's left hand before he decided to answer.

"Relationship overstates it, but there is *something* there." He met David's eyes. "I'd maybe like there to be more, but it isn't possible. You're right to raise the issue, though. As Christian was talking, I was imagining Jack's response to each demand. Was it too aggressive? Would he be disappointed I ask so much?" He ran a hand over his smooth scalp. "I don't know that I can be objective enough to negotiate something like this."

David looked sympathetic. "Believe me, I understand wanting someone you don't think you should have. It can make you do crazy things. Sometimes that's good if it shakes up your life. Sometimes it's tough if you can't reconcile your wants and your needs."

"Yeah?"

"Yes." David glanced down at the ring on his finger. "I came very close, twice, to losing the man I love. My husband Brandon is quite a bit younger than me." He flicked a sheepish look at Randy. "Twenty-two years actually. It took me a long time to understand how much Brandon loved me, and that I was being an idiot to let something like age threaten that." He blushed. "We just got married in September. I wouldn't have that if I'd let my pride stand in our way."

Randy had to frown. "You think pride is my issue?"

David shook his head. "I can't tell you that. We just met, but I know something about who you are. I remember the news stories, when you helped save the life of Thomas's partner. The kind of decisive action I read about doesn't jibe with the hesitancy I hear when you talk about Jack."

Randy thought about David's words. "I get that. I'm not sure how to handle the thing between us. I mean Jack and me. Or even if I should." He studied the conference table and ran a thumb over the grain as he admitted, "I don't like that feeling."

"Look, here's what I'd suggest. Hire us, get Jack's museum to pay the legal fees, then let Christian do his job and negotiate the best deal for you that he can, whether that's with Jack or with a lawyer for the museum. Keep your personal relationship out of it. That will give you the time you need to figure out what you want from Jack, and the confidence that whatever deal you end up with isn't colored by your attraction."

"That's smart. Let's do that."

David stood. "Excellent. You should have the initial conversation with Jack to get the ball rolling, and then we'll take over. I'll wait to hear from you." Randy rose and they shook hands. "You know, Joe's been trying to get Brandon and me to come down to Mata Hari. Maybe we'll make it in one night soon."

They said their goodbyes, and Randy checked his watch as he left the law firm, deciding he didn't have enough time to get home for a workout and still make it back to Mata Hari to prepare for opening. He slid behind the wheel of his truck in the parking garage and tapped the leather cover on the steering wheel as he thought. Well, warred with himself.

It's lunch. No mixed signals at all. Just a chance to talk to him about the entrustment issues.

And whether Monday night meant anything more than a hook-up.

And why he wants a wealthy fiancée from the family that owns one of the largest auction houses in the world when he could have a slightly-used up bartender with a kink for leather.

Randy snorted at his own bullshit but pulled out his phone to dial Jack's hotel. When the receptionist put him through to the room, no one picked up. *Well fuck. All that nonsense for nothing.* He debated leaving a message, but hung up at the beep. He had Jack's cell on a card somewhere but it was a UK number and he couldn't remember how to make an international call on his phone.

He still needed to have lunch, but he didn't want to eat alone. As he pulled out of the garage, he wondered if Danny would like to come help out at the bar, for something to do. He put the phone on speaker and gave the voice command to call his home number. No answer.

Strike two. He should probably buy a cell phone for Danny, since it looked like he'd be sticking around for a while.

Fine. He'd just go grab a sandwich and then head to Mata Hari early.

● ● ●

THAT EVENING, THE bar was unusually busy for a Wednesday. Randy was pleased at the extra customers because it signaled he was doing something right. As soon as six o'clock hit, he and Malcolm slung drinks steadily for what seemed like two hours straight. He'd understaffed because he expected the usual level of business, and his crew was having trouble keeping up with bussing and washing glasses.

Miss Ethel was on fire at the piano, and her band of admirers sang along lustily to the score of *Les Misérables*. Randy took a short break at seven to call Danny again to see if he'd come help out, but once again the home number went unanswered. A tingle of unease crawled through Randy's gut, but he dismissed it. Danny wasn't accountable to him for every minute of his day. Maybe he'd made some friends, or gone to another movie.

Around eight-thirty, the crowd slowed enough that Malcolm said to Randy, "Get some dinner, boss. I got this."

"You sure, Mal?"

"Yeah, no sweat. Besides, the extra tips today will come in handy." Malcolm grinned at him. "Got a date tonight after we close up."

"Where are you taking Sarah?"

"Oh shit, I thought I told you. Sarah and I broke up. I'm seeing Latoya now."

"Should I say I'm sorry, or congratulations?"

"It's all good, boss. Sarah started pushing for something more serious, but I just want to play around while I can."

"Well, as long as you're being careful."

Malcolm gave him a toothy grin. "Are you gonna tell me to wrap it up?"

"Fuck no. Surely you're smart enough to know that already."

"Yes, Dad. I always use a pecker checker." Randy swatted backhand at Malcolm's shoulder and he ducked away, laughing. "Hey, bring me back something to eat? Whatever you get is fine."

"Yeah, sure. I'm in the mood for a gyro from the place across P Street. No onions for you, right?"

Randy pulled on his jacket and walked through the parking lot in front of Mata Hari to P Street, then crossed to the small Greek deli. As he waited for his order, he tried Danny again, and then Jack's hotel. No answer at either place, but this time he left a message on the hotel system.

He tried for an impersonal business tone. "Um, hi, Jack. It's Randy Vaughan. I talked to a lawyer today, and I'd like to circle up with you to discuss next steps." He hesitated, then went on more softly. "And I want to see if you're okay, after the way we left things."

Immediately he wished for a way to erase the message, but when he started pressing buttons on his phone he heard a recording announce, "The message has been left for the guest you called." *Ah shit.*

Randy took the bag of food when it was ready and headed back to Mata Hari. No sooner had he reached the parking lot than his phone rang in his pocket. He pulled it out quickly, hoping to see either his own home number or Jack's hotel. The number displayed was unfamiliar, though it did show the two-oh-two area code for DC. He accepted the call. "Randy Vaughan."

Danny's frantic voice filled his ear. "Randy? Please. I need help!"

Chapter Seventeen

RANDY DROPPED THE bag of food on the pavement.

"Danny? What's going on? Where are you?"

"He's got a gun. I'm scared." Danny sobbed. "He says you have to come here or he'll… He'll…"

"I'm coming. Nothing's going to happen to you. Tell me where."

There was the sound of a slap and a moan, then the rustle of paper. Danny choked out, "I'm in a warehouse in Northeast Washington." He read an address on Florida Avenue. "And Randy? He says don't tell anyone else. Unless you're alone, he's gonna… Oh God."

"I'll come alone. I'll be there as fast as I can." The call ended abruptly, and Randy scooped up the food bag before running inside Mata Hari. He pulled Malcolm aside, shoved the bag at him, and said, "I have to take off. It's urgent. Can you hold the fort? If not, go ahead and call in Wilson or anyone else available."

As he talked, he pulled his .357 Magnum from its storage space under the bar and ignored Malcolm's shocked expression. A quick check showed the gun was loaded, so he decided against taking the time to grab extra bullets. Instead, he ran for his truck.

Danny had said he wasn't supposed to call anyone. *Fuck that.* He put his phone on speaker and called Maria Torres's cell phone. She didn't pick up—*sure, why break the streak of unanswered phones today?*—but he left a message. It was a professional call, and he found himself falling back into the habit of treating her as a police detective rather than a friend.

"Torres, it's Randy Vaughan. I need help. I'm on my way to a warehouse. This kid I've been helping has been grabbed and threatened. He says the person who took him has a gun, and I'm going in armed. I hope you get this and can send help." He left the address for the warehouse, then disconnected.

Should he call the regular police, or 911? He trusted Torres but retained his snobbishness about DC's Metropolitan Police Department. Or really, any law enforcement other than the Secret Service. He could imagine unprepared officers rolling into the warehouse without proper surveillance and Danny getting killed in the crossfire.

No. He had confidence in his twenty-five years of federal experience. He'd handle this.

Traffic was brutal as he made his way through the busy streets. Once upon a time Washington had been a sleepy little town, but it was booming with new construction replacing long-abandoned and derelict buildings. Whether prosperity brought an influx of drivers or the other way around, road congestion grew worse every year. Like that evening, when jam after jam had Randy pounding his steering wheel in frustration. He was still about ten blocks from his destination when "La Vida Loca" sounded from his phone.

"Randy, don't be an idiot," Torres said immediately when he connected the call. "You can't go in alone. You have no way of knowing if there's more than one person, or what you're walking into. Wait until I can get a squad car there at least."

"I can't wait, Torres. It could take another thirty minutes or more to get someone there, but if I know backup is coming, then I can play for time."

"Do you think this is tied to the break-in at your bar?"

"Well shit. That never even occurred to me." The pieces started to fit together in his head. Whoever broke in took nothing, but he'd had the impression his artwork had been disturbed. Like someone was looking for something specific and didn't find it.

"You're too emotional, or you'd have thought of that first thing. So who is this kid? Tell me what's going on." He explained to Torres about helping Danny when he was being mugged, and how he'd given him a place to stay.

"So why would someone grab a homeless boy to force you to go to a meeting like this?" When Randy delayed answering, she prompted him. "You need to tell me what's happening, Vaughan. Right now."

"Okay. Remember that painting I told you that Fraser was asking about? I just found out recently that it may be extremely valuable. It could be worth millions. If whoever grabbed Danny knows that, then maybe this is a play to get me to ransom Danny with the painting."

"*Mierda*," Torres breathed out heavily. "How would they know this Danny means anything to you, that a trade would be plausible?"

Randy didn't like the ideas that began to percolate in his head. Someone who knew how much the painting was worth. Someone who had seen Danny at Mata Hari on multiple occasions. Someone who could play on Randy's weakness for helping wherever he could. Someone Randy had refused access to the painting, multiple times.

Torres might have been reading his mind. "Do you think this could have anything to do with Fraser? You were suspicious of him after the break-in."

Shit, she had to go and just say it like that. Randy huffed, "I don't know." More quietly, he said, "I hope not." He finally turned onto the street for the warehouse. "I'm here, Torres. It's been forty minutes since Danny called. I have to go in and see if he's all right."

"Randy, please don't. My guys are getting closer but they're probably fifteen minutes out even with sirens. No one in this goddamn city gets out of the way for the flashers."

"I'll be fine. I told you, I'm packing."

"Listen. I picked up this trick recently. You have an iPhone, right? Tell me your account and password. I can try to track your phone if anything goes wrong."

"Um, sure." He rattled off his information without another thought. Maria Torres was someone he'd trust with his life, so account privacy was pretty small potatoes to him.

"Leave your phone someplace inconspicuous, if you can. Like, tuck it in your boot. And put it on silent, dumbass."

He disconnected the call, hesitating with the phone in his hand. He turned off the ringer, then took it out of its protective case to make it as small and light as possible before sliding it into his jockey shorts. The cover glass was cold against his belly and genitals, but he took some comfort in Torres's suggestion. He checked the safety on his pistol again and climbed out of his truck. His was the only vehicle in the parking area.

The warehouse looked empty and abandoned, though a large sign plastered over the front indicated it would soon be part of a reconstruction project. The squat building was probably five stories tall, and made of an ugly grayish brick. Street lamps revealed large windows with a vaguely purple tint seemed to glare down at him, adding to the sense of oppression.

Traffic hummed on Florida Avenue. He strained to catch the wail of a police siren, but nothing more than honking horns came to his ears. He couldn't delay any longer.

Randy approached the building carefully. The main entrance

seemed to be double doors up a flight of concrete steps, but a chain was padlocked around the handles. He moved along the walk in front of the building, and where it turned a corner, he spotted what looked like a service entrance. Cautiously, he approached the metal door and tried the handle. It was unlocked.

A god-awful screech of rusty hinges made him wince as he pulled open the door. *So much for an unobtrusive entrance.* A small room beyond still contained metal racks to hold time cards and an ancient clock for punching in. He crossed the sticky linoleum floor to a second, interior door. A small window was inset, with wire crisscrossing inside the glass. Peering through, he had an impression of a long, dark hallway. No movement, but a light showed at the far end.

Carefully, he opened the door and looked around, then stepped through to the interior. The place had a dry, dusty smell that made him think of rats, and his hackles rose. He hated fucking rats. Nothing else moved in the hall, and as his eyes adjusted to the gloom, he was reasonably sure he was alone there. He began to walk slowly toward the light. The source wasn't visible, but appeared to be coming from around the corner.

A small sound, like a chair leg scraping the floor, hit Randy's ears. He froze. The sound didn't repeat, but he became aware of another smell mixed with the stale air of the warehouse. It was faint, but distinctive. It was something tart, dark and earthy, entirely delicious.

It smelled like Jack's cologne.

Mother fucker, Randy swore to himself. It was happening again. Just like with Trevor.

He drew his .357 and moved quietly down the hallway, only to pause when he reached the end. Cautiously, he leaned around the corner.

Twenty feet away, a floor lamp with no shade glowed next to

a wooden chair. Danny sat in the chair, facing the junction where whoever took him obviously expected Randy to enter. It looked like his hands were tied behind him, and his head hung down. As Randy scoped the rest of the area, Danny moved in his chair to rock it. The same scraping noise came again.

He saw no one else near, though he could still smell that damn cologne. His concern about Danny warred with his anger, and the mix of emotions threatened to choke him. He stepped into the corridor, and stopped when Danny's head jolted upright.

Expressive eyes wide, Danny didn't speak but licked his lips. Randy put a finger to his own mouth. Danny looked pale and scared, but no obvious bruise or blood showed on his face. His purple sweatshirt was also clean. Whatever had happened when Danny was grabbed, apparently the person (*not Jack, please, not Jack*) hadn't hurt him badly. Randy took a step forward and had a moment to register alarm as Danny's eyes shifted to something behind him.

A needle jabbed into his neck. Intense warmth at the injection site began to spread, and Randy whirled around too late. He couldn't seem to speak or yell. He swung his arms wildly and brushed against a slick fabric of some kind. It seemed to slide through his fingers. His knees gave out as the warmth moved down his chest, and then he collapsed on his back.

He wasn't completely unconscious but that seemed only seconds away. He should be fighting but he couldn't muster the energy to resist. The pistol was pried loose from his fingers. *Oh yeah. I should have shot.*

He was almost under when he heard a distinctly English accent say, "Grab his feet and hoist him onto the cart," and then he was out.

*   *   *

THERE WAS SOMETHING heavy around his wrists.

Randy was lying on cold concrete, still clothed though his boots were gone. He had no idea how much time had passed or where he was when he opened his eyes, but realized he was handcuffed with his arms in front. His head ached, and he fought off nausea.

He staggered to his feet, and when he pulled on the cuffs, he registered that they had been secured through posts in a metal railing. He could slide them up and down as far as a cross-bar set about waist-high, but he couldn't pull away from the structure. He looked around to get his bearings. The room was big, bigger than the hallway where he'd found Danny. And the smell seemed different to him—more like sawdust, or freshly cut wood. And that other smell again, the one of Jack's pomegranate cologne.

Lying son of a bitch. I should have known. Should have known he'd never wanted me at all. Just like Trevor.

Randy choked down the hurt and rage. No, he had to be smart now since he'd been dumb enough to trust Jack and get himself drugged. Clearly he should have waited for the cops since he was useless.

Two closed doors were visible, one directly ahead of him and the other to his right. A row of windows stretched high overhead. No light came in through the panes, so it must be night time. Still? Again? He didn't know. But from what he could see and smell, Randy was pretty sure he had been brought someplace other than the warehouse where he was ambushed. He thought about the cops Torres had sent after him, but they'd be looking in the wrong place.

There was no sight of Danny, but the fact that Randy was alive must be a good sign. His brain was fuzzy, but he pulled on the cuffs until his wrists ached. The pain seemed to help him focus. Finally, he became aware someone was standing near. He blinked until the blurriness passed. "Holy shit."

The man watching him had white hair and a mustache, ruddy cheeks, and was slightly pear-shaped. His khaki pants and button-down shirt were neatly pressed, and he even wore a tie. On a chair next to him rested what looked like a rain slicker. The handle of Randy's pistol protruded from a pocket in the discarded coat.

The man facing him looked less like a criminal mastermind than someone's grandfather. Or, more correctly, the owner of an art gallery in London.

"Bernard Gates," Randy said with a sigh to the man who had sold him the *Sunrise* painting years earlier.

"Mr. Vaughan," Gates replied in his proper English tones with a quick tip of the head. "So sorry we meet again in these circumstances."

Randy tugged feebly on his cuffs again. "All this to get back a painting," he muttered.

Gates didn't deny it. "To be fair, I did offer to repurchase *Sunrise* from you. We could all have avoided a great deal of unpleasantness if you had simply restored my property."

Randy frowned. "*Your* property? I bought it from you."

"Ah, but I didn't know what I was selling, did I? It was a mutual misunderstanding, and it wouldn't be proper for you to take advantage of my ignorance to escape with a treasure." Gates rocked on his heels and gazed quite earnestly at him, as if he actually expected that Randy would buy his bullshit. "In fact, I recall you were a devotee of Brousseau. Perhaps you knew even then." Gates nodded rapidly. "Yes, that could be it. Even then, you knew. So it wasn't just misunderstanding. You took advantage of me and stole the sunrise painting for a pittance."

"What the fuck are you talking about?"

"You know. Don't pretend you don't." Gates leaned toward

him but stayed well out of reach. "A previously unknown work by Jean-Pierre Brousseau. It's worth many, many millions of pounds. Handled properly, *tens* of millions." He hissed, "That's rightly my painting, Mr. Vaughan. I've come to get it back."

"Where's Danny? What have you done with him?"

"He'll be well as long as you cooperate. Now, can we resolve this like gentlemen? Will you return my property?"

"You're crazy," Randy snarled and jerked harder on his cuffs. The movement tightened his stomach, and cold glass pressed against his skin. He had no idea if Torres's trick of tracking his phone would really work, but it was his best hope. He needed to buy time for Torres to locate him, so he opted for ignorance. "There are no unknown Brousseaus. The painting you sold me is just a hack job by an imitator."

Gates grew agitated. "That's not so. The evidence is compelling. Once the painting can be examined by an appropriate appraiser and compared to the paper trail, the conclusion will be unmistakable. Jean-Pierre Brousseau painted that work, and any museum in the world will pay dearly to own it." He rubbed his hands. "I might even make more from a private collector. The Russian prime minister, for example, has paid unbelievable amounts of money for great works of art."

"Great work," Randy jeered. "It's a poorly executed painting in a nice frame. That's why I bought it."

"Ha! The provenance is impeccably assembled." Gates shook his head. "I can't believe I didn't see it myself."

"You sell shoddy hand-me-downs and castoffs in a tiny shop," Randy sneered. If he could make Gates angry enough to try to hit him, that would bring him in reach of Randy's handcuffed arms. "No wonder you're unable to see how ridiculous this idea is."

The little man kept himself at a distance but Randy had obviously found a sore spot because his face flushed a bright red.

"Shoddy. Exactly," Gates fumed. "I've made errors. Poor choices over the years. Items I bought, items I let pass by. After thirty-four years, I'm on the brink of losing everything." His brow furrowed. "*Everything.* But this Brousseau, the *Sunrise at the Abbey of Chaalis*. This is the one I've waited for all my life."

"To hear you tell it, it's just another bad idea in a lifetime of bad ideas," Randy taunted. "How could you possibly prove the provenance? Even if it existed."

Gates stilled, then smiled at him. "Oh, it exists. In fact, I have it in my possession." He lifted the slicker and retrieved a thick leather portfolio from the chair underneath. "It's all in here, Mr. Vaughan. The original appraisal. A photo of the location where Brousseau painted the sunrise and the abbey. The correspond-ence. I have it all."

That folder. There was only one person who had been able to assemble the information Gates was itemizing. But…No. Jack wouldn't share that information with anyone. It was vital to everything he hoped to accomplish professionally. No way in hell would he give that to a pissant like Bernard Gates.

"Where did you get that?" Randy asked hoarsely, nodding to the leather folder.

Gates's smile stretched wider and grew more manic. "My associate provided it to me. I'm delighted you admit that you know what this is. We can stop playing your little game." He carefully replaced the folder on the chair. "If you know about these materials, then Mr. Fraser must have shared it with you, which means you already know the painting is authentic."

Clearly someone had helped Gates move him while he was unconscious, as the little aged man would never have been able to handle Randy's heavy body. If Torres did find him, if the police raided, he needed to be able to warn them to take into account two people at least. "What associate?" Randy asked.

Please don't be Jack. Please let me be wrong.

Gates rocked back and forth, so obviously pleased with himself that he couldn't keep quiet any longer. "There's nothing to be gained by further delay, I suppose. You'll find out anyway as part of the negotiation we need to undertake about *Sunrise*." He turned his head and called out, "Mr. Winiarski? Please come meet Mr. Vaughan properly."

Randy's blood ran cold, his gut clenching painfully. Winiarski? That name was etched in his memory with acid, but it wasn't possible...

Then Danny stepped into the light.

Chapter Eighteen

"OH NO," RANDY moaned. He couldn't help it. "Danny?"

He sank to his knees and leaned his forehead against the metal railing to which he was cuffed. All that time together, and he had never seen this coming. Just like with Trevor. Randy clenched his eyes shut as waves of grief and fury crashed together and drowned his heart. He had believed in Danny, and it had all been another lie.

The cold seeped into his knees and wrists to remind him of the danger, so he forced his eyes open again. He pushed aside the pain for another time and focused on Danny, who was standing rigidly with his hands flexing at his sides nervously. Emotions as strong as those tearing up Randy raced across Danny's face, his big eyes tormented. Randy saw shame, fear, anger. Maybe regret?

If there was regret, there was hope. Cuffed as he was, with no way of knowing if Torres could track him, Danny might still be his way out of this.

Gates rested a hand on Danny's shoulder as he smirked at Randy. "Danny has been a big help to me. His acting skills are top notch, wouldn't you say? It was his idea to wait in the chair and look tied up to draw your attention. And I certainly couldn't have gotten that bulk of yours onto the motorized cart without his help."

Danny seemed to shy away at the touch of Gates's hand, but he didn't disengage completely. Randy tried to draw his attention.

"Danny? Why are you working with him?" Randy asked sadly. Danny met his eyes then, and Randy understood for the first time why he looked so familiar when they met. He sighed. "Winiarski. You're related to Henry."

Henry Winiarski. The man who'd killed Kevin in a PCP-induced mania. The man who took apart Randy's life, and who made Luc a widower.

"He's my dad," Danny blurted. "He's been in prison my entire life because you keep him there."

Randy shook his head. "I didn't put him in prison. He did that to himself when he killed a police officer."

Desperation temporarily won the battle on Danny's face and he hollered, "He paid for what he did. Long ago! But every time he came up for resentencing, *you* were there to make sure he didn't get out." He scrubbed his hands against his jeans. "I saw you there once. I went to the hearing two years ago. You didn't even notice me, but I remember you. So big and imposing. All clean cut in a black suit. I listened while you told the sentencing judge about how great your uncle Kevin was and how you tried to do good in the Secret Service to honor him." His eyes filled. "The lawyer wouldn't even let me talk and the judge was all '*Agent* Vaughan' and 'the court is so grateful for your service' and 'thank you for flying to Portland for this civic duty.' My father never had a chance."

It was true—Randy didn't remember seeing Danny. He didn't even really look at Henry there in the courtroom. He never had. "Danny, he had a chance before he took those drugs."

Danny was practically crying. "He was a kid! Nineteen then, not much older than me. He made a mistake and he's been paying in prison for decades."

Randy frowned at that. "You're right. It's been more than

thirty years. I don't understand how Henry could have a son your age."

"He met my mom when he was in prison. She was a librarian there, part time, and they got married after a year of visits and writing back and forth. A case worker bent the rules to get him furlough once, and that's where I came from. Man, my mom really loved him, but all they ever had was a monthly visit. He had to watch my birth on a recording his sister made when Mom went into labor."

Guilt bloomed in Randy. He hated Henry Winiarski with a passion, yes. Had for thirty years. He did everything in his power to make sure the son of a bitch never got out. And yet, it had never crossed his mind to wonder about Henry's family. Whether there was someone waiting at home. Whether he had a child who might hunger for his dad.

"I didn't know about this, Danny. That Henry had a son."

Gates spoke up. "And would you have done anything differently, Mr. Vaughan? If you had met Danny Winiarski and seen a young man desperate for his father to be free, would you have relented?"

"I don't know," Randy admitted.

"You've come to trust Danny. You know him now. You let him into your home and into your business establishment." Gates's tone was wheedling, and it made Randy narrow his eyes. What was he up to?

"It's what I promised," Gates said to Danny. "Didn't I keep my word?"

Danny glared back at Gates sullenly. "He hasn't agreed to anything."

"Oh, but I think he will." Gates looked again at Randy. "When I found Danny, his mother had just died. That's absolutely true. People in his community knew about the father,

and were unwilling to take a chance on the son. The few relatives
he had were either dead or had moved away. Danny was on the
edge of starvation and his choices were grim. Sell drugs? Prosti-
tute himself? Rob a convenience store? When I approached him,
he thought he was going to have to suck my todger."

Danny turned his head away. Randy snarled at Gates despite
himself. "You better not have touched him or I'll break your arm
when I get out of these cuffs."

Gates laughed. "I assure you, my tastes lie elsewhere. But I
offered Danny a better path. Didn't I, young man?"

Danny looked directly at Randy. "I didn't have sex with
him." His voice was softer when he spoke again, and the flare of
anger and despair seemed to have died away to be replaced by
shame. "I would have with you," he confessed.

Randy frowned as he tried to piece the mess together. "And if
I had slept with you, you were, what? Going to blackmail me?"

Gates said, "Well, that was certainly among the possibilities
we discussed, though I was reasonably confident we wouldn't
have to go there." He patted Danny's back solicitously. "We
knew about your savior complex, you see. The news coverage of
your aid to Zachary Hall, combined with the testimony you gave
over the years to the court to keep Henry behind bars, was highly
revealing. You seem to have a pathologic need to save any stray
kitten or wounded puppy in your path, so we decided to put
Danny in peril and let your nature run its course."

Randy exhaled his disgust. "The mugging in front of Mata
Hari. It was all a setup." God *damn* but he was a fool. He was so
easy to manipulate. Trevor had known how to do it. That prick
Gates too. All it took was to show Randy someone weak, and his
ego dragged him to the rescue. It made his stomach churn to
think about.

Was Jack in on this too? Randy burned to know, but wasn't

about to give Gates the satisfaction of asking.

Danny couldn't look at him, but Gates bobbed his head up and down in gleeful agreement, seemingly unaware of the pain he had inflicted. "Good, wasn't it? We watched the bar for a week to learn your rhythms, paid a few lads to make it look good, and next thing you know, Danny was safely ensconced in your house."

The last traces of drug in Randy's system must have cleared, because he finally understood many things. The sense he'd had of being watched. The items mislaid in his house. "This has nothing to do with Henry. You had Danny go through my house and studio to look for the painting so you could steal it. When it wasn't there, you had him search at Mata Hari." His eyes narrowed again. "Wait though. Danny was with me when the break-in happened so that must have been you in the bar Sunday night. It's all about the painting."

Danny shot a panicked look at Gates, but he patted Danny's shoulder. "Not exactly. True, *I* was looking for the painting but Henry is part of the negotiation."

"You've said that already," Randy snarled. "What negotiation?"

"The negotiation we are about to undertake. Do you know the hallmark of a successful businessman, Mr. Vaughan?"

Randy didn't try to conceal the scorn that curled his lip. "I'm sorry, are you calling yourself a successful businessman? You run a tiny, failing shop and you let a valuable painting pass right under your nose."

Gates turned red. "I have a highly reputable gallery and an enviable client list. And everyone missed the truth about that painting. *Everyone.*" He turned away, breathing heavily. Randy caught Danny looking intently at him, and read concern and fear in his eyes. Danny seemed to be trying to give him a message of some kind. Before Randy could figure out what to do with that, Gates turned back around.

He was more in control of himself. "Well done, Mr. Vaughan. You managed to set me on the wrong foot. I'll have to be more alert to your tricks." He drew another deep breath, then let it out. "As I was saying, the key to a successful negotiation is knowing the other side in intimate detail. When you responded to my overture with an exorbitant price, I realized I would have to make a study of you. So I hired a private detective who unearthed a great deal of useful background." He smiled. "Frankly, it's shocking how much information is available for one with the motivation to look. That's how I learned about Henry Winiarski. Your submissions to the court in Maine were public records. It was in reviewing those submissions and the other court documents that I learned of the existence of Danny here."

"And you decided to use a young boy to do your dirty work?" Randy heaped disgust on Gates. His voice had always been his best tool. "Got him beat up by thugs? Yeah, what a great businessman you are."

Danny turned defensive. "Don't, Randy. If I got a split lip out of it, so what? I've had a lot worse. Bernard said he would get the painting he wants and you'd..." He choked off what he was going to say, though he was trembling with the effort.

"I'd what, Danny?" Randy prompted as the kid rocked on his heels. Tension built in every line of Danny's body and he gnawed on his lower lip. "Tell me. He'd get a painting worth millions of dollars, and what would you get?"

Danny finally erupted. "You'd help me get my dad out of prison!"

"What?" Randy was stunned, and Danny stepped closer.

"Please, Randy. I need him to get out." He couldn't seem to stop himself from begging. "I *need...*"

"Enough, Danny." Gates patted his back. "Let the adults talk now, and I'll keep my promise to you." He turned back to face Randy. "So. Allow me to make the opening bid in our negotiation. I will undertake the effort to authenticate the *Sunrise at the Abbey of Chaalis* as an original work of art by Brousseau and to achieve the very highest possible price for it. You will persuade the Maine judge that your opposition to Henry Winiarski's release has been withdrawn. In exchange, you will receive twenty-five percent of the sale proceeds. I think that is exceedingly generous, since your investment is no more than a few thousand dollars. What do you say?"

Randy blinked. "Are you serious? You fucking moron."

Gates flushed. "You Yanks are always rude with no cause. Let's discuss this like reasonable men without the name calling."

"Reasonable?" Randy barked out. He rattled his cuffs and was gratified when Gates took a step backward. "You endangered Danny. You committed a felony when you broke into my bar. You kidnapped me and are holding me captive." He was all but roaring by that point. "And how did you get the provenance records from Jack?"

Gates faltered under his rage, but Randy saw Danny flick a fearful glance at the metal door opposite. Another piece clicked into place. What Danny had been trying to tell him with his eyes. Why he could smell Jack's distinctive cologne. How Gates had obtained Jack's research. *Oh no, no, no.*

To Danny, he said in a strangled voice, "What did you do to him?"

"Nothing. I mean, he's okay," Danny choked out. He held his hands wide as if trying to convince Randy of his sincerity. "Bernard knocked him out, right? But it's like with you. It'll wear off."

"Oh, Danny." Randy shook his head sadly. "You're so young

still. So foolish."

"What...what do you mean?"

Gates tried to interject. "This is all off topic. We have an offer on the table and we must discuss—"

"How do you think Gates is going to get away with selling a stolen painting based on another man's research?" Randy continued to Danny. "Think."

Danny looked at Gates nervously. "Well, we can give him some of the money too."

Gates snarled, "Fraser gets nothing. All he did was put together a few scraps of paper."

"So what are you going to do? What are you going to do with Jack?" Randy asked. He let the question burn in the air for Danny's benefit before saying, "And even if you do kill Jack, his fiancée knows about his research. His museum does as well. Too many people know for you to ever be able to pass the provenance off as your own work."

Danny was pale and Gates was sputtering, but Randy pressed on.

"Jesus Christ, Gates. Did you steal your plot from an episode of *CSI: London* or something?" Gates flushed even more deeply and opened his mouth to respond, but Randy barreled on over his objections. "What are you going to do with me when I refuse to cooperate? Are you going to shoot me too? Let's say you do. You don't know where the painting is, and it will become part of my estate if I'm dead. No way to get your hands on it then."

Danny licked his lips, then said to Gates, "Bernard, you told me no one would really get hurt."

Gates started pacing back and forth. "No. I've thought about this. This is a negotiation. You just have to be reasonable."

"Are you going to kill Danny too, after you kill me and Jack?" Randy interrupted, though his eyes were on Danny and not

Gates. Danny looked truly shocked. His own danger had never even occurred to him. Randy grimaced sadly at him. "Think about it. You're the link to all Gates's crimes."

Gates howled in anger and yanked Randy's Magnum from the coat pocket where he'd left it. He brandished the pistol and yelled, "Stop muddling everything! You're confusing the boy and making problems where there should be none. This is a negotiation, dammit. What do you want? We'll make a deal and this will all be over."

Randy shook his head. "Don't be ridiculous, you sad little man. There is no deal. You can't keep your promise to Danny and you can't get to the painting. Ever."

Gates froze, then looked at the pistol in his hand. His chest heaved, but then he stood straighter. Randy realized that even a dumbass like Gates could be dangerous when backed into a corner. The little man said, "The negotiation is not concluded. I have another bargaining chip." He strode to the metal door across from Randy, turned a key in the lock, and pulled it open with a flourish.

Jack lay on the floor on his back in just a white T-shirt, untucked from his pants. His hands were taped together and more tape covered his mouth. Someone had at least shoved a sweater under his head, but he seemed to be unconscious. He was pale and sweat shone on his face though his body was shivering.

"What did you do to him?" Randy bellowed. "Jack!"

Danny rubbed his hands against his jeans nervously. "Bernard gave him the same drug he gave you."

Gates frowned. "I gave him a second injection while you were still out, to keep him quiet."

"Look at him," Randy ordered. "He's having a bad reaction. What did you shoot me up with?"

Gates seemed as surprised at Jack's condition as Danny. He

muttered, "It's a combination of fentanyl and some other narcotic. I found a supplier on the internet."

"Is that where you found your scheme too, asshole? I out-weigh Jack by seventy fucking pounds at least. If you gave him two loads of the same amount you gave me, he's overdosing."

Danny tried to move into the room to check on Jack, but Gates suddenly waved the gun at both of them. "No. Stand back, Danny. This is what we need."

Gates looked straight at Randy but pointed the pistol at Jack's prone form. "Your last chance, Mr. Vaughan. Make a deal or you can watch Mr. Fraser die right now."

"Bernard!" Danny protested. "No!"

"Shut up, Danny. Mr. Vaughan, he doesn't look well at all. If you let him die, how will you live with yourself?"

Bastard. Randy gritted his teeth. There was no sign of Torres. The way Gates was waving the pistol around, he'd never held a gun before; it could go off at any moment, hitting Randy or Danny. Or Jack.

On the concrete floor, Jack moaned and started to shake. "Fine," Randy spit out. "Get medical help for Jack and I'll give you the painting."

Chapter Nineteen

"**S**EE, I KNEW you'd eventually be reasonable," Gates gloated, and Randy wanted to put a fist in his smiling face. "Excellent."

Jack twitched violently, maybe on the verge of convulsing, and Randy's training kicked in. "Danny, you have to position him so he doesn't hurt himself if he seizes." Gates waved the gun to indicate permission to Danny. Randy winced and yelled at Gates, "Stop doing that, you moron. You're going to shoot someone accidentally and then you'll face the death penalty."

Gates obviously was unaware that DC didn't have that punishment, but he was nonplussed by Randy's threat and he looked at the gun in his hand. Randy hoped vindictively that it would go off in his face, but no such luck. At least he held the gun more gingerly and kept it pointed to the ground.

"Fine," Gates said grudgingly. "Danny, do as he says."

Danny rushed into the cell and crouched so he could face Randy with Jack's prostrate body between them. "What do I do?"

The twitching seemed to quiet down, so Randy said, "Roll his body gently toward you." Danny put a hand on Jack's leg and another on his shoulder and tugged until Jack was on his side facing Danny. The risk of aspiration on vomit was lessened with that position. "Pull the tape off his mouth. Good. Now use your knee as a brace so he doesn't roll too far forward. Pull up his bottom arm—yes, like that—and put his hand on his cheek. It will help keep him in that position."

What else? Think, Vaughan.

"Check his belt. Make sure it isn't tight." Danny complied and Randy breathed a little easier. That would hopefully keep Jack from hurting himself if he did seize.

He looked at Gates with loathing. "How are you going to play this?"

"What do you mean?"

Randy rolled his eyes. "I'm not giving you the painting until I know Jack is safe. You going to call an ambulance? Where will you tell them to come? How are you going to get him out of here? Jesus, what kind of criminal mastermind do you think you are?"

Gates grew increasingly red with Randy's insults. "Shut up," he yelled. "I have to think."

Danny said, "He's sweating really bad. I think he needs a doctor right away, Bernard."

Gates pulled at his hair with the hand not holding the pistol. He was pacing back and forth, muttering to himself. He clearly hadn't thought anything through, and Randy decided that was his best opportunity—to keep Gates reeling. "If he dies, there's no deal. You'll have to kill all of us. You ready for that?"

Gates flinched and paled. Danny looked at him fearfully, as if the peril they were all in finally got to him. "Bernard..." he began carefully.

"No. Hush." Gates stiffened. He stalked into the room where Jack lay on his side and waved the gun at Danny. "Go stand over there. Near Vaughan. But not too close." Danny rose to his feet carefully, stepped over Jack and sidled around Gates. His eyes were terrified as he approached Randy, but he kept out of arm's length.

Gates turned his body so he was staring Randy in the eye and raised the gun in his hand to point at Jack's leg. "It occurs to me, Mr. Vaughan, that you may need more motivation to conclude our transaction. So here's what is going to happen.

"In five minutes, I'm going to shoot Mr. Fraser in the leg, which I expect will hurt him quite badly. You should have just enough time until he bleeds to death to get the Brousseau delivered here. Once the painting is in my possession, I'll load it on my cart and be gone. I will leave Danny with the key to the handcuffs, and he can free you and help get Mr. Fraser to hospital. That should give me enough time to disappear."

He looked at Danny. "Apparently, I won't be able to deliver the release to your father that we'd hoped for, but I am grateful for your help. Now, please give Mr. Vaughan your mobile so he can arrange for delivery of the painting." He paused, then pointed the pistol at Randy. "And in case you think about giving the police our location, you should understand that I am quite prepared to shoot you, Danny, and Mr. Fraser. Now how does that sound?"

Terrible, but Randy could see no other option. Not yet. The gun trembled slightly, but the desperation in Gates's eyes left Randy convinced the man had reached his limits and would shoot if pushed much farther. He nodded slowly.

"Excellent. Danny?"

Danny reached into his pocket and pulled out a cell phone Randy had never seen before. He entered his pass code but stared at the screen. "There's no signal in here, Bernard. I can't make a call out."

That explained why Torres hadn't yet been able to use Randy's cell phone to find them. A glimmer of an idea appeared.

Randy said to Gates, "Uncuff me and let me get close to a window or something. You still have Jack hostage so I won't be able to do anything." He sneered. "And I'm not a fucking coward like you. I won't run and leave Jack or Danny in danger."

Gates grunted and looked back and forth between Randy and Jack where he lay on the floor. Jack seemed to have calmed and the shivers had stopped. Randy couldn't tell if he was still breathing, but had to assume so. There was nothing else to do at the moment.

"Fine," Gates said. "Danny, you will take the key from me, unlock Mr. Vaughan from the pipe and then relock the handcuffs." He looked at the row of windows that spilled a small amount of street light into the warehouse. "There should be a better signal over there, and I can keep a close watch on you. Remember, Mr. Vaughan." He pointed the gun again, this time at Jack's head. "Mr. Fraser is depending upon your cooperation."

Danny edged over to Gates and took a small silver key, then hurried back to Randy. He leaned over the cuffs so his back was to Gates and muttered, "I'm so sorry, Randy. I never thought it would go like this."

Randy said nothing, but stared at the auburn head bent over his wrists. Danny unlocked the cuff from his left wrist and waited for him to step clear of the pipe to which he had been chained. Randy caught his eyes and continued to stare, making Danny flush as he again secured the wrists. Randy yanked on the cuffs sharply to make Danny jump.

He held out his hand for the phone, then walked slowly to the wall of windows. His eyes were on the phone's signal meter. *C'mon, c'mon.* Just as it showed one bar, the phone hidden in his underwear vibrated slightly. Incoming messages, maybe. Both phones had a signal, so everything depended on whether Torres could indeed track his location, and was close enough to make a difference.

He turned back to Gates. "Where do I tell them to bring the painting?" Gates rattled off an address Randy recognized as being just four or five blocks from the warehouse where he'd been captured. He dialed Thomas's number from memory.

Gates said, "Put it on speaker."

It rang just twice before Thomas picked up, and Randy immediately pressed the button to turn on the speakerphone function. He heard urgency as Thomas said, "Hello?"

Randy cleared his throat. "Jason? It's Randy Vaughan. You're on speaker. Please listen." He gambled using Thomas's given name would make him focus and understand what was happening. Maria Torres was one of the few people who knew that Thomas had dropped the name when he moved away from Seattle.

"Randy! Where are you? Are you all right?"

"Listen, Jason. Please. I need you to do something very important for me. Bring the big painting in your bedroom to me." He gave the location. "Do you have that address? Jason, don't call the police." *Call the police*, he thought frantically. "This will all be fine, but we need to proceed carefully."

"I think I understand, Randy. But the painting is big. It won't fit in my Maserati."

"Fair point. Hold on." To Gates, Randy said, "He doesn't have a vehicle big enough to transport it."

"Bollocks," Gates muttered. Then he brightened. "Call one of those Uber things. A big one."

"That will take some more time. If you shoot in five minutes then Jack will be dead. I'm not doing that deal."

"Fine. I'll wait an extra twenty minutes."

Better. Every few minutes help.

Randy said into the phone again, "Jason? Can you call an Uber big enough to transport the painting?"

"Yes. I'll do that as soon as we hang up."

"Thank you, Jason. Please remember. No police."

"Understood." Thomas disconnected the call and Randy passed the phone back to Danny. The three men stared at each other as precious minutes passed, and the silence built uncomfortably.

Gates kept the pistol pointed at Jack but eventually raised his other wrist to glance at his watch. "Fifteen more minutes and I *will* shoot."

Randy growled deep in his throat as the last conversation with Jack filled him with remorse. He'd wanted to explore if there was a way to make a connection even though Jack lived in England, but his own pain at discovering nothing more could happen than a one-night stand had made Randy cruel. His feeble attempts to guard his heart had led Randy to wrong Jack, even if just by his doubts in the man. What if Jack died without knowing how sorry Randy was, that his disappointment in Jack's engagement had caused him to lash out? Even if they all survived Gates's trap, Randy might never again get to kiss his soft mouth or stroke his beard or help him fly, but he racked his brain for a way to get Jack out of this mess.

More minutes ticked away. Danny chewed on his lip and hugged himself in the fraught, chilly air of the warehouse. Randy was painfully aware of how still Jack was laying. It might already be too late. He gritted his teeth and asked, "Is he breathing?"

Gates glanced down quickly. "Yes."

"How did you know what the painting was?" Randy eventually asked to break the heavy atmosphere.

Gates preened. "I know you think I'm a hack as an art dealer, but when Mr. Fraser approached me to ask about the sunrise painting, I grew curious. He never told me why he was looking for it, but I did some research into Mr. Fraser and the puzzle grew more enticing. After all, a representative of a museum with a renowned collection of Brousseaus, showing interest in a work that was in the style of Brousseau, would be enough to pique anyone's interest. When I made a casual inquiry to the family that had consigned the work to me initially, I learned that Mr. Fraser had also contacted them to ask about the painting and in particular about an old appraisal. Well, at that point, I was reasonably sure what I had let slip through my fingers.

"I had declined to give your contact information to Mr. Fraser, but I immediately wrote in hopes I'd reach you before he did. When you replied with your demand for forty thousand dollars, I feared I had given an inkling of its true worth so I grew cautious. Once I found the news reports about your escapade involving Zachary Hall, I realized an ally would be essential. Then when I chanced upon Danny here, the pieces came together."

"How did you arrange the fake mugging?" When Danny glanced up at him, red-faced, he continued. "It's not likely you brought a posse over from London."

Gates rocked on his heels again, obviously pleased with himself. "Oh that was fun. I created an account on Craigslist in your name and using your picture from the news reports. I pretended I was looking for someone to help me fulfill a fantasy for my young lover."

He almost giggled as he looked at Danny. "I said that your boy wanted to be rescued by his big, strong hero, so I needed a few people willing to act it out. The man who contacted me was able to round up a few friends and I paid them two hundred dollars each for the scene. I told them when to show up at your bar and sent them a picture of Danny." His grin faded and turned rueful. "It went as expected until you thrashed one of the men pretty well and took his knife. He threatened to go to the police unless I paid extra, so your heroics cost me another five hundred there."

"Put it on my tab," Randy scoffed. He looked around the vast room and thought about the other location where he'd initially been caught with his guard down. "How did you learn about these warehouses?" he asked.

"Through internet searches about the historical records of your city. I've been in Washington for several weeks following you and then Mr. Fraser, you see. I wandered by these warehouses once and I had an inspiration when I saw the construction signs. I waited near this warehouse until I saw a man approach with a roll of architectural drawings under his arm, then I struck up a conversation with him in my most charming manner. Even played up a bit of a cockney accent. Well, you know how the Yanks are for a kindly English bloke. He thought I was charming and, Bob's your uncle, he was showing me through his site. Even pointed out that tunnels used to be important to connect the various warehouses to the railway for deliveries. Clever, yes?"

"Yeah, you're the next Laurence Olivier," Randy snarled. "Or maybe the next Mr. Bean. You just keep racking up the potential witnesses, don't you?" Gates flushed angrily.

Danny had been standing quietly but stiffly near Randy. Suddenly he jerked his head as if surprised. He glanced at Randy, then back at Gates. In an unusually loud voice, Danny practically yelled out, "You just used me, didn't you? All this time. You had no intention of trying to help my dad."

Gates frowned at him. "Calm down. I did try. You heard me ask Mr. Vaughan to support his release."

Danny took a step toward Gates and balled his hands into fists. His face contorted as he shouted, "You're a monster and I was such an idiot. If you didn't have that gun, I'd... I'd hit you. I should never have trusted you."

Randy heard it then. A slight squeal of metal. The scuff of a boot. Danny had been trying to cover the sounds with his own shouting.

Randy bellowed out, "Danny, get down!" and jumped forward just as officers in flak jackets burst into the room. Gates whirled and raised his pistol, but Jack rolled himself over to collide with Gates's legs, sending him sprawling.

"No!" Gates yelled from the floor. "Get away. Get back!"

He swung the pistol wildly as he tried to regain his feet, and Randy could do nothing but track the barrel as it moved through space and came to a stop pointing directly at him. He heard Jack scream out his name, mixed with the roar of the large gun going off, and was unable to comprehend why he was knocked sideways and off his feet in a blur of auburn and purple.

He was still cuffed, unable to break his fall as the concrete rushed to meet him. He hit hard and expected even more pain as heaviness settled on his side. It took him a moment to realize that he hadn't been shot but that a limp bundle weighted him down. A bundle that wasn't moving.

"Danny!" He scrambled to free himself from under the boy and lay him gently on the ground. Danny was pale as blood darkened his purple sweatshirt. Randy pressed a hand to the hole in the shoulder to try to staunch the bleeding. The wet, red stuff oozed between his fingers as it pumped from the wound.

"We need an ambulance," Randy yelled. He heard one of the officers speaking into a radio, but he couldn't take his eyes off Danny's white face. Dimly, Randy was aware of two police officers securing Gates while another helped Jack to his feet. One of the officers hurried over to do what he could with the gunshot wound.

Randy scooted back to let the officer help but he couldn't look away. Jack was there to pull off his own T-shirt and offer it as a makeshift bandage. He became aware of Torres speaking in his ear. "Ambulance is on its way, Randy. I don't know who the hell the guy with the white hair is, but he's with my team heading to the station. Are you hurt? Do you need a doctor?"

Randy blinked slowly and turned to look up at Torres, bending over him. He was unable to think clearly, and all he could say was, "That bullet was meant for me."

Jack sank to the ground next to him, shivering as he sagged and croaked out in his burr, "Randy, ay up, duck." Randy needed badly to hold Jack and stretched out his arms, only then realizing he was still in cuffs.

Jack managed a ghost of a smile. "And it's Detective Torres, I believe? We met recently when you asked me about the break-in. I think the key to the handcuffs is in the young 'un's pocket."

"Mr. Fraser. Are you all right?" She reached into Danny's jeans, careful not to jostle his unconscious body, and pulled out the small silver key.

As soon as she unlocked Randy, he reached for Jack to lend him warmth. The smaller Jack fit perfectly into the shelter he offered, relaxing into Randy's body and dropping his head back against Randy's shoulder. Randy flashed to the contentment he'd known when he woke up at Cuir with Jack safely under his protective arm.

To Torres, Jack said, "I was given an injection of some kind that knocked me out and, frankly, I'm feelin' like 'angin' right now." He gave a small shrug at Torres's confusion. "It means I feel like shite. I believe they gave the same drug to Randy."

Torres called out instructions and one of the officers found a spare shirt for Jack. Another turned up Randy's boots. A team of EMTs arrived. One determined that Randy was physically fine but declared him in shock so he sat wrapped in a warm blanket while a second EMT did what she could for Danny. Jack slouched with his eyes closed, wrapped in a blanket of his own, his head drooped.

Randy rasped out, "Are you really all right, Jack? How did

they get to you?"

Jack opened his eyes and straightened his head to look at Randy. "I received a call that said you wanted to meet me to discuss the painting. It was Gates, I realize now, but he sounded calm and I suspected nowt until I took a taxi to the address he gave me. I was foolish, I know, but I walked into the warehouse anyway and, well, I was injected with something. Everything was hazy an' all for a long time after that, but I became aware of you telling Danny to position me on my side. I think that was when I really started to come back awake, but I kept still until I could understand what was going on."

"I'm glad you're safe. When I saw you in that cell…" His stomach churned at the memory.

"You as well, Randy." Jack paused, then said softly, "I'm very sorry about what happened with Danny."

Randy watched intently as the EMT stabilized Danny. He knew Jack wasn't talking about the gunshot, but about the betrayal. Now that the danger was passed, he found himself replaying the previous week with Danny. *How was I so foolish a second time? What did I miss?*

As if Randy had voiced his questions out loud, Jack said, "You did nowt wrong here. You tried to help someone in need. Yes, he took advantage of your nature. He's young and no doubt Gates confused him. But Randy? I was looking right at the two of you when Gates fired. I was sure you'd be shot, and then Danny was there, pushing you away. He wanted to save you. Let that sink in. He made a terrible mistake, but he cared enough for you to risk his life."

Randy only nodded because he was unable to speak, but Jack's words helped. As the EMTs loaded Danny's stretcher into an ambulance, he reached out to take Danny's limp hand in his own while he tried to remember a prayer from his childhood.

Chapter Twenty

RANDY AND JACK were driven to the same hospital as Danny in a second ambulance. When they arrived, Torres was already there and told them that Danny was in surgery.

They were taken into the ER and placed in adjoining cubicles to be checked over by a doctor. The police had found vials of the fentanyl-based compound with which Gates had sedated them, and the doctor was able to determine they should have no lasting ill effects. She pronounced them both fit to leave, though she advised rest and fluids for at least twenty-four hours.

Torres was in the hospital waiting room when they both emerged from the ER. Her gray wool coat hung open over jeans and a blouse that showed a surprising amount of dirt, and the normally neat ponytail in which she kept her long black hair was coming loose.

She saw Randy's raised eyebrow and bared her teeth at him. "No smart comments, *pendejo*. When I dressed for work this morning I didn't expect to be hunting through abandoned warehouses." Randy chuffed as she looked him up and down critically, then glanced at Jack. "I was going to take your statements, but you both look like crap. We can do this tomorrow."

Randy twisted his body to stretch out his back. "I don't mind doing it now. I want to wait for word of Danny's surgery anyway. Jack, you can go back to your hotel, maybe get some rest." But

Randy hoped he'd stay. His quiet demeanor was soothing and helped keep Randy's anxiety down.

Jack cocked his head and gave Randy a small smile as he sat on a plastic chair. "I've slept enough today. I dunna think I could rest anyway until I understand what just happened."

Randy dropped into a chair next to him. Their arms brushed, but Jack made no move to pull away. *I was so close to losing him.* Then he recalled sadly, *He's not mine to lose.*

He sighed and asked, "Where do you want to start, Torres?"

She dragged over a third chair to face them and pulled out her notebook. "Let's start with you, Mr. Fraser—"

"Jack, please."

"All right. Jack. How did you end up in the warehouse?"

Succinctly, Jack described the call he'd received and what happened afterward. With a glance for permission to Randy, he also detailed the circumstances of his initial meeting with Bernard Gates and expanded on the reason he was in Washington. Torres asked probing questions to elicit details, including how he had located Randy in the first place.

"When I spoke to Gates, he wouldn't reveal the name of the purchaser," Jack explained. "But I knew from talking to the family who had consigned *Sunrise* to the Gates Gallery the date of the sale and that the painting had been shipped to America. When artwork over a certain monetary value is shipped internationally, a customs form must be filed. I submitted a request under your Freedom of Information Act for all such forms filed within a week on either side of the sale date. It took quite a long time to receive the responses, and when I did, all I had to go on were the descriptions of the painting being shipped or, in a few cases, a photo of the work that was attached to the customs form. From that, I eventually was able to identify four works of about the right size, value and description. I went to Boston and eliminated one such possibility, then I came to see Randy. I had his home address, but when he didn't respond to my letter requesting a meeting, an internet search led me to Mata Hari. Eventually, it turned out Randy's was the correct work of art."

Randy was impressed. Even though Jack had told him about the FOIA request, he realized he'd never understood the extent of his investigation. "That's a lot of legwork."

Jack smiled at him. "Well, yes. Being an art historian is a bit like being a detective, without the guns." Randy winced and Jack covered his hand with his own. "That was thoughtless. I'm sorry." Randy shrugged, but he looked down the hallway, hoping for a glimpse of Danny's doctor.

Torres turned her attention to Randy and had him fill in what details he could. Randy relayed the things Gates had revealed to him and what had happened as they waited for rescue. He frowned. "I don't really know how I ended up in a different warehouse. Gates said something about tunnels and a cart?"

"We found a motorized flatbed cart that I guess was originally used to move inventory," she said. "It turns out there's a system of underground tunnels to connect various warehouses to the railroad, so I think Gates and Winiarski probably used those tunnels to haul first Jack and then you to the other location."

Torres leaned forward and rested her elbows on her thighs. "I'm sorry it took us so long, Randy. My squad was all over the initial meet point, but we didn't spot the entrance to the tunnels. I had another team going building to building in the neighborhood but they hadn't made it as far as your warehouse before the phone app kicked in and narrowed your location. We were mobilizing to break in when Scarborough called me about your request."

She smiled admiringly. "That was smart. When he heard you call him 'Jason' he guessed right away you were giving him a signal to call me. You made sure he could alert us there were hostages at gunpoint, so we went in quietly. You know the rest. I already called back to let Scarborough know that you're safe, by the way."

Randy hung his head. "Danny heard you coming in before I did. He was actually great. He created a big distraction for Gates to cover the sounds your guys were making." He tried for a grin but his teeth were clenched so it probably looked more like a grimace. "It wasn't much noise, but I'm telling you, a few training sessions for your team in stealth entries might be a good idea." Pain flickered through his chest then. "Danny was between me and Gates when they came in. Gates panicked and fired…" He rubbed his face, and was surprised when Jack's arm fell around his shoulders.

"He'll make it through," Jack murmured. "You heard the woman before he was taken in the ambulance. The bullet missed his heart and lungs."

Randy realized he was leaning into the comfort Jack offered, and he was suddenly so tired that he couldn't remember why that was a bad idea. "I know. There was just so much *blood*, though, and he's so thin."

"We should talk about Winiarski," Torres said. "He's an accessory to kidnapping, at a minimum. The district attorney will probably come up with more charges."

"Ah shit," Randy groaned. "I didn't even think about that. Look, you won't arrest him while he's in recovery, right?" he asked Torres. "I'd really like to talk to him before he's taken into custody. Can you give me that?"

She looked troubled as she tapped her pen against her note-book. Finally she closed the book and shrugged. "I'll do what I can, but I'm going to have to put a uniformed officer outside his door to make sure he doesn't run."

"That's fair. I just need to understand. Once the wheels are turning, I think it will be too late."

Torres looked up as movement caught her eye, and she brought Randy and Jack's attention to a man in scrubs approaching them.

"Detective Torres?" he asked. "I'm Dr. Gannon. I was asked to give you an update that Daniel Winiarski is out of surgery." He frowned at Randy and Jack, but Torres signaled for him to go on. "Well, the surgery went well. The bullet lodged in his shoulder but we extracted it successfully. We don't expect permanent nerve damage, though rehabilitation may take some time. He's under anesthesia right now but he should be awake in a few hours. Would you like us to call when he's conscious?"

Torres walked a short distance away with Dr. Gannon to discuss arrangements for guarding Danny's room, while Jack pulled Randy into a hug.

"You see? I told you he'd be well," Jack said, looking up at Randy with a smile.

Randy allowed his head to loll against Jack's shoulder. "You were right." He was more relaxed now that Danny was out of danger and found himself murmuring, "You were also right about the paintings in Mata Hari. The way I have them displayed sucks."

Jack laughed affectionately. "We'd better get back to that doctor. I'm sure you'd never admit that in your right state."

Randy pulled back to look Jack in the eye. "Thank you," he said, but then turned uncharacteristically shy. "For staying here. For what you said about Danny. You're the only one who knows about, I mean, why that hurt so much. To find out Danny was using me."

Jack brushed a thumb along Randy's cheek. "I'm glad I was of help to you. And by the way," he added acerbically, "thank you for rescuing me. I didn't care for being the damsel in distress." That made Randy grin. "Good. I like your smile. Now please go home and get some rest. You won't be able to talk to Danny for a while anyway, and you'll be able to handle the conversation better when you're fresh."

"That's good advice." Suddenly Randy couldn't face the idea of the empty house in Arlington. He knew he'd wander the floor, looking at Danny's things and the signs of his habitation. He'd let himself into his studio and stare at the portrait of a young man he had thought he understood but didn't really know at all.

Perhaps Jack could tell Randy's heart was heavy and troubled because he bent his head and said quietly in Randy's ear, "I suspect you'd rest better with me. Come back to my hotel room. Please."

Comfort. Warmth. Kindness. Randy ached for what Jack was offering. He wanted to wrap his arms around Jack's slender frame and keep him close as they drifted away, then wake up with his face buried in Jack's soft, dark hair. But he didn't know if he could trust himself.

Jack brushed his hand along Randy's cheek. "Just to sleep. I respect your convictions." Randy could sense Jack's slight smile, hear the gentleness, as he added, "I promise to keep my hands to myself."

Randy closed his eyes. It was a fucking terrible idea, but he knew he would give in. Even if one night of comfort would make it hurt worse when Jack returned to England, and would leave Randy feeling like shit for seeking intimacy with a man engaged to be married. He nodded. "Okay. Just sleep."

Randy put on his jacket as he considered their options. Torres would arrange a police car for them and he could deal with his truck, parked back at the warehouse, the next day. She was still talking to the doctor, though, so he took Jack's hand in his big paw and left the hospital to find a cab.

They were quiet in the back of the taxi until Randy started. "Shit. I need to let Thomas know what happened." He pulled out his phone; the battery was low and it was the middle of the night, but he figured his friend would be awake and eager to hear from him so he dialed anyway. Sure enough, Thomas picked up on the first ring.

"Randy! Jesus, man. Are you okay?"

"I am, buddy. You really helped me by alerting Torres."

"Well, I figured that was what you meant when you said 'Jason.' From when you, Torres, and I talked about my old life in Seattle. She gave me the highlights a few hours ago, but what happened?"

Randy summarized the events briefly, including the fact that Danny had been playing him. Jack squeezed his hand as he told about Danny getting shot, and Thomas exhaled heavily across the line.

"Aw no. That must hurt. I know you were trying to help him, and then to get stabbed in the back like that. Fuck."

"Yeah, that's about right." Randy hesitated before continuing, but finally confessed, "Even with that shit Danny pulled, I don't want to see him in jail. Does that make sense?"

Thomas was silent for a long moment. "Knowing you? Yes, it does make sense. You're my best friend, so I hope you don't take this wrong. When you give your loyalty, that's a bond for you. Even if the loyalty isn't deserved, I don't think you can withdraw it."

Randy thought about Thomas's words, and Trevor came to mind. Even with all the crap that went down there, a part of Randy still wondered about him. He didn't even carry much anger anymore. He just wondered occasionally, was Trevor all right? Did he ever get to see his wife?

"I see that, brother," Randy said. "I don't know if it's a good or a bad thing though."

"Believe me, it's good. You want my opinion? I think you'll need closure with this Danny kid, no matter what happens. Go talk to him. See if he can be honest with you, and trust your instincts like you always do."

Randy sighed. His instincts... they'd failed him with Trevor, and again with Danny, but he didn't have a better plan. "Okay, I'll do that. Talk to you soon."

At the hotel, Jack obtained a replacement key card since the one he'd been carrying was evidence. He leaned against Randy in the elevator as it rose. He opened the door and gestured Randy inside.

A maid had apparently turned down the bed for the evening, and a low light burned. Randy's heart beat faster as he turned to Jack. He hoped he was equal to the temptation facing him, because all he wanted at that moment was to bury his sadness and relief and loneliness inside the man before him.

Jack watched his face closely, his whiskey eyes darting back and forth to gauge Randy's emotions. Finally he said in a low voice, "I wish things were different. If you met Sophie–" He cut himself off and shook his head. "Never mind. I understand. I'll be back in a moment."

He went into the bathroom, the shower ran, and a few minutes later he emerged in loose-fitting sleep pants. The bathroom light behind him cast his slim body in silhouette, but as he moved to the bed, the lamp there shone on his bare chest with its swirls of soft hair, still looking damp from his shower. Randy wanted to comb his fingers through it, to grasp and tug just hard enough to awaken the senses, and then to roll Jack's nipples between thumb and forefinger until his back arched and he gave himself over to Randy's touch. The curl of desire in his belly flexed and grew as he watched Jack's lithe body slide into the sheets. He remembered penetrating Jack as he bent over a chair and then the sensation, as he sank deep, that he was home. Jack said Sophie understood...

No. This can't happen. He took his turn in the bathroom to rinse the weariness of the day, and the traces of Danny's blood, down the drain. He hesitated before returning to the bedroom, but finally pulled his white cotton T-shirt and jockey shorts back on. Jack held the blankets open to him and Randy climbed into the big luxurious bed, sliding close over smooth, cool sheets.

They lay facing each other, not touching. Randy stuffed one hand under his pillow to keep from reaching out. Jack gave him a sad smile and silently mouthed the words, "Mighty bear" before he rolled over, facing away.

A sense of expectation remained in the room and Jack's breathing was controlled. Tense. Randy studied the shape of his lean body under the draped bedclothes. *This much won't hurt anything,* Randy lied to himself as he shifted closer and draped his free arm over Jack's waist. Jack gave a contented huff and adjusted himself with a small grunt so they were spooned together. He fit into the curve of Randy's body like the missing piece of a puzzle.

"Good night, Randy," he heard, and then Jack clicked off the lamp. The stress of the day faded as exhaustion stilled Randy's body. He began to drift away, and the last thing he remembered was Jack taking his wrist and pulling his arm even more tightly around.

Chapter Twenty-One

RANDY WOKE A few hours later in the darkened room, momentarily confused until he heard Jack snuffle in his sleep. Jack had rolled over so he faced Randy, knees crooked and dark head bent. Randy longed to stroke his hair and run hands over the lean muscle of his body, but fought off the impulse. Jack needed to rest after the things that had happened to him.

What was left of Randy's night was full of chaotic thoughts and self-recrimination. He found himself replaying every day with Danny as he tried to understand. So many clues had been right in front of him, and bile burned his throat as he added up his errors. He had asked too few questions. He had assumed Danny was attracted to him, and the nervousness the kid showed was about handling a crush.

Instead, Danny was actually working a con and was probably just afraid he'd be caught. Only Randy's colossal ego had kept him from seeing it. He had no more idea whether Danny was really even gay than he did about Trevor.

God, what if Randy had done it? What if he had let Danny into his bed? He'd be a monster instead of just an idiot. Not that he would ever have sex with an underage boy, but he still buried his face in his pillow in humiliation at the thought.

But then Jack's words about Randy being caught between two men came back to him in the lonely darkness. Kevin had taught him so much, but most importantly, he had taught Randy about honor. Trevor didn't take away that honor; he just exposed Randy's weakness and his vulnerability.

It wasn't bad that Randy wanted to protect, and if it sometimes made him a target for manipulative men like Trevor or Gates, well, he'd have to accept that risk as a consequence. The alternative—a closed heart, a cold shoulder to the world—would have made Kevin ashamed of him. And that would be a true tragedy.

His thoughts circled around Jack as he slept inches away in the big bed. The man was so insightful. Randy's side of the king mattress was sad and empty, and he wished he could forget what he knew about Sophie and London and everything else that occupied Jack's life and marked him as off limits.

To hell with principles, Randy thought savagely. What had those gotten him? He'd proven to be a fool, time and time again. What did he have to show for it all but an empty house and a closet full of leather?

What might have happened if, on one of his strolls through London, he had run across a younger, unattached Jack? Would they have recognized something in one another then, something that would have brought them together before Sophie and Danny and Gates?

Randy snorted softly at himself. Might-have-beens were useless. He was drawn to Jack, but the man was taken. He tried to help Danny, but the boy lied to him. All he could do was hold on to his honor, keep his friends safe, and live as a man Kevin and Luc would be proud to call their son. Anything less would mean he wasn't worthy of Jack in any case.

But when Jack woke and his sleepy brown eyes found Randy's, his first thought was that principle did very little to protect one's heart. A smolder started in Jack's face. He could tell that Jack was hard under the covers, and he fought with everything in him to keep away. *Please don't push this. I'm not strong enough.*

The desire in Jack's eyes melted away to sadness and understanding. He leaned in just enough to kiss Randy with his lips closed, then rolled the other way and got out of bed. As he closed the bathroom door behind him he called out, "Perhaps you'd like to have some coffee and breakfast sent up?"

Randy considered it, but he was frayed from the restless night and the turmoil in his stomach over Danny. *Is he all right after the surgery? Why did he do it?* He pulled on his own clothes, rank as they were, and ran hands over his scalp. His skin felt too tight as anxiety crawled into his gut.

Suddenly he regretted staying the night with Jack. It was too close to the line he swore he wouldn't cross, and it left him dirty. His voice sounded raspy and harsh to him when he called back, "I think I just need to get to the hospital."

Jack opened the bathroom door, a toothbrush in his hand. "Of course." His smile didn't reach his eyes. He crooked his head slightly as he seemed to take in Randy's tension and softly asked, "Can we talk soon?"

"Sure." Randy's skin itched and he had to get away. That was probably why he added, "We still have to discuss the painting."

Jack inhaled sharply. "That isn't what I... Never mind." He looked away at the rumpled bed and refused to meet Randy's eyes any longer. "Please let me know if Danny will be all right. You can leave a message here at the hotel if I'm out." Hurt radiated from him but Randy didn't know how to fix it. How to fix *anything.*

In his poshest tone, Jack said, "When you're up to it, we can schedule a time to address the painting. I expect the police would like me to be available, so I'll arrange with my museum to stay in Washington another week or so."

RANDY ROLLED INTO the hospital later, sure that he looked like shit but not caring, to find Torres already there and talking to Dr. Gannon. He approached in time to hear the doctor say, "He'll be weak from blood loss for several days, but recovery from the wound will take considerably longer than that. I assume you're going to put him in an infirmary at the Central Detention Facility. It would be a good idea to let me or someone on my team handle the transfer and communicate directly with the attending physician there."

When Torres spotted Randy, she excused herself and escorted him to Danny's room. To the uniformed man outside, she said, "Officer Carson, this is Mr. Vaughan. He's authorized to speak with Winiarski." As Carson held the door open to the room, Torres touched Randy compassionately on the shoulder but let him enter alone.

Danny lay with a clear IV dripping to one arm and a bag of blood to the other. His right wrist was cuffed to the hospital bed. His eyes were closed, so Randy said nothing and just grabbed a padded vinyl chair from the wall and moved it next to the bed. He sat and waited.

Without opening his eyes, Danny said, "I didn't figure I'd ever see you again."

Randy cleared his throat. "I need to understand. I think you owe me that much."

Danny rolled his head toward the sound of Randy's voice but kept his eyes squeezed shut. He said roughly, "I can't look at you, Randy. I'm so ashamed."

"Keep 'em closed then. Just explain." More softly, he added, "Please."

Danny sighed. "You know most of it. My mom and me, we

always struggled. People knew she was married to a con and that made it hard for her to get a good job. But she wouldn't move away because she wanted to be able to see my dad as much as she could. They really loved each other. She wanted me to know him, even though he was in jail.

"I always understood what he did. I mean about the drugs and the shooting. They were both honest with me. But the man I got to meet once a month, he tried so hard to be better. He worked in the prison library and got a degree online. He became a drug counselor to other inmates. I bet you never knew any of that, did you?"

"No. I checked every so often to see if he was still in prison, to make sure I didn't miss a hearing or anything. When the Maine authorities contacted me about his requests for resentencing, I went to be heard by the court. I went for my uncle and for his partner Luc, because he couldn't make himself face your father after what he did."

Finally Danny opened his eyes and they were shiny with unshed tears. "I'm so sorry my father took Kevin from you. But my dad was a kid when that happened. Almost the same age I am now. He made a terrible mistake and he's paid for it. He's still paying for it. When my mom died, he couldn't come to the funeral. He..." Danny choked off with a sob.

Randy waited while he got himself together. When Danny was able to speak again he continued. "I told you the truth about losing the place we rented. I didn't know what to do. I didn't want to move away and abandon my dad, but I didn't know how to keep my head above water. I kind of hated you, because I knew you made sure he didn't get released and there I was, poor, homeless, and with no family. I thought I'd have to.... Well, it was a bad time."

Randy waited but Danny went silent. Finally, he prompted,

"Was that when Gates found you?"

"Yes. He told me he needed help getting something from you and that he believed he'd be able to persuade you to change your mind about my dad. I had nothing to lose, and I didn't know you except for pieces of paper in my dad's file and that one time I saw you at the resentencing hearing.

"So Bernard got it set up. Everything made sense when he explained it at first. Bernard wanted me to have sex with you because he figured we could blackmail you." Danny reddened. "I didn't lie to you about my age, but he thought pictures of you having sex with a teenager would be enough to get you to do what he wanted. Anyway, it didn't work. You didn't want me.

"Then he said I should try to be friends with you so maybe you'd offer me a job and I could nose around. He hung around outside Mata Hari to watch you but he didn't want to go into the bar as a customer in case you recognized him. He thought maybe you hung the painting there, or maybe I'd be able to get more out of you."

Danny stopped talking and just stared at Randy for a long stretch before he said, "The thing was, even though Bernard had done all this research into you, he didn't take it seriously. You know? He didn't get that the protective thing is really *you*. When you asked me to come to your house, no strings attached, I already knew I'd made a big mistake. But I didn't know how to get out of it. If I told you the mugging was staged, you'd kick me out and there was no way Bernard would help me at that point. I figured I'd stick around and get some information and maybe…"

He paused again, and Randy asked softly, "What did you think would happen?"

Danny blushed. "I was hoping maybe you'd start to like me. Like I liked you. That wasn't an act. I've never met anyone as kind as you and I thought, maybe if you wanted me, I could tell you the truth and you'd help me."

Randy blew out a breath in frustration. "You could have told me the truth anyway, Danny."

"I was scared how you'd react," he mumbled. "At first, I didn't think I was going to have to do anything really bad. I looked around the house and your workshop when I was alone but I couldn't find the painting Bernard wanted. He'd already stolen the letter from Fraser but I told him about the visits to you at Mata Hari. I asked you about art to get you talking, but it was also because I was really interested. I gave Bernard information about the bar. I didn't know he was going to break in, I swear. When you took off Sunday night after the alarm I called his cell to warn him you were coming, but it was because I was afraid *you'd* get hurt. Like, he'd ambush you or something."

Randy shook his head. "Danny, how can you say you weren't doing anything bad? You had to understand what was happening when you lured me to the warehouse."

He turned his head toward the pillow to hide from Randy's direct gaze. He whispered, "I knew that was bad. I didn't know Bernard was going to knock Jack out. When he called me to come meet him, Jack was already unconscious and Bernard told me to go to his hotel to look for his proven-whatever. I didn't know what to do."

He rolled his head back to look at Randy. "I was sure you could fix it, if you were there. So I called you and then I… I sat there like a Judas." Tears welled in his eyes and began to run down his cheeks. "You did so much for me. You fed me and gave me money and clothes and you wanted me to go to college and I *still* let Bernard stick that needle into you." He started sobbing and threw his uncuffed arm over his eyes, heedless of the IV needle.

Randy didn't know what to do or how to feel, but he couldn't take the misery pouring out of the boy. Thomas was right. Once he gave his loyalty, he didn't know how to withdraw it.

He leaned forward and scooped Danny awkwardly into a hug. Danny threw his free arm around Randy's neck and clung to him like he was drowning. Maybe he was. He just kept saying against Randy's neck, "I'm sorry. I'm so sorry."

Minutes passed, and eventually the storm ebbed. When Danny seemed to have stopped crying, Randy let him down so he could wipe his cheeks with the heel of his hand. He seemed more focused after the emotional jag and Randy pressed on. "Can you tell me the rest?" he asked. "I really need to know."

Danny blinked at him with red-rimmed eyes. "Okay." He exhaled heavily. "It was the only way I could think to help Jack. Bernard needed your help, so I figured he couldn't really hurt you. Once he stuck you, I helped him load the cart, but it was so I could bring you to where Jack was. Please believe me."

Randy's voice was rough when he answered. "I get it. If you warned me, Gates could have done something else to Jack maybe. Something worse."

Danny nodded. "I tried, though. When I took Jack's key card and went to the hotel to search for his, what'd ya call it, provenance papers, I left a note."

"Why didn't you call me when you were away from Gates?"

Danny blinked. "I was in so far I didn't know how to explain." He sniffled. "I'm so dumb. All I can say is, I was scared and I just thought—"

"You had to get me there." Randy focused on the toe of his boot. "Why'd you jump in front of me, when Gates was waving the gun around? You must have known you could get shot."

When he looked up, Danny was staring at the foot of his bed. Finally he mumbled, "You see someone you can help, you do it."

Randy's throat hurt. He remembered saying those words the

night they met, when he brought Danny into his home.

He couldn't know exactly what had been happening in Danny's head when Gates pointed the gun, but maybe, just maybe, Randy had made a difference to him after all. Maybe it wasn't all an act. Thomas said to trust his instincts, and they told him Danny was telling the truth.

Danny looked at the cuff around his wrist. "I know I'll probably go to jail for helping Bernard. I deserve that for what I did to you and Jack. But if you could just meet with my dad, just once, it would mean everything to me. I'll plead guilty or whatever you need so I don't make any more trouble than I already have. But please. Please don't hold what I did against my dad."

Randy stared at him for a long while. Even with all the shit running through his head, he came back to one thing, over and over again. "You took a bullet for me. I don't know if I can help you with the DC police, but I'll do what you want. I'll go meet your father and see what I think. No promises, but I'll at least meet with him."

Danny grabbed for his hand, though the cuff pulled him up short. Randy met him halfway in a clasp. "Thank you. I don't deserve it but thank you for doing this."

Do any of us get what we deserve? Randy wondered. Kevin spent his life trying to help people and died for it. Danny wanted a father, but Randy denied him. Randy finally admitted to himself that he craved a future with someone, but the man he would choose was claimed.

It isn't about what we deserve, but whether we can help.

He released Danny's hand and brushed away hair that fell over his eyes. "Get some rest now. I'll see what I can do."

Chapter Twenty-Two

RANDY CALLED TORRES when he left Danny's hospital room and asked her to think about talking to the prosecutor regarding a plea deal for Danny. "He fucked up, but he's a kid. Look, will you check with Jack to see if it's true that Danny left a note in his hotel room? I know it's not much, but he was trying to find a way to help."

Torres sighed. "You're a pain in my ass. Can't you just let the little bastard go to jail and move on?"

"You know I can't, Maria."

"I know." She was silent for a beat, then said, "Okay. I'll check with Fraser and if this pans out, I'll at least talk to my captain. See what he thinks about me bringing it to the prosecutor."

Next he called Christian Fong at the law firm to ask him to set up a meeting with Jack about a custodial arrangement for the painting. "Do whatever's smart," he instructed his lawyer, "but I'm ready to let this happen. If there are good reasons for taking the canvas to England instead of testing it at the Smithsonian, I'll trust your judgment."

Christian said, "Understood. I'll call Mr. Fraser right away, and we'll start with having his museum agree to foot the legal bill."

"Hey, while I have you, do you know any criminal lawyers in town? I, um, I want to help someone out. I don't think I can afford someone at your firm's level, but if there's a smaller law firm you know, maybe I could swing that."

"Hmm. Actually, a law school colleague of mine recently decided to hang out a shingle and start his own criminal defense practice. He's done a fair amount of cases in what we call biglaw, meaning the large law firms. But since he's newly on his own he might be willing to take on a matter for a reasonable fee." Christian read him a name and phone number, then Randy signed off with his thanks.

That left one call he needed to make.

He dialed Jack's hotel, and this time, Jack picked up in his room. As the smooth English voice said hello, Randy instantly grew more calm. "Jack, it's Randy."

"I'm glad you called. How did it go with Danny?"

"I, uh, I think he'll be all right. Physically anyway. Legally, well, that's up in the air. Oh, heads up. You're going to get calls from Detective Torres about whether Danny left a note in your room, and from a lawyer named Christian Fong to talk about the painting."

"Actually, Detective Torres called me already. There was a note, sitting on the chest of drawers. I suppose we didn't see it when we got in last night." An awkward silence descended. Randy was sorry for the way he'd left things earlier, but he didn't know how to make anything better. Jack cleared his throat and continued, "I've set it aside to deliver to the police. Danny wrote down where I'd been moved after the first warehouse. The handwriting is shaky, so I'd imagine he was terrified when he wrote it."

Randy gave a sigh. "I'm glad he did that. I don't know if it will make a difference, and it was feeble, but it was at least something. He tried."

He could almost sense Jack nodding. "I agree. I don't blame

him for what happened to me, not really. He seems a naïve chap who had no idea what idiocy Gates got him involved in."

"You're a good man, Jack."

"It's the company I've kept this week. It inspires me to be more trusting, more open."

Randy chuckled, then fell silent for a few moments. He couldn't explain it, not after only knowing the man for a matter of days, but he was going to miss Jack like hell. "So my lawyer Fong is going to negotiate a custodial arrangement for *Sunrise*."

"Will you be at the negotiation?" Jack asked softly.

"I don't think so." *I don't trust myself around you.* "I've got too many irons in the fire, and I need to plan a trip up to Portland."

"Is that about Danny's father?"

"Yeah. I said I'd meet him and make up my own mind about whether… I don't know."

"Whether he's paid enough for the pain he caused you and your uncle Luc." Jack said it with such certainty that Randy was amazed.

"That's pretty intuitive for someone who's spent as little time with me as you have. But I guess I shouldn't be surprised. You put together things in a way that impresses me."

Jack huffed a laugh. "Not always. We got off to a pretty rocky start because I had trouble connecting the man who would pick a Brousseau out of a rundown gallery in Whitechapel with the grizzly bear in a *fierce* white shirt serving drinks at a bar." Randy snorted at that. "And I'll never forget the way you led me to that corner in Cuir before I had a meltdown in public. And the way you held me in bed after, when I felt I'd fly apart. Honestly, I never guessed you'd be such a cuddler."

"Well that tears it. I guess I've lost my tough guy rep." Randy smiled to hear Jack's soft chuckle, and he was glad they were having this conversation by phone.

He promised himself that he would avoid meeting Jack in person again. The man saw too much that Randy wanted to hide. Like the way he could picture Jack in his leather harness, wanton and begging for Randy's touch. The wiry strength of him, spooned in Randy's arms. Randy was too raw and he didn't trust himself to keep his principles. Not if they had even one more night together.

Jack was quiet and careful when he spoke again. "I don't think anyone else would notice, so your reputation is safe. I just paid close attention. As did you, to me." Silence for a beat. "I like you very much, Randy. I wish—"

"Yeah, me too." Randy cut him off, then cleared his throat. "Look, I gotta go. Play nice with Fong and I'm sure you'll make a reasonable arrangement I'll be happy to support."

"Very well. Goodbye, Randy."

"Bye, Jack."

* * *

ALMOST A WEEK later, Randy sat next to Luc in a small room in the state prison in Warren, Maine. Luc had never been tall and hearty like Kevin, but his once-black hair had gone gray, his hazel eyes were too large, and he'd shrunk with age. As they waited, he was fretful and nervous, so Randy put a hand on his thin shoulder.

"You ready for this?" he asked.

Luc shook his head slightly, but then he pulled himself straighter in his chair. "No, I'm good. It's been more than thirty years. It's time."

"You can wait outside if you want," Randy offered, but at that moment the door opened and Henry Winiarski was led in. Luc sucked in a breath but otherwise kept still. Randy stood and met the guard, who waited until Henry sat down and then positioned himself in a corner of the room.

Henry was awkward and pale. His auburn hair was thinning, but his eyes were almost the same shape as Danny's. In fact, he looked so much like his son that Randy couldn't believe he hadn't seen the connection right away. On the other hand, he'd probably never before looked at Henry that closely as a *person*. He was a boogeyman, the monster who had taken away Kevin all those years ago. Randy had never gotten past the shooting to wonder about the boy who had pulled the trigger and became a man in prison.

Henry cleared his throat and spoke first. "Thank you for meeting me, Mr. Simard. Mr. Vaughan."

Luc answered first. "This isn't easy but…." He shook his head and tried again. "Yeah, it isn't easy."

"Have you been able to speak with Danny?" Randy asked.

Henry nodded. "Three days ago. He told me what happened; what he did." Henry's eyes filled with tears. "I need to apologize for my boy, for him hurting you again. It's no excuse, but I didn't know what he was up to. I would have tried to stop him."

"Danny got in over his head, and then he didn't know how to get out. He may have told you I got him a lawyer. I think they're going to be able to work out a deal where Danny will get probation or maybe even a suspended sentence in exchange for testifying against Bernard Gates."

Tears slid down Henry's cheeks. "I didn't know you did that. Thank you. We…" He bent his head over his folded hands. "We owe you for many things."

Luc leaned forward. "Your son saved my son's life." He glanced up at Randy and said as if embarrassed, "You know what I mean."

Randy squeezed Luc's neck lightly. Kevin and Luc had always been better parents to him than his own mom and dad, and he had called them his fathers. But hearing Luc claim him as his son, well, he didn't know he still wanted that until he heard the word.

To the unspoken question and alarm in Henry's wide eyes, Randy responded, "It's true. Maybe Danny didn't tell you everything, but he was shot in the shoulder. The bullet was meant for me."

"Is he all right?" Henry asked quickly, and Randy nodded.

"He's healing fine. No permanent damage. We have him in physical therapy with a great guy in DC."

Henry exhaled hard in relief. "My poor boy. Once his mother died, he was lost. I tried to help, but there was so little I could do from a cell." He must have thought that sounded like a criticism, because he quickly looked between Luc and Randy. "I deserve to be here. I do. I just wish there had been someone for Danny to turn to after Sheila died. I tried to talk her into a divorce when Danny was about eight so she could give him a new father, but she wouldn't hear of it. She kept bringing him here, one day a month. She wanted him to know his dad, even if this was all we'd ever have."

Luc said, "It must have been hard for all of you. Wanting to be together with your family. Knowing you couldn't be."

"Like you." Henry leaned forward again to meet Luc's gaze. "I know what Danny asked you to do, about meeting me and what he wants. I'm not asking for that, Mr. Simard. I know what I did to you when I took your friend away all those years ago. I think about it every night. I can't make it right, but I can try to prevent others from making such a terrible choice. That's why I became a counselor here."

"Danny mentioned that," Randy said. "Tell us more."

The hour went quickly, and Randy was surprised when the guard said, "Time's up, Winiarski. Gentlemen."

Henry stood, and Luc and Randy rose to face him. "I can

never tell you enough just how sorry I am for what I did to Kevin and to you, or how grateful I am for what you've done for my boy. If you can give him some guidance, some direction, then that's more than we deserve. Thank you for coming." They weren't permitted to shake hands with Henry, but Randy found to his surprise that he wanted to.

In the car driving back to Portland, Luc spoke first. "I'm glad we finally did that. I had so many bad dreams over the years." Luc shivered as he trailed off. "He's not a monster, just a sad man who hurt many people through foolish choices when he was young."

"What do you think, Luc?" Randy asked. "Can you forgive him?"

Luc whooshed out a breath. "Forgive. That's a big word." He looked at the passing towns for a while. "Kevin would want me to. Forgive him, I mean. Henry's done everything in his power to make amends. Keeping him in prison will never bring back our Kevin, and it led indirectly to you nearly being killed." More silence, and then Randy saw Luc's shoulders heave a bit as he fought and controlled his emotions.

Randy was quiet for several more miles. He glanced at the man sitting next to him. "You and Kevin, you gave me everything. I chose my path in life to make you both proud, and to show the world I was proud of you. I've done some good as a result, I think. I'd like Danny to have the chance to know his dad too, and see what choices he makes from that."

Finally Luc seemed able to speak again. His voice was hoarse when he said, "You're our son in every way that matters. Since you have faith in Danny, maybe the best thing we can do to honor Kevin is give Danny his dad while there's still time."

Chapter Twenty-Three

AS RANDY PULLED his truck into the driveway, the headlights swept over Thanksgiving decorations Danny had insisted upon. A stuffed scarecrow waved from the front of Randy's studio, and sheaves of corn lined the walk to the side entrance. He wasn't sure how the jack o'lantern lights left over from Halloween fit the holiday theme, but Danny had been unwilling to abandon them so he just worked them into a vaguely autumnal tableau. It made Randy tease that Danny might become an artist yet.

Three weeks had passed since Randy's trip to meet Henry Winiarski, and it surprised him that he'd gotten so comfortable with Danny's presence again. With Randy's agreement to be responsible for him, Danny had been able to return to Randy's house rather than spend time in jail while the criminal prosecution moved forward. After his hospital discharge, Randy brought him back to Arlington. The defense attorney Randy hired had worked a deal with the prosecutor to get probation for Danny in exchange for cooperation with the case against Gates.

The first few days back at the house were tense and awkward, but Danny did everything he could to atone. It had been Danny's idea to perform his community service with the LGBT shelter Rainbow Space. Even though he was the same age as the oldest residents, Joe always had chores and jobs that needed to be done and he kept Danny busy. It also meant that Randy and Danny didn't see a lot of each other during the week because of their conflicting schedules, and that was probably a good thing as the bruises on Randy's heart healed. A few weeks into their new arrangement and Randy optimistically believed their relationship would continue to mend.

He was hungry and hoped Danny had left something in the warming oven for him. Tuesdays had really picked up at Mata Hari recently; the bar had been packed until closing. With Thanksgiving just two days away, Randy expected to be busy the rest of the week as well, and the thought exhausted him in advance. He was ready for a shower, a quick bite, and then maybe some time in his studio with his canvas of Danny sitting in Del's Diner and staring out the window.

The lights were on in the kitchen when he entered the house so Randy figured Danny was still awake. He called out, "Hey kid. Got anything around for me to eat?" He jumped when he heard a low chuckle, whirling to find Jack standing near the fireplace in a dark sweater and black pants.

He hadn't seen Jack in person since the morning in his hotel room when everything had been awkward, and they hadn't spoken for weeks once Jack left for London. A few quick text exchanges had been the extent of their communication, and Randy had missed Jack every bit as much as he'd feared. Before he could even think about it, he took quick strides over and hauled Jack into a hug. Sure enough, he still smelled of pomegranates and earthy, delicious things.

Jack returned the hug, but almost immediately Randy recollected himself and let go. He stood back and reached to clout Jack lightly on the shoulder. "You look great. What are you doing here?"

"Danny let me in." Jack looked shy but pleased with himself. "I got in touch with him a few days ago to ask for his help once I knew when I was returning to the States. I wanted to surprise you."

"Well, mission accomplished. Is Danny here?"

"No, but he left some food for you. He warned me you come home hungry from the bar." Jack scratched his head sheepishly. "I, uh, gave him taxi money. He's spending the night with your friends Thomas and Zachary."

As happy as he was to see Jack, Randy was instantly wary. Jack had arranged for the two of them to be alone in Randy's house. With a fire burning and sending up sparks. Principle was one thing, but with Jack so near... Randy wasn't sure he was strong enough to face that trial a second time.

He struggled to ignore the erection that had begun to form when he hugged Jack and began, "You know I won't—"

Jack interrupted to pull him toward the fireplace. "Can we catch up before you eat, Randy? I really want that."

Randy let himself be led over, and he sank into one of the comfortable chairs there. The fire crackled and hissed in the grate, filling the room pleasantly with the scent of wood smoke. Jack sat on the raised hearth facing him and leaned forward earnestly with his hands clasped between his knees.

"There are two things I need to tell you. The first and most important one is..." Jack stopped and chuckled nervously. His burr crept in when he spoke again to mutter, "Christ, I dunna know how you're going to take this." He steeled himself and captured Randy's gaze. "Okay. Sophie and I broke it off. Our engagement, I mean."

Randy's jaw dropped. The words echoed strangely in his ears over his pounding heart, and all he could wonder was, *what did Jack mean*?

Maybe Jack saw something encouraging, because he bobbed his head nervously and kept talking. "When I got back to

England, Sophie knew right away that something was different. We talked a lot and, well, we took the decision to end the sham."

Randy asked hoarsely, "For me?"

"Yes," Jack said firmly. "Well, sort of. Look," he scooted closer to the edge of the hearth and reached out to take one of Randy's big hands. "I realize we don't know each other very well yet. It was such a short time when I was last in Washington. But being with you was everything I didn't know I was missing. Do you understand?"

"I think so," Randy answered cautiously, then gave up trying to pretend he had any resistance and admitted, "Jack, I've never been so attuned to another human being in my life."

"Exactly. It's not just the sex, though the sex that night at Cuir was magic." Jack groaned and rolled his eyes to make Randy chuckle. "But it was so much larger. When I was alone those last few days, I probably went by the outside of Mata Hari every day, just to think about you and maybe catch a glimpse. The way you made me safe, the *care* you took with me." He shook his head. "Well, it ruined me. In a good way. When I was back in London, I knew I needed you to be happy more than I needed sunshine. And I want to be the one to make *you* happy, the way you deserve. Sophie told me if I didn't try, then I was an arsehole and should be assigned to clean graffiti off the Tube walls."

Randy chuckled even as he tried to reel in what was happening. "How could anything between us even work, Jack?" His blood was thundering in his ears but he was fifty-one, not fifteen. He needed to be practical even though his heart had left his mind in the dust and was flying around the moon. "I want it too, but realistically—"

"Here's the thing," Jack cut him off. "I got a job with the Smithsonian as a curator. I'll start as soon as the work visa goes through. I also went online and found a flat to let in some neighborhood called Adams Morgan."

Randy had no idea what to say. "A job here, an apartment. Jack, we barely know each other."

"That's why I'm doing this. I think we're going to be stunning together, but it's too early to be sure. With me in Washington, we can spend time together, hopefully without anesthetic." Randy grinned ruefully and touched the spot on his neck where he'd felt Gates's sting as Jack added, "If I'm wrong and it dunna work, well, at least we wunna spend our lives wondering.

"Because that's the thing, Randy." Jack tugged on the hand he held in his own. "From the evening I met you I *wondered*. Even when you would barely give me the time of day. 'What if?' I asked me sen, I mean myself. What if this grizzly bear with a passion for art and a *desperate* need for someone to help curate his collection is who I've been missing all this time? What if I take a chance to be proud as I *am* instead of who I thought I needed to be to succeed? What if the one man who is perfect for me is just an ocean away and I lose him over something as silly as geography?" Softly, Jack added, "I have to know, Randy."

In answer, Randy stood and pulled Jack to his feet. He brushed past his objections, his nerves, and just let himself embrace the moment. Arms tightly wound around Jack's lean body, he bent his head to claim the kiss he'd dreamt of for weeks. Jack was pliant and welcoming in his arms, taking in Randy's warmth, his tongue, his breath.

It was so good that Randy didn't recognize the trembling in his legs for a moment. It wasn't until it spread to his hands and froze his mouth that Jack leaned back and asked, "What's happening?"

"I, uh…" Randy's eyes darted around the room. He couldn't settle on any one thing. Jack put a hand on his cheek and drew back his attention. Looking down into those whiskey-colored eyes, concerned and suddenly nervous, Randy knew he had to answer. "I never thought about this for myself. Not really. Jack, you could do a lot better than me."

Surprise flared, then Jack narrowed his gaze. "Do you na want me here?"

"What? I do want you. Here, I mean. It's just..." His eyes were shifting around again and he wanted very much to go somewhere else right then. *But Jack came all this way, made all these arrangements.* That took enormous courage, and Randy owed him honesty.

"I'm not good enough for you."

Jack made a soft sound that drew Randy's eyes to him. To his surprise, Jack was nodding. "Of course you are. Mighty bear, so big and confident. But no one really gets to see it, do they?"

Randy licked his lips before asking cautiously, "See what?"

"The fear you carry." Randy blinked, but Jack didn't let him interrupt. "You fear that you can't protect the people you love. Or that you won't be there in time. You fear that you'll be made to look foolish by those you trust."

"How do you do that?" Randy hissed.

"I *see* you, about as well as you saw the real me. And Randy? It's human to know fear. What makes you special is that you dunna let fear *control* you. You charged into that warehouse alone, no idea what was facing you, to protect Danny. You did the same for your friend Zachary. You bargained recklessly for my life when I might have overdosed."

Jack wrapped himself around Randy again. "You're afraid this wunna work out between us. I understand that. I canna give you a guarantee, but I tell you that I've wanted nowt in my life as much as I want you. I believe in us, Randy. Please, take a chance. Believe in us too."

What else could he do? This handsome man moved his entire life across the Atlantic Ocean to take a chance on someone he'd known for a week. How could Randy let himself be any less brave? Certainty began to grow and to push aside the doubts and fear that had knocked him for a loop.

"I do believe," he said slowly. "I believe in you. And in us." He surrendered to the arms around him and kissed the smile that spread across Jack's lips. He grew warmer than the fire at his back, happier than Christmas, brighter than Times Square on New Year's Eve. Randy threw back his head and whooped for joy.

· · ·

THEY FINALLY BROKE apart long enough for Randy to take Jack's hand and lead him upstairs to his bedroom, his late-night dinner forgotten. Jack kissed him again when they stood by the bed and then rested his forehead against Randy's chest as he murmured, "I can smell the leather. Will you show it to me?"

Randy turned nervous again, though nothing like he'd experienced minutes earlier. Of course he'd seen Jack at Cuir in that sexy-as-fuck harness, but it wasn't like they'd had time to explore each other's desires. Jack might be a tourist for all Randy knew, but leather was important in a way he couldn't explain even to his best friend. Pulling it on made him sexy and invincible and strong.

Yet paradoxically, at the moment it made him insecure. What would they do if Jack were turned off by the depth of Randy's need?

Well, this is what Jack wants. For us to get to know each other.

Randy stiffened his spine and walked over to his closet where he kept his gear. A light came on automatically when he opened the door, and there it all was. Harnesses, vests, chaps. Three pairs of boots. Arm bands and jock straps. A row of hats. A police uniform made out of dark blue leather. Hung along the wall were an assortment of crops and floggers. Soft white ropes, color-coded to indicate length, were bound in coils and stacked on a shelf.

Randy took in a steadying breath scented with tanned hide as he gestured at it all with a firm hand. "I don't know if this means anything to you, or if it's just a fantasy you were trying out. But this is me, Jack." He waited for a long moment, trying to gauge the look on Jack's face. "Is it okay?"

Jack exhaled shakily as he walked toward the closet. "Oh Randy," he moaned. "It's glorious." He stepped right into the closet, spread his arms wide and leaned to gather the garments to his chest. "Leather must speak deeply for you to have so much."

Randy cleared his throat and answered hoarsely. "It does. It feels... I don't know."

Jack smiled at him. "It feels like the real you."

Randy looked away, raw and exposed. "How about you, Jack? What does all *this* say to you?"

"It says that we correspond." Randy tilted his head quizzically as Jack pulled a harness down from the rack to hug against his body with one arm. He bent his head to inhale deeply, then reached to stroke a coil of silken rope with his free hand. "Randy, I love the touch, the scent of leather. And I love to be restrained. I'm more intrigued by the B and D than the S and M, if you follow? I want to be tied, held—" Jack paused as desire crossed his face and ran down his body in a ripple that fired Randy's blood. He added in a deeper register, "Maybe even compelled."

Randy was hard already in his black pants. The mental picture of Jack, bound before him, waiting for whatever Randy might want to do with his body... Yes, there was correspondence. He said heatedly, "I can do that for you. What about the rest?" He flicked a meaningful glance at the crops and floggers.

Jack said with certainty, "I can take anything for you if you get me in the right headspace. I would serve you any way you'd like." Randy heard some hesitancy, though, as Jack trailed off. He sounded a bit shaky. Nervous.

"But?" Randy prompted, just as he realized something that should have been obvious. Although he'd been into the leather scene for most of his adult life, Jack had only occasionally permitted himself to explore it. From the little he'd said, it might be no more than a handful of times that he'd ever acted on his desires. Randy could make a gift of his experience, and bring Jack the things he had craved yet denied himself.

Apparently unaware of Randy's thoughts, Jack stammered on. "That inna something I *need* all the time. To serve you, I mean. In my fantasies, we're able to put it on and off like you do this harness. When it's you and me, I'll have no hard limits because you wunna ask me for the impossible. I just trust that. Whatever you want from me, whatever you want me to do—that's what I want to do."

"Outside the private scene, though?"

"Outside, I want to be equals. I dunna think I could be in a full-time submissive relationship. Maybe it's cowardly, something I built up after all those years of hiding, but—"

Randy said, "Stop." At Jack's stricken expression, he reached out and pulled him close, leather harness included. "Don't apologize or explain. That's what I want too. I can't imagine myself as a Dom all the time. It's too damn much work." Jack chuffed a laugh against his chest. "But you and me, sharing this thing, exploring in private? Oh yeah." He ground his erection against Jack's belly. "That will work."

Jack looked up at him shyly. "Well, you say private."

"Yes?"

"I have to admit that Cuir was exciting to me. I've never been involved in any kind of public scene, but in a space like that, with you taking me in front of a group of men…" Randy didn't mean to purr as Jack moved sinuously against his body, but the thought of Jack, naked and waiting for Randy's touch under one of the spotlights at Cuir, set fire to his blood.

Jack asked, "Do you think you might enjoy that too?"

"Displaying you in front of those hungry eyes? Showing them how you respond to my touch and my voice? Oh yes, Jack. You could serve me that way." He made his tone commanding and straightened to his full height. "But here? Now? It's just you and me."

Jack's eyes flared at the change in tone. He stepped back from Randy's embrace and rehung the harness where it belonged. Eyes on the carpet, he took three steps away from the closet and came to rest with his hands clasped behind his back and his head down. He waited.

"Take off your clothes," Randy ordered.

Chapter Twenty-Four

JACK SHIVERED BEFORE he moved quickly to obey. Soon his clothes were folded on a chair, and he came back to attention with his legs slightly spread. Randy focused on the leather band around Jack's bicep. It was the one he'd put there the night at Cuir, and the sight of it moved him deeply.

Jack caught his eyes. "I've worn it every day since I left Washington."

Randy swelled with pride in Jack as he walked around his naked body, trailing a hand along his chest, then shoulders, then back. He stopped behind to run a hand down Jack's spine and over the swell of that high, firm ass.

He then repeated the stroke from neck down but raked his fingernails with just enough pressure to bring out faint traces along his back. A third, stronger pass and Jack moaned softly as Randy watched the streaks turn white again before reddening.

Jack responded like a concert piano to a maestro. His skin pebbled under Randy's touch, and his sighs and moans were almost musical as Randy played him. A spasm of excitement ran through Jack's body, and Randy said quietly, "I'm never going to yell at you, or demean you, or stress you unless we discuss it in advance. In here, it's safe." He slowed the cadence further as he stroked Jack's skin. "Trust in me. You know I won't abuse it." Jack gave a low, deep groan, and his shoulders sagged as he surrendered into the scene.

"Tonight will be easy, because I want that, but sometimes I will be more demanding," Randy said into Jack's ear. "Do you understand?" A short pause, and Jack's head moved slightly in acknowledgment. "Same safewords?"

"Yes, sir." He sounded so trusting that Randy reached over his shoulder to run fingers through his soft beard. Jack smiled and rubbed his cheek against the hand.

"Do you have any injuries, or problem joints I should know about?" Randy asked. Jack shivered slightly at the implications but shook his head decisively. "Now tell me. What is one thing you've always wanted to do but never let yourself experience?"

Jack licked his lips, then flicked a glance to the closet. "I want... I've na been properly tied up. Just handcuffs once but nowt else."

Randy bent to kiss his shoulder before saying firmly, "I want you to retrieve the soft rope with the green tips from the closet and bring it back to me." Jack moved silently across the room, found the coiled rope and held it out across his palms as an offering.

"Thank you, Jack." His voice was a caress, and he could see the reaction in blown pupils as his lover began to sink deeply into his own head. Randy set the rope on the bed, then began to remove his own clothes efficiently as he ordered, "Watch me."

Jack's eyes were hot as Randy bared his chest, removed his shoes, then unbuckled his belt. He opened his pants next and bent smoothly from the waist to remove them, showing off his supple body. Jack gave a small sound of appreciation as Randy returned to full display. He spread his arms and his stance, exposing himself fully, and said, "Tell me what you see."

Jack licked his lips. In a slurred tone that sounded drugged with hunger, he said, "I see a mountain of a man. Big, thick chest. Brown nipples with a silver bar worked through one. I see shoulders bigger than my hands and I know the muscle will be smooth." He swallowed and his erection twitched and flexed as he continued.

"I see a broad, masculine body, covered in soft hair that I want to brush with my lips. I see a tight belly tapering down to a gorgeous dick that's hard and long and flushed. For me. I see legs like oak trees, straight and solid and massive. I see feet that I want to caress with my tongue." He slid his gaze back up Randy's body and found his eyes. "And on top of all that, I see the proud head and face of a nobleman, more beautiful to me than any bust in the finest museum."

Randy's heart swelled at the devotion in his words. He could feel eyes on him as he went to the closet and selected a harness, a pair of gauntlets, and a thin strap. He beckoned Jack over and silently handed him the treasures.

Jack buckled a gauntlet onto Randy's left forearm, then his right. He worked the straps of the harness over Randy's hairy chest and carefully secured it, then drifted his palms over Randy's torso and down the leather. He looked curiously at the strap until Randy took it and efficiently ran it up around Jack's balls and over his hard cock before snapping it closed. A soft whimper filled the room as Randy adjusted the strap and then tugged on Jack's sac.

Randy leaned down and saw Jack's nostrils flare as he scented the leather on Randy's body. Softly, Randy said, "There's a collar in there I've never used on anyone." Jack quivered, and longing appeared in his eyes. "But I expect you to earn it first."

Randy watched Jack's hunger grow into determination. It wouldn't happen that night, but his blood hummed at the promise of helping Jack discover his pleasure and test his limits as they moved toward the intimacy and bond implied by the collar.

He permitted them both another deep kiss before he retrieved a large pair of shears from the closet, set them on the dresser in easy reach, and made sure Jack knew they were there should he safeword. When he was satisfied, he picked up the rope from the bed. Jack's eyes on him were eager as Randy gave a flick of his wrist and the neat coil unraveled smoothly.

Locating the mark he'd placed previously on the middle of the rope, he began with that centered against the middle of Jack's back so the final binding would be even. The symmetry of Western-style bondage was Randy's favorite, and the flexibility in Jack's limbs made him a dream to position.

Randy folded his arms behind his back with bent elbows, so that the fingertips of each hand cupped the opposite elbow, then secured the position with hitches connecting bicep to bicep and around the wrists to keep the arms as placed. The restraint forced Jack to arch and flex his chest as Randy wove a harness around front to form a diamond pattern over Jack's lean pectorals and down his torso. Efficiently, calmly, he wove and wrapped and restrained, tying intricate knots along Jack's body. He was slow and careful, and described what he was doing as he went so that Jack grew more and more slack as his measured voice carried Jack down into a deep space within his own head. He checked joints carefully as he worked his art and made sure nothing would interfere with circulation.

He paused with lengths of rope crisscrossing Jack's tight belly and meeting at the back of his waist, then made a quick knot in one length. He drew the rope down the crack of Jack's ass so the knot rested against his hole, then gently pulled the rope through his legs. Holding his gaze, Randy looped it around and over the cockstrap and sharply tugged. Jack gasped at the sensation in his ass from the knot pressing against him. He squirmed a little, clearly chasing the feeling again, and Randy smiled.

"Test the rope," he instructed. "You won't get out of this."

Jack moved more intentionally, trying to slip free even as he pleasured himself with the knot against his asshole and the rope looped around his dick and balls. He began to pant in excitement as he realized just how completely he was bound, and his hard cock flushed red as precome dripped silvery threads down to the carpet. His eyes were glassy and his jaw slack even though he trembled and quivered in the ropes.

Randy was sure he could make Jack come right then without ever touching him, but it would be much more pleasurable for both of them to draw the evening out.

"Stop," he ordered, and Jack stilled instantly. Randy dropped the loose ends of the rope and moved around Jack's body, using his hands to pat against exposed skin. He stopped short of spanking Jack, but he wanted the light impact and noise of his strikes to draw focus away from an orgasm. After a few minutes Jack's level of arousal was back to where Randy wanted it.

Before he moved on to the legs, he put his fingers into Jack's left hand. "Squeeze," he directed, and nodded in satisfaction when the grip was firm. Then he laid Jack safely down on the bed and continued weaving his web.

When Randy was done, Jack lay on his side, arms behind his back, thighs bound to his calves to keep his legs bent and drawn toward his chest. The position left his hole vulnerable and exposed to the knot that pressed against his opening. Randy slid a pillow under his head, then asked softly, "Are you comfortable?"

"Oh yes," Jack murmured contentedly and his eyes shone. "I feel like a slave boy on display for his prince."

Randy asked a few more questions to be sure Jack was in a good space before stepping back to admire the picture he had created. The wiry, strong body, limned in soft white rope, was a work of art all on its own. Randy's dick was aching. He pondered getting out a paddle or maybe a cane. That ass would look even better with a warm red flush or a few neat stripes.

Plenty of time to explore later. For that night, he wanted to claim Jack with nothing more than his mouth, his hands, and his cock. He crouched at the side of the bed and ran the pad of his finger all along Jack's crease before returning to nudge the knot away from his hole and circle around the ring of muscle. Jack made a low noise of approval and visibly relaxed even more.

Randy leaned forward to stroke the coral-colored opening with the flat of his tongue while he scratched his stubble against the delicate skin of the crevice. Jack's rim tasted fresh and sweet, and Randy lapped around the edges before he narrowed his tongue to breach the opening.

Jack sighed contentedly as he pressed his hips back and ground against Randy's mouth. Randy gave him what he wanted for a few minutes longer, alternating between light surface licks and deep thrusts of his tongue into that velvet interior. Jack tightened his muscles and alternately strained and sagged against his bindings, while Randy stroked along the knots and cords around his thighs to share the sensation of the soft rope that secured Jack in place. His cries became guttural as he strained and urged Randy for more.

Wickedly, Randy reached around and stroked the head of Jack's cock. He smeared the precome he found all around the shaft using just the tips of his fingers and the lightest of touches. Jack bucked and tried to thrust faster, so Randy stopped what he was doing entirely until Jack whimpered and settled down.

When he was still again, Randy repeated the whole torturous process, bringing Jack even closer to orgasm before once again cutting off all contact. Jack rolled and flexed in the ropes, panting and pleading for Randy to help him come.

Randy rested a hand on his hip, leaned over to caress the shell of an ear with his tongue, and murmured, "No." He grinned at the desperate, heartfelt groan that rose from Jack's chest.

Since Jack had never done rope play before, Randy was aware that he shouldn't keep him restrained for long. He retrieved a condom and lube from his bedside table, then stretched out along Jack's body and rolled the latex down his shaft. He drew in Jack's scent as he nudged away the rope knot again and found his hole, wet with spit. He pressed inward with two fingers until Jack grunted deep in his chest but didn't protest or move away.

Randy fucked him that way for the sheer joy of coaxing his lover open from the inside out while Jack shook and trembled with pleasure. When he finally moved the head of his cock into position, he hovered there, right at the edge of penetration, until he slipped one arm beneath and tugged the bound body closer to his own.

Slowly, so slowly, he slid forward and into Jack's ass as he begged and rucked his hips back to try to get more. If Jack had any discomfort from the penetration, no sign of it showed in his eager, desperate, welcoming body. Randy took his time, sliding inside inch by inch, leisurely but relentlessly. Finally his balls brushed against Jack's ass but he kept going to drive the final half-inch as deep as possible.

Jack stretched and thrashed and tried to impale himself even farther. His eyes fluttered open and he rolled his head back to look at Randy. The embers in his eyes almost glowed as he moaned, "You're inside my soul."

Randy's lust blazed up and he had to move. His deliberate strokes quickly grew more intense as Jack pushed back against him to meet each thrust in a beautiful rhythm. Randy wrapped a lube-covered palm around Jack's dick to twist and stroke. The juice leaking from him mixed with the lube to create a slick glide that drove Jack crazy. In minutes he was screaming his need for Randy to fuck him harder, deeper, *faster*.

"Please, sir. There, oh right there, fuck me right there," he sobbed and Randy did, until his orgasm became inevitable. Jack knew it too and whimpered and babbled as he rocked against Randy's body. "Ah, sir. Please stroke me. Please, may I come?"

"Not yet," Randy said, and Jack almost sobbed. He reached down to Jack's ass and ran a fingertip around the ring of muscle where it stretched around his girth. When Jack pressed his head back to Randy's chest and moaned at the sensation, he slid his index finger in, filling Jack even more than his thick cock already did. Jack stiffened for a moment and then gasped, "Give it all to me. I want it."

Randy considered further testing Jack's limits, but his mind's eye pictured a clock. As much as he took pleasure from Jack's body, his responsibilities as the top man came first. He withdrew his finger so he could again grab Jack's lovely slender dick and run his hand up and down the shaft in a twisting motion that made Jack cry out.

He began to pump, faster and harder. "Now," Randy growled as he tightened his slick palm around the head and created a cage of sorts. It took only a few more strokes before Jack gasped and cried out as his come shot into Randy's palm, hot and sticky. Randy let go too, filling the rubber buried deep inside Jack's ass. "Aah, Jack," he boomed as his balls emptied. "So good."

"Don't stop, sir," Jack begged, reduced to a wild creature by the sensations Randy brought him. He twisted and shook in his ropes, still not trying to get free but clearly reveling in being bound as they came together. "Please keep fucking me."

Randy brought his palm to Jack's mouth and let him lick the come off with broad swipes of his tongue over the skin and between the fingers while Randy kept moving in his ass until he softened naturally.

Jack finally stopped thrashing to sag down again into his

arms. "My god. That was fucking incredible," he gasped weakly. Randy rubbed his cheek against Jack's beard and held him for another minute before withdrawing slowly, discarding the condom, and untying the ropes. He held Jack close while rubbing circulation into his limbs to make sure there had been no loss of blood flow, then rearranged them both under the covers.

As Jack gradually came back together from his shattering orgasm, Randy stroked his body, murmuring in his ear. Occasional tremors ran through Jack, but after ten minutes or so, he was all melted and limp under Randy's roaming hands. He muttered, "I'll give you a year to stop doing that."

"What, just a year?" Randy teased, though his heart was pounding. He knew already that a year wouldn't be enough.

Jack shifted around and rested his cheek on Randy's chest, wrapping an arm around his waist. "The things we're going to do to each other. I can't wait," Jack murmured, and Randy kissed the top of his head.

After a pause, Jack asked quietly, "I havna right to ask, but did you go back to Cuir after I left for London?"

Randy smiled at the touch of jealousy he could hear, though Jack was carefully looking away from him and at the foot of his bed. "I did." Jack immediately tensed but Randy gave him no time to stew. "To talk with Liam and other friends. That's it. I was lonely when you left and I needed some company, but even thinking you and I'd never be together, I wasn't ready for anyone else."

Jack tipped his head up. His eyes sparkled in the low light as he exhaled heavily. "Would you have come after me? If I hadn't returned to Washington?"

Randy hesitated, but his heart was already laid bare. "Yes, I think I would have. I fought myself damn near every day not to call you, but I was losing the fight. You remember the movie *Love*

Actually? Where the guy in love with Keira Knightly pretends to be a bunch of carolers and shows her poster after poster?"

Jack grinned and said, "Oh no."

"Yeah," Randy said sheepishly. "I *might* have been checking into where in London to get a boombox or hire a troop of itinerant carolers."

Jack's eyes glistened as he smiled. "I should have waited then. That would have been something to see."

Randy kissed his head again. "No, this is better."

Almost nervously, Jack asked, "Are we...exclusive? I suspect so, given your principles, but perhaps I shouldn't presume—"

"Absolutely," Randy cut him off with a playful growl. "I wunna share you, and I dunna want you to share me."

"Good Potteries," Jack murmured, and he sounded pleased both about the attempted accent and the message. "We dinna talk about it but I'm on Truvada. Not that I've done all that much, only when I traveled, but—"

"Just in case. I am too," Randy said.

"Oh, wonderful. So, if you want to skip the condom next time?"

"We can talk about it." Even though Randy'd been on PrEP for a few years, he hadn't barebacked anyone in a long, long time. The idea of doing that with Jack made his dick twitch and attempt to come back to life.

Jack noticed and laughed. "My insatiable grizzly bear," he murmured as he burrowed more deeply against Randy. Then, in an abrupt change of tone, he added, "Danny told me about what you did for him and his father."

Randy was surprised at the shift, but he went with it. "I didn't do that much. Danny's lawyer reached a great deal with the prosecutor, and as a result Gates also took a plea. That note Danny left in your hotel room was enough to persuade the judge of his sincere attempt to stop Gates, so he accepted the recommendation of a suspended sentence. If Danny completes probation and community service he'll have no criminal record at all."

"That's brilliant news," Jack said. "They contacted me in England as well, you know, before recommending the deal to the court. I told them I supported it."

Randy pulled Jack's chin up and kissed him hard on the mouth. "Thank you. You had even more right than me to want to see Danny behind bars."

"It's na where he belongs. What'll happen with Danny's father?"

"We don't know yet. Luc and I agreed to support a change to probation for the remainder of Henry's sentence, and his lawyer has started the wheels turning. It isn't clear when the next court hearing will take place or if our support will be enough to persuade the judge to alter the sentence, but the lawyer's hopeful."

"What will Danny do if his father does get out? I mean, will they have to stay in different states because they're both court-supervised?"

"Nope. Part of the recommendation in Danny's case was that, if his father's released, he can do his probation and community service in Maine. Luc agreed to give him and Henry a place to live if all that comes together while they get established. He thinks that's what Kevin would want him to do."

"Oof," Jack grunted, then eventually said, "Your Luc sounds a remarkable man."

"He is. You'll like him."

"As I think you'll like Sophie."

Randy raised his head and looked at Jack in surprise. "Is she coming here? With you?"

Jack chuckled. "Not exactly. She's coming for a visit in two weeks to help me get settled in the flat, and she wants to meet you of course." He mouthed at the piercing through Randy's nipple until he elicited a moan. "She wants to meet the man who stole me away from her."

Things started to heat up for a second round, but Randy abruptly stopped what he was doing with his hand pressed against Jack's wet hole. "Wait a minute. I just remembered. Before, you said there were two things you wanted to tell me. One was that you're moving here. What was the second thing?"

"Can't you guess?" Jack teased as he rutted shamelessly against Randy's fingers.

"Tell me or I'll make your beautiful ass so pink you won't be able to sit for a week," Randy snarled playfully.

"Is that a threat or a promise? Anyway, it's about how I got my position at the Smithsonian so quickly. Do you know what kind of demand exists for jobs there?"

"Did Sophie or her father pull some strings?"

"Not exactly, though they helped with the introduction. Ultimately, what made the difference was my scholarship in identifying and authenticating a previously unknown work by Jean-Pierre Brousseau." Randy froze as Jack continued with a touch of smugness. "I shall be quite the commodity on the lecture circuit for a while, and the Smithsonian board leapt at the chance to hire me on before the public reveal."

Randy croaked out, "Are you serious, Jack? It's really a painting by—?" He couldn't say the name. It was beyond impossible. Even after all the talk, deep down he hadn't been sure it could be true.

Jack scooted up in bed so they were sitting side by side. "Beyond question. The tests on the canvas, on the pigments used, even the frame, all bore out my research. We found the number

François wrote on the back of the canvas, just covered up. Combined with the paper trail I assembled, the Valcoates appraisers were persuaded of the error and have formally withdrawn the incorrect report that denied authenticity."

Jack was so proud he looked like he'd combust as he declared, "You, my dear, are the sole owner of a genuine Brousseau."

Randy had known he'd look like that. He had known that Jack's fire would shine out like a beacon when he proved without a doubt that he alone had identified an unknown work by Jean-Pierre Brousseau, and Randy was grateful he could see it. He pulled Jack to him and tasted as much of that passion and joy as he could capture.

Once Randy was able to think again, he put a hand to his head. "Oh my god. I actually own a priceless work of art. I don't even know what to do about that."

"You don't need to make any decisions yet. The custodial agreement your lawyer Christian negotiated allows for private disclosures for professional purposes, but is quite explicit about your rights to determine whether and when a public disclosure is made. Of course my museum, well, my former museum, is hopeful they can persuade you to make a big production out of it. They'll want to have press conferences and a gala opening. Pomp and circumstance an' all. But you have the final say." He smiled. "And since I no longer work for the Kensington, they canna use me to persuade you to go one way or t'other."

Randy was reeling. It wouldn't sink in. He owned a painting potentially worth many, many millions of dollars. "Do I need to sell it?" he fretted. "How will I protect it if I don't?"

Jack soothed him and pulled Randy's head down to his own shoulder. "Shh. There's no rush. The painting is safe and you've as much time as you want to take advice and think this through."

"What about your new job? Won't that depend on when the

unveiling happens? And you deserve the recognition."

"My new director at the Smithsonian is confident the reveal will happen at some time, and she's sufficiently impressed with my work that she has ideas about other lost mysteries she'd like to investigate. As for me, yes, I have the satisfaction of knowing that I proved my scholarship was correct."

Jack cupped Randy's face between his hands. "But much more important than that, I found my life. Whether the painting turned out to be genuine or imitation ultimately made little difference." His eyes glistened and his voice was rough. "My own sweet bear. You are the true masterpiece."

Epilogue

"LEFT," JACK SAID. Sophie adjusted the landscape slightly on the left side and waited for Jack's approval. He nodded.

Randy watched the two of them work with his arms folded across his burly chest as he tried to keep amusement off his face. Jack and Sophie were like two halves of a whole. They didn't need to talk much but seemed to communicate in eyebrows and grunts and one-word comments. Jack turned and saw the glint in Randy's eye.

"What?"

"Nothing," Randy said with a shake of his head. "It's just I get a kick out of watching you together."

Sophie slipped through Mata Hari to join them near the bar. She had golden hair pulled back from her heart-shaped face and was willow-thin, so the slinky silk dresses and strappy heels she favored made Randy think of a femme fatale in a movie from the forties. She and Jack were about the same height, and when she twined her long, bare arms around Jack's waist they looked almost like siblings. As the two of them surveyed the curated walls of Mata Hari, the tilt of their heads was so similar Randy thought they might calibrate it with a protractor.

With a nod of satisfaction, Sophie rested her head on Jack's shoulder and smiled over at Randy. "Twins from different wombs," she murmured before continuing her study of the walls, and Randy laughed. Despite how intimately Jack and Sophie stood together, Randy had realized instantly upon meeting Sophie that not a touch of sexual attraction existed between the pair. Sophie might have no sex drive to speak of, but she craved physical contact. Randy didn't quite understand yet how that worked, but then, it didn't matter. It worked for Sophie.

He followed their gaze over the walls. Sophie and Jack had spent all morning rearranging Randy's art collection into vignettes that each told a story, then directing his staff to move the bar's furniture in order to complement the works on the wall. Even though he'd looked at many of the pieces for years on end, combining them in a new way made him appreciate them all over again.

"Damn, you're good," he said happily as he studied the nearest grouping. "I never would have made these connections."

Sophie languidly turned her green eyes back to him. "You selected each work with love, Randy. It's like they're all your children. You didn't want to play favorites, so you tried to showcase each one individually."

Jack shrugged. "Sometimes it takes an unbiased eye to see how the personalities fit together, and how certain pieces can support each other. That's all we did here."

"Well, it's fantastic," Randy said.

Sophie slipped free of Jack and took Randy's hand to tug him into the side room on the left of the bar. "Come see what we did," she urged.

Randy and Jack had been together for two weeks when Sophie arrived from London to help Jack settle into his apartment. The three of them had spent a lot of time together each day before Randy headed to open the bar, exploring the museums of Washington like noisy, chattering magpies, full of opinions and reactions to everything they saw. Randy noticed that around Sophie, Jack's accent stayed posh. It was only in private with

Randy that he slipped into his more natural way of speaking.

A few nights she and Jack had been waiting up for him at Randy's house after he closed Mata Hari, and they'd lazed around the fire with a bottle of wine to talk about favorite painters and new artistic movements. Sophie had taken to pushing Jack onto the floor so she could curl up against Randy. When Jack teasingly complained one evening that he'd been replaced, she'd looked at him under her lids and murmured, "Randy is far warmer than your scrawny bum."

Over the past weeks, Randy had discussed the *Sunrise* painting at length with Jack and Sophie, Christian, Thomas, a director from the Kensington museum, and Luc before finally deciding to put it up for sale. The plan was to attract publicity with a gala reception at the Kensington, and the museum had already begun to tease a big, mysterious discovery. That would give Jack his well-deserved moment in the sun, and his colleagues and the museum patrons bubbled already with questions.

Sophie had persuaded Randy that, once the gala was concluded, the time would be ideal for a vigorous auction of the previously unknown Brousseau to capitalize on the publicity. With Jack's help, Christian negotiated an auction arrangement in which the house waived the seller's commission and also agreed to split with Randy the buyer's fees—which Jack explained were typically added as a percentage of the hammer price—in a careful ladder structure.

The potential bid floor they were discussing staggered Randy. He didn't want to get ahead of himself, but at even *half* what the auction house intended to ask, he'd be set for life. He'd pay off his loan from Thomas right away. There would be money for a new house for Luc, and perhaps for Danny to go to college. Maybe he'd talk to Joe about expanding Rainbow Space or opening a transition shelter for kids who aged out yet still needed job placement training or other kinds of counseling. The possibilities made his mind reel.

The logistics of Randy and Danny and Jack and Sophie could have been awkward, but on the second night of Sophie's visit, when they had all eaten a very late dinner prepared by Danny and were relaxing at the mission table in Randy's dining room, Sophie stood gracefully and stretched out a hand to Danny.

"Little waif, I think you should come back to Jack's apartment with me tonight to let these men enjoy themselves, and tomorrow I will take you shopping. Your hair is gorgeous and I should very much like to see you in an amethyst blazer. Jack will summon a taxi for us while you grab a few things for the night. Fair warning—I'm going to have you brush my hair while we discuss your life in embarrassing detail."

Danny had blushed but ran upstairs delightedly while Jack stood to hug her, saying softly, "Thanks for giving us some time alone."

"I've never seen you so happy, darling. Hold on to your bear with both hands." She'd winked at Randy.

When he saw Danny again, his hair was styled and he had a new but serviceable wardrobe. Sophie left him with enough practical clothes so he could carry out his community service hours at Rainbow Space, but otherwise she was ruthless in consigning his sweatshirts and other used things to Goodwill.

The next time she'd pulled Danny off into the night to let Jack and Randy be together, Randy heard her grill Danny about what he might like to do with his future. He'd been unreasonably proud when he heard Danny say as he walked out the door, "I've been thinking I'd like to know more about computers."

It was probably too soon to think in terms of a life with Jack, but if that developed the way Randy hoped, he knew Sophie would become his sister every bit as much as she was already

Jack's.

Randy snapped out of his reverie as he reached the side room and stopped in his tracks. Jack and Sophie had assembled a collection of portraits on the walls, but the most prominent pieces were his portrait of Thomas and his painting of Danny looking forlornly out the window of Del's Diner. He'd only completed the canvas a week earlier, but Jack had managed to get the piece framed in a way that echoed Thomas's portrait.

Embarrassment and pride warred in Randy as warmth crept up his neck and probably turned his scalp red. Jack wrapped arms around him from behind. "They're really good, Randy. You need to display them."

Randy turned his head to nuzzle Jack's scented neck. "I never told you I painted that one," he said, indicating the picture of Thomas.

"You didn't have to. Your style is mature and consistent with the portrait of Danny. Particularly the melancholia in their eyes."

Sophie chimed in, "I think you could find an audience, if you want to display or sell your work." She gave him a sweet, teasing grin. "I have an 'in' with the Valcoates Auction House if you'd like to pursue this."

Jack kissed Randy's cheek. "Maybe when we're in London next month you should meet with Sophie's father. He handles acquisitions. I could arrange to ship a few pieces over for you."

"I think there'll be plenty of drama next month without adding that kind of stress," Randy said. "The unveiling of *Sunrise*, your lecture, then the auction. Whew! That's enough."

The auction would take place two weeks after the reveal gala, so Randy and Jack planned to stay in Sophie's apparently enormous flat as a base for side trips as Jack led Randy around England on a guided tour.

They were even going to visit Stoke-on-Trent, and Randy

looked forward to seeing Jack's home town. He'd like to thank Jack's mother for the love and support she'd shown when Jack decided to pursue art history. On the other hand, Jack's father and brothers sounded like pieces of work; Randy probably shouldn't hope for the opportunity to make out with his boyfriend in front of them and dare them to pull some shit.

"You're growling, love," Jack murmured as he leaned into Randy's body and brought him back to Mata Hari.

"Sorry. Just thinking about our trip to England next month."

"Speaking of," Jack said with a glance at his watch, "it's about time we leave for the airport to bring Danny to Portland. Yes?"

"Five minutes and we're out of here." He hugged Sophie, as she was returning to London later that day. "See you soon," he promised, then left Jack and Sophie to their goodbyes while he rounded up Danny.

He found him showing the new bar manager, Rudy, how to use the computer Danny had persuaded Randy to install as an upgrade to the piece of shit in place since Mata Hari opened. Rudy was seated in Randy's chair with Danny hovering over his shoulder, but he jumped up when Randy poked his head into the office.

"Oh! I'm so sorry—" Rudy started to say but Randy cut him off.

"Don't be. It's your office now. I'll get my personal stuff out when I return next week."

Rudy sank back into the office chair and grinned as it squeaked. "What do you think, *Danielito*? Do you think the *guapo dueño* will mind if I replace this chair?" His grin lit up his eyes, and Randy figured that his outgoing personality and confidence meant he'd do just fine managing the bar.

With everything that was changing in Randy's life—not least the potential to find himself with a large nest egg if *Sunrise* did well at auction—he'd let Thomas persuade him it was time to step back and see Mata Hari continue to grow under a new manager.

A year of working from four in the afternoon until two in the morning had gotten old, especially now he had Jack in his life. Jack would be starting his job at the Smithsonian when the two of them returned from England, and Randy could see no way to make Jack's conventional work schedule jibe with a bartender's life. Randy and Thomas would remain co-owners of Mata Hari, and Randy was sure he'd be in often because he really loved the place. But yeah, he was ready to go back to life at more normal times.

He'd talked to Malcolm about moving to bar manager, but the young man had just grinned at him. "Shit, boss man, I appreciate the offer but I don't want that kind of responsibility. Let me bartend for you, and I'll show whoever you hire how you like things to run."

So Randy had met Rudy Portillo, a handsome man originally from El Salvador, and they hit it off right away. Thomas's friend David and his husband Brandon, who had finally come by the bar one night with Joe, put in good words for the flirtatious young man they knew from Provincetown.

"Go ahead, order a new chair if you want," Randy said. "Danny, it's time to hit the road. Rudy, you've got all the phone numbers in case anything comes up?"

"I'm all set. Have a good trip and I'll try not to bother you."

Danny carried his luggage to the front door and paused to look around Mata Hari. "I'm going to miss this place," he said hoarsely and then turned away before he teared up. Randy patted his shoulder, scooped up his bags, and carried them to the truck.

Jack already had it running and waited beside it. Randy threw the luggage in the back as Danny said, "I almost forgot, Jack. I left you a folder of recipes of things Randy likes to eat."

Jack laughed. "I'm no cook. Randy is going to have to get used to takeaway again, or fire up his own range." He shot a heated look toward Randy. "I have to find other ways to keep him happy than through his belly."

Danny looked troubled, but Randy chuckled. "You know, I did take care of myself before you moved in."

"Yeah, burgers at Del's Diner at three in the morning isn't taking care of yourself," Danny muttered, then he smiled shyly when the other two men laughed. "Okay, I'll let it go. But I'm coming back to check you're eating right."

"Any time, kid. You know that."

Grinning, Danny climbed into the passenger side. Randy and Jack looked at each other, their breath fogging in the cold air. Jack threw his arms around Randy and hugged him tightly. "I hope your Luc will like me," he confessed into Randy's chest.

Randy kissed the top of his head. "Not a doubt in my mind. He still has an eye for a handsome face so you've got no worries there." Jack laughed before Randy said softly, "Anyway, all that really matters to him is that you make me happy. And you do."

He bent his head to take Jack's lips and warmth, to taste his clever tongue and claim the moan of pleasure he drew forth. Yet even as Randy gathered his lover to himself and asserted his control, he knew that, in truth, he belonged to Jack body and soul.

• • •

SIX HOURS LATER, Danny fidgeted next to Randy in the rental car as they pulled into the prison's visitor lot. Jack had stayed behind in Portland, getting to know Luc. Randy hoped Luc would keep the embarrassing pictures and stories to a minimum, but since Jack was the only man Randy had brought home in decades, there was little chance of that kind of restraint happening.

"Ready?" Randy asked and Danny nodded nervously. They climbed out and walked through the entrance to sign in. The linoleum floor, vinyl-covered chairs, and scattered wooden tables of the waiting room were clean but sterile. The receptionist was pleasant enough, though a guard hovering on the other side of a barred gate left no illusions that they were anywhere but a prison. Danny settled on the edge of a chair and chewed a fingernail while Randy got sodas out of a machine.

Everything had happened so quickly. Maybe it was the fact Christmas was coming up, but Judge Rhodes had scheduled the resentencing petition for a hearing just two weeks after Henry's lawyer filed it. Luc and Randy had both attended, and while the judge had been surprised they now supported Henry's release, she'd agreed to commute his sentence to ten years' probation.

And now less than two weeks after that, Randy and Danny were at the Maine State Prison. They didn't have to wait long. A gate buzzed, the guard pulled it open, and Henry walked through to meet them. He had on a thick but worn coat over street clothes, and carried a small suitcase in his hand.

As Henry looked around the waiting room to find them, he gnawed on his lower lip the same way Danny did. A blur of purple and auburn charged forward and Henry barely had time to drop his case before Danny wrapped arms around him like a boa constrictor.

"Dad," he choked out as he buried his face in Henry's neck.

Henry hugged him back and closed his eyes. "Danny," he whispered while he rocked to and fro. "My boy."

Randy wiped at his own eyes as he stepped forward to pick up the suitcase. Henry disengaged gently from Danny and held out his hand. When Randy took it, Henry looked up at him with those amber eyes so much like his son's and said, "I don't know how to thank you for this chance. I'll never ask for your forgiveness because that's not something I deserve, but I want you to know, I will do everything in my power to make you proud of your choice and of Danny."

Danny pulled Randy into a three-way hug with his father. "Hero," he mumbled.

Randy demurred. "No, Danny. I'm just a man who made many mistakes of his own, but meeting you helped me finally face them. One of those was holding on to blind anger and not letting myself see that your dad isn't the same guy who made his mistake over thirty years ago."

Randy's eyes threatened to fill and he didn't bother to hide the tears, even if he could have gotten free from Danny's embrace. He had lived a lot of life to come to a place he couldn't believe was real. He had good friends, a bar that meant a lot to him, and apparently a small fortune on its way.

And he had Jack.

He had the love he'd dreamed of all his life but had given up on finding. They hadn't *quite* said the words yet, they hadn't *quite* figured out the living arrangements, but in his heart, Randy knew they would, and soon. The way they fit together gave him a quiet, fierce joy.

And life had somehow even given to him a son of sorts in Danny, one he shared with Henry. Perhaps it was because of the other good things in his life that he was able to let go of the betrayal and acknowledge that Danny was every bit as human as Randy. They'd both made terrible errors, and they'd both let themselves and others down.

But that wasn't the end of either of their stories. If Randy could respect those truths about Danny, then maybe he could also live more easily with his own past while he and Jack built their future.

Entangled as the three of them were, there in the sterile waiting room of a prison in Maine, it was hard to catch Henry's eye but he did. "You raised your son to own his mistakes and make them right where he can. I think that with you two together, you'll help him do wonderful things with his life. You don't have to ask for my forgiveness, Henry. I know Uncle Kevin would forgive you, and so do I."

He thought of Jack and Luc waiting, and kissed the top of Danny's auburn hair. "Now let's go home."

THE END

Thank you for reading *Lying Eyes*. I hope you enjoyed it!

Subscribe to my newsletter at *robertwinterauthor.com* for giveaways, my latest book news, LGBT romance recs and deals, and more! I won't spam or share your email address.

If you did enjoy the book, **please consider writing a review** on Amazon, Goodreads or other sites that discuss MM romance. I appreciate any feedback, no matter how long or short. It's a great way to let other romance fans know what you thought about this book. Being an independent author means that every review really does make a huge difference, and I'd be grateful if you take a minute to share your opinion with others.

Author's Acknowledgments

Jean-Pierre Brousseau, the artist who created *Sunrise at the Abbey of Chaalis*, is fictional and therefore, sadly, so is *Sunrise*. I based Jack Fraser's research and scholarship on the fascinating discovery of a previously unknown work by Vincent van Gogh. In 2013, Louis van Tilborgh and Teio Meedendorp, two senior researchers of the Van Gogh Museum, were credited with identifying an unsigned canvas as the painting *Sunset at Montmajour*. The story can be found at www.vangoghmuseum.nl/en/news-and-press/news/new-discovery-sunset-at-montmajour.

Jack lives in London but he comes from Stoke-on-Trent. "Stokies" speak what is referred to as Potteries dialect, full of interesting and unusual words. My favorite is probably "mon-stink", which means a pretentious young person. Jack straddles the two places—London and Stoke-on-Trent—and his native voice tends to slip out when he is exceptionally angry or exceptionally relaxed. I am grateful for the help of Kimi Saunders and Michelle Sims in my use of Potteries; any errors are entirely mine. Readers interested in the lexicon of this district might find these references useful: "North Staffordshire Dialect – Words and Phrases" at www.thepotteries.org/dialect1.html and "Potteries 101: 84 words and phrases to help a non-Stokie understand the Potteries dialect" at www.stokesentinel.co.uk/potteries-101/story-24534365-detail/story.html.

I am humbled and grateful for the help I received in learning how to publish this book on my own. Thank you especially to Leta

Blake and Keira Andrews for their generous assistance and unstinting support. Thanks also to Brandon Witt, Devon McCormack and Lori Blantin for answering my questions.

Thank you to SB for his invaluable assistance in commenting on my descriptions of rope play and the leather community. Again, errors are all mine.

I have taken some liberties with the Maine corrections system to avoid distractions in the story.

If there are no tunnels connecting DC warehouses to the railroad, there ought to be.

Readers love *September* by Robert Winter

2017 Rainbow Award honorable mention

"September is a book filled with hurt and comfort, moving on and finding love, and living your best life."
—Joyfully Jay

"The emotional pull in this story is unbelievable. … The writing was captivating and the characters were remarkable."
—Love Bytes

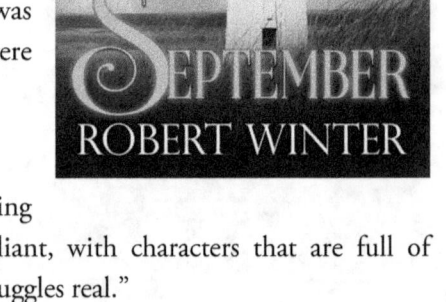

"[Winter'] writing and storytelling
ability are both beautifully brilliant, with characters that are full of emotion, and their plight and struggles real."
—Alpha Book Club

Reader Praise for *Every Breath You Take* by Robert Winter

2017 Rainbow Award honorable mention

"[T]he tension that Winter creates and builds combines perfectly with the other areas of the story, always leaving the reader with an apprehension about the next move of the perpetrator. For me, Every Breath You Take and Robert Winter deserve a full five-star rating!"
—Joyfully Jay

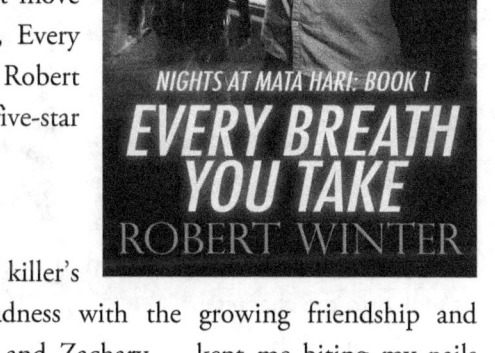

"The juxtaposition of the killer's stalking and escalating madness with the growing friendship and attraction between Thomas and Zachary … kept me biting my nails right up until the end."
—Scattered Thoughts and Rogue Words

"This story starts out on a murderous note, with the prologue leaving me absolutely needing to know how its dark events were going to figure in the lives of the main characters."
—It's About the Book

Excitement for *Lying Eyes* by Robert Winter

Five stars
"Every book gets better… This is an easy recommendation, even more so if you're a romantic mystery and/or suspense maven."
—Hearts on Fire

"Robert Winter is now an auto-buy author for me. Spectacular writing!!!"
—Amazon reviewer

"There are pulse-racing action scenes to go along with the intrigue and building romance, and an ending that goes above and beyond to supply gratification to the reader, as well as to the characters."
—It's About the Book

"4.5 stars!!"
—Bayou Book Junkies

"Robert Winter has definitely made it onto my favorite author list. This is his third book, and they just keep getting better!"
—Scattered Thoughts and Rogue Words

Vampire Claus by Robert Winter

'Twas the night before Christmas, but what's stirring is a little more dangerous than a mouse.

Taviano is nearly two hundred years old and never wakes in the same place twice. Weary and jaded, the vampire still indulges in memories of childhood Christmases in Naples. He lingers in shadow, spying on mortals as they enjoy the holiday.

When Taviano spots a handsome young man in Boston loaded down with presents and about to be mugged, he can't help but intervene. Soon he's talking to joyous, naïve, strong-willed and funny Paul, a short-order cook who raised funds to buy Christmas presents for LGBTQ children. Before he knows what's happened, Taviano is wrapped up in Paul's arms and then in his schemes to get the presents delivered by Christmas morning.

A vampire turned into a Christmas elf… What could go wrong?

Vampire Claus is a 30,000-word standalone gay romance about a lonely vampire and a fearless mortal with no instinct for self-preservation. A heartwarming ending, no cliffhanger, and a young man who discovers he has a thing for fangs. Isn't that what Christmas is all about?

About the Author

Robert Winter lives and writes in Provincetown. He is a recovering lawyer who prefers writing about hot men in love much more than drafting a legal brief. He left behind the (allegedly) glamorous world of an international law firm to sit in his home office and dream up ways to torment his characters until they realize they are perfect for each other.

When he isn't writing, Robert likes to cook Indian food and explore new restaurants. He splits his attention between Andy, his partner of sixteen years, and Ling the Adventure Cat, who likes to fly in airplanes and explore the backyard jungle as long as the temperature and humidity are just right.

Contact Robert at the following links:

Website:
www.robertwinterauthor.com

Facebook:
facebook.com/robert.winter.921230

Goodreads:
goodreads.com/author/show/16068736.Robert_Winter

Twitter:
twitter.com/@RWinterAuthor

Email:
RobertWinterAuthor@comcast.net

Photo by Brad Fowler,
Song of Myself Photography